waking the witch

KELLEY ARMSTRONG

waking the witch

orbit

www.orbitbooks.net

ORBIT

First published in Great Britain in 2010 by Orbit

Copyright © 2010 by K. L. A. Fricke, Inc.

The moral right of the author has been asserted.

A CIP catalogue record for this book
is available from the British Library.

ISBN 978-1-84149-805-8

Printed and bound in Great Britain by Clays Ltd, St Ives plc

Papers used by Orbit are natural, renewable and recyclable
products sourced from well-managed forests and certified
in accordance with the rules of the Forest Stewardship Council.

Mixed Sources
Product group from well-managed
forests and other controlled sources
www.fsc.org Cert no. SGS-COC-004081
© 1996 Forest Stewardship Council

Orbit
An imprint of
Little, Brown Book Group
100 Victoria Embankment
London EC4Y 0DY

An Hachette UK Company
www.hachette.co.uk

www.orbitbooks.net

To Jeff

ACKNOWLEDGMENTS

I had a new editor on this one, so I'd like to give a huge thanks to Carrie Thorton at Dutton US for all her help. And, of course, thanks to those who've been with me from the start: my agent, Helen Heller, and editors Anne Collins of Random House Canada, and Antonia Hodgson of Warner Orbit. As always, I'm indebted to my beta readers: Ang Yan Ming, Xaviere Daumarie, Terri Giesbrecht, Laura Stutts, Raina Toomey, Lesley W, and Danielle Wegner. Thanks, guys!

PROLOGUE

FOR THE FIRST TIME SINCE CLAIRE KENNEDY DIED LAST WEEK, there wasn't a police officer guarding the site of her murder.

Kayla peered out from behind the boarded-up beauty salon. Seeing no one, she hoisted her backpack and set out, kicking stones, her gaze fixed on the ground. She was careful to walk slowly. If you ran, grown-ups paid attention. Kayla hated it when they paid attention. She liked being invisible.

Until her mom was murdered last year, Kayla had always been invisible. But now it wasn't just the other kids who whispered behind her back, calling her weird or—in grown-up language—"an odd little thing." Adults did, too. It wouldn't help if they found her sneaking into the place where her mom had been murdered.

Kayla knew the rear door would be locked. She had lock picks from her Junior Detective kit, but they were just toys. She knew a way in, though. A boarded-up window on the first floor with a gap big enough for a nine-year-old to squeeze through. Concrete blocks scattered behind the building made a good stepladder.

She pushed her backpack in first. It hit the floor with a thump. As she hoisted herself through the window, she avoided the broken glass she'd cut herself on last time. Grandma had flipped out and taken her to the clinic. Grandma was like that. She worried a lot. After Mom died, Kayla thought Grandma would have less to worry about. No such luck.

She dropped to the floor and rummaged in her backpack for her flashlight. Plastic, of course. She'd considered asking Grandma for a real one for her birthday, but hadn't figured out yet how to explain why she needed it.

Kayla shone the flashlight around. Empty. No, that was the wrong word. The building was only empty of *people*. Abandoned.

There was tons of crap here, all of it dirty and old and broken, but Kayla barely needed the flashlight to get where she was going. She'd been here five times since her mom had died. She'd recorded every visit in her notebook. There hadn't been much to see, though. By the time she thought of coming, the police had cleared the place out.

This time it would be different. If Claire Kennedy had been killed here just over a week ago, there had to be a connection to the murder of her mother and her mother's best friend. There just had to be.

She opened the basement door and shone her light into blackness. She went down one step, then stopped, working up her nerve as she always did, before shutting the door and letting the darkness of the basement envelop her, her plastic flashlight barely strong enough to cast a pale, distant circle.

Halfway down the stairs, she heard the thump of a door shutting above. An officer back on duty? That was okay. He'd peek inside the main floor, assure himself all was clear, then sit outside in his pickup. Kayla knew the routine.

Still she listened for a minute. When no more noises came, she resumed her descent. Down into the basement, where the chill was enough to make her wish she'd brought her jacket. Lissa would say it was the chill of death.

Lissa talked like that. When Kayla confided that she came here, her friend's eyes had gone round and she'd said, "Are you trying to contact her ghost?"

"Whose ghost?"

"Your mother's, dummy. If you could talk to her, she could tell you who killed her."

Kayla thought that was silly, but she didn't say so. Lissa was the only friend she had.

It was just a dark, cold, smelly basement. Where her mom had died. And no one knew who'd done it or why. That's why Kayla kept coming back. To find out what had happened to her mom. And to Brandi, though really she didn't much care what had happened to Brandi. But Grandma would say she shouldn't think like that. She did want to find out what happened to Claire Kennedy, though. She hadn't really known Claire—she was one of the girls from the cookie place—but she'd seen her around town a few times, and she'd seemed nice, always smiling and waving, even though they'd never met.

From the bottom of the basement stairs, Kayla picked her way around piles of junk until she saw the yellow crime-scene tape wrapped around a pillar, the broken end trailing across the floor.

She stopped. It was exactly the same spot where her mother's and Brandi's bodies had been found. She shivered and maybe it wasn't the cold this time, but she told herself it was.

She crept forward. There was blood on the cement floor. The spot wasn't very big, not like the big stains she could still see, almost hidden under a layer of dust.

She shone the flashlight on those old blood stains and, for a second, she could see her mother lying there, her eyes open, her—

Kayla shook her head sharply and swung the beam away. She wasn't here to think about her mother. She was here to find out who killed her. And she didn't need ghosts for that. She needed science.

She took her backpack off and unzipped it. Inside was her Junior Detective kit. She had a camera, too. A real one. It was on her mom's old cell phone, which Grandma let her keep for emergencies. She took it out for a picture of the blood. Blood stains were important. They could tell you—

A creak overhead. Kayla froze. Then she shook her head. Just a noisy old building. She aimed the flashlight with one hand, holding the cell with the other—

This time footsteps sounded above her, crossing the first floor, the distinct *thump-thump* of someone walking.

She swallowed.

Just the police officer. Or maybe Chief Bruyn, come back to check something. Or someone from town, also trying to sneak a peek at the crime scene.

But what if it was someone else?

Kayla had read every book in the library on murder investigations. One line came back to her now. *The killer may return to the scene of the crime.*

It seemed crazy to come back after you'd gotten away, but Kayla trusted the books, and listening to those footsteps, her heart hammered.

Then it hit her. If this *was* the killer, maybe she really could solve her mother's death. All she had to do was hide and see who showed up.

A click from upstairs—the basement door opening.

Kayla turned off her flashlight and tucked herself into the shadows beside the old furnace.

ONE

FOR FIVE YEARS, I'D TOILED AS EXECUTIVE ASSISTANT SLAVE to Lucas and Paige and now, finally, I was in charge. For the next week anyway.

The plaque still read Cortez-Winterbourne Investigations, but that could be easily changed with the deft use of an energy-bolt spell. Levine Investigations rolled off the tongue so much more easily. At one time, I would have done it, if only as a joke, but there are things you can get away with at sixteen that just don't fly at twenty-one.

I used my key card, then crept through the lobby, trying to squelch the click of my heels.

"Savannah!" a voice chirped behind me. "I thought I heard you come in."

I started a cover spell, but Tina had already spotted me. I considered a knockback spell—make her trip and give me time to escape. But that would, sadly, not be a good way to launch my week playing a responsible adult.

When Paige said we were getting an accountant for a tenant, I'd thought, *Great, someone nice and quiet.* That was the stereotype, but apparently, no one had told Tina.

"I'm so glad I caught you," she said. "It's almost ten and no one's in the office yet."

It was 9:14.

"There was a man here looking for Lucas," she continued. "I called upstairs and the phone rang and rang. Did he and Paige leave on vacation already? I know Adam is at a conference. In Spokane, isn't he?"

I made a noncommittal noise. Tina might be human, but she had a supernatural sense for snooping. Adam said we should hire her. I threatened to give her his home address and that shut him up.

"I hate to tell you kids how to run your business, but you really need to have someone up there during business hours. It's no wonder you have hardly any clients. You need a full-time receptionist." She patted my arm. "Yes, I know, dear, you're the receptionist, but you're always flitting off, doing God-knows-what. I could—"

"Oh, my cell phone's vibrating," I lied. "Could be a client. I'll talk to Paige about drop-ins."

"It's no bother, dear. I wanted to speak to you anyway. I think I have a job for you." Tina lowered her voice, though we were the only ones in the lobby. "I started dating this man. A widower I met online."

"And you want me to run a background check? Good idea."

"Oh, no. A man has the right to his privacy. It's just . . . Well, I was watching this show on private investigators, about a firm of women hired by other women to test their mate's loyalty."

It took me a second to catch her drift. "You want me to try to seduce your boyfriend?"

Her lips pursed. "Certainly not. Just get dolled up, talk to him, flirt with him, and see whether he'll flirt back."

"I'm probably half his age. I'd be worried if he *didn't* flirt back."

A muffled snort made me glance down the hall. A guy a couple of years older than me leaned out of the stairwell doorway. Light hair just past his collar, denim jacket, boots, and a pair of snug-fitting worn blue jeans. He lifted a finger to his lips, shushing me, and I tried not to stare even if he was definitely stare-worthy.

I turned back to Tina. "That guy who wanted to speak to Lucas. Did you let him in?"

"Certainly not." She lowered her voice. "He looked a little dodgy."

"Was he in his midtwenties? Dark blond hair? Looks like he lost contact with his razor a few days ago?"

The guy arched his brows, mock-indignant.

"Yes, that's him," Tina said. "Now about my job offer . . ."

"Spend the money on a shopping spree at Victoria's Secret and make sure he's too exhausted to look at twenty-year-olds."

Before she recovered from that suggestion, I took off.

The guy waited until she was safely in her office, then strolled to meet me.

"Dodgy?" he said. "I'm not the one wanting a hot chick to try seducing my new boyfriend." He extended his hand. "Jesse Aanes."

I'd heard of him. A half-demon PI out of Seattle who'd worked with Lucas a few times. Lucas said he was a good guy, which was the only seal of approval I needed.

"What brings you to Portland?" I asked.

"Cases. One that I'm working now and a new one I wanted to run past Lucas. Two birds, one stone. I left him a message, but he hasn't returned it, which isn't like him."

"He's on vacation with Paige. I confiscated their cell phones and the only messages I'm passing on are well wishes and death notices."

He laughed. "Good idea. They can use the break. Did that woman say Adam isn't around either?"

"He's at a conference. It's just me for the rest of the week."

Jesse hesitated and I knew what he was thinking—he needed help, but I wasn't what he had in mind.

"Why don't you come up to the office," I said. "Tell me what you've got."

I used my key card to unlock the stairwell door. Yes, we have key card entry everywhere, plus a shitload of protective spells for the second floor. I undid them under my breath as we walked.

As Tina said, we don't get a lot of drop-in clients. We don't want to. While we rarely turn away paying human customers, our clientele is almost exclusively supernatural and they don't need an ad in the Yellow Pages to find us. Given that Lucas is heir to the Cortez Cabal, though, not everyone who finds us wants to hire us. Hence the heavy security.

Jesse followed me up the stairs. "I guess the daughter of Eve Levine and Kristof Nast doesn't need to worry about strangers attacking her in an empty office."

"If they do, I can always use them for my next ritual sacrifice. Volunteers are so hard to come by."

It's not the sort of crack you should make when you have a notorious dark witch for a mother and an equally notorious cutthroat sorcerer for a father. It was a test of sorts, and Jesse passed, just laughing and saying, "I'll watch my step then."

"So what's your power? I know you're a half-demon."

"Agito."

Telekinesis, then. Agito was the second of the three levels, meaning he had mediocre abilities. Having dealt with a high-level Volo before, I was much more comfortable with an Agito.

His powers explained how he'd snuck past Tina. Using telekinesis, he'd caught the door before it closed. I'd have to talk to Lucas about that. Yet another argument against human tenants.

I led Jesse into the meeting room. He didn't sit down—didn't even take off his jacket—just strode straight to the table and pulled files from his satchel.

He set a crime-scene photo on the table. "Six months ago, two young women were murdered in Columbus, Washington, about an hour over the Oregon border. I doubt it made the Portland news. Nothing all that hinky about the killings. No sign of a serial killer or sexual sadism. Just the shooting death of two twenty-five-year-olds who led the kind of lives where you sort of figure, sooner or later"—he gestured at the photo of the two women—"this is how they're going to end up."

"Hookers?"

He shook his head. "Just not exactly sterling members of society."

"Drugs?" I said. "Booze? Petty crime? All of the above?"

"You got it. Nothing you haven't seen a million times before. I was on that path myself until Lucas got me out of some trouble and persuaded me there were legal ways to use my skills. Anyway, these girls didn't run into a Lucas. They were high school dropouts. Never held a job more than a few months. One had a kid at sixteen. Both had short rap sheets, and a string of boyfriends with longer ones."

I lifted the photo to take a closer look. The two bodies lay on a floor. Both were fully dressed, T-shirts covered in blood, each bearing a hole. Single gunshot wounds to the chest. One was on her back, eyes open, arms akimbo, legs twisted, a pool of blood under her. The other was stretched out, arms and legs only slightly bent, eyes closed. The blood under her was smeared.

"Both shot, as you see," Jesse said. "A through-and-through for the first, the bullet apparently lodging in the wall over there." He pointed to the edge of the photo. "They recovered another bullet from inside the second victim. The first one died immediately. The second didn't."

"Doesn't look like she tried to get away, though. Drugged?"

"I don't have tox screens."

"No sign of rape or torture, like you said. Looks execution style. A classic case of 'Hey, bitch, you gonna pay for that dope or what?' The answer, apparently, being 'or what.' "

"Yep, that's what it looks like."

When he didn't go on, I glanced at him. "So what's your interest? Is one of these girls a supernatural?"

"Not as far as I know."

He set a second photo on the table. It was another murdered young woman, also early twenties, though one glance told me *this* girl didn't sell herself for dime bags.

I put the two photos side by side. All three bodies had been left in the same place.

"Basement?" I asked.

"Of an abandoned building."

I could hear Lucas's voice. *The fact that the deceased are found in a common location may speak less to a connection than to a simple matter of convenience.* Yes, Lucas really did talk that way. Drove me nuts, especially when I found myself slipping into the same speech patterns. On the plus side, I may not be an A student, but I sure as hell can sound like one.

When I told Jesse my theory—small town, not a lot of places to put a body, someone had already used this one, so the second killer followed suit—he shrugged. "Possible, but in this particular small town, there's no shortage of abandoned buildings."

"What's the local murder rate?"

"You're looking at it. This double killing last fall, then the single one ten days ago. Before that, the last homicide was a domestic incident in 1999."

"Lot of drug activity in town?"

"It has its share, maybe a little more. You can blame that on a depressed economy, though. It's not exactly a hotbed of gangsta activity. Mostly kids selling pot from their lockers, the laid-off guy down the road dealing out of his garage, that sort of thing."

"Do the police think it's the same killer for all three?"

"Yep, but only because otherwise they'd need to catch two murderers, and that's more work than they care to contemplate."

"You're going to make me guess what the supernatural connection is, aren't you."

"I was just seeing if you'd pick it up. It's—"

I lifted a hand to cut him off. "Is the answer here?" I asked, pointing at the photos.

He nodded.

"Give me a minute."

TWO

I STUDIED THE VICTIMS FOR SOME SIGN THEY'D BEEN KILLED by a supernatural—puncture wounds, gnaw marks, weird burn patterns. But the only sign of trauma was the bullet holes.

Next I looked at the background for evidence that the victims had been used ritualistically. If so, then we probably *weren't* dealing with a supernatural killer. There were black art rituals involving human sacrifice—usually high-level protection spells that required a life in forfeit for a life protected—but that's a lot more rare among witches and sorcerers than Hollywood would have people believe.

If these were indeed ritual murders, then the most likely culprit was Hollywood itself, for suggesting that it's possible to harness the forces of darkness through sacrifice. As if a demon really gives a rat's ass about a dead human or two.

When humans ritually kill, though, they're rarely subtle. Pentacles in blood are a particular favorite. Apparently, if you're going to the trouble of proving what a badass occultist you are, you want to make sure the whole world gets it.

However, even if the killer was human, that was a concern for us. The agency takes a few calls a year from supernaturals freaked out because some lowlife in their city drained a victim's blood or left occult paraphernalia at a crime scene. I tell them to chill—most humans are smart enough to know vampires and witches and demons are the products of overactive imaginations, and the police will quickly turn their attention to more plausible explanations.

Sometimes, though, exposure threats do bear investigating. We can never be too—

I stopped. I lifted the photos and squinted at them. Was that a faint line under each body? Part of a circle drawn in chalk and hastily erased?

"Do you have a better picture of this?" I asked, pointing at the line.

Jesse shook his head.

"What does the police report say about it?"

"As far as I know, nothing. I haven't seen it myself, but my contact says it wasn't mentioned."

"Okay. But since it's in a covered, unused area, the marks under the latest victim should still be there."

"That's what I'm hoping."

All the magical races—witch, sorcerer, shaman, necromancer— had rituals that used chalk circles. The important part was the symbol presumably underneath these bodies. Once I'd noticed those chalk lines, I started picking up other very discreet signs of a true dark art ritual—flakes on the concrete that looked like dried herbs, a black smudge on the wall that I recognized as smoke from a burning brazier, an edge of silver, almost hidden in the latest victim's clenched hand. A coin? An amulet?

"The cops must have seen that," I said, pointing to the silver. "Or the coroner did."

"I'm guessing yes, and I'm really hoping they'll tell me what it is, but they may hold on to the information to weed out the killer from the cranks."

I looked at the two earlier victims. One had her left hand fisted and the other's right hand was palm down on the ground. Either could have been holding something.

"Who's the client?" I asked.

"Me."

When I glanced up, he looked faintly embarrassed. "See, that's the problem with knowing Lucas. You get this urge to do pro bono work."

"It's called guilt."

"No kidding, huh? I'm not a crusader, but every now and then something like this crosses my radar. A necromancer buddy with the Washington state police recognized signs of what looked like a real ritual. He can't jump in without raising eyebrows, so he passed it to me."

I took out my iPhone and logged in to our database, tapping the virtual keypad as he continued.

"Officially, though, the mother of the last victim hired me. I tracked her down and offered to investigate in return for her confirming that to anyone who asks."

"A free PI. Bet she was happy."

"I wouldn't say *happy*. It took a lot of fast-talking to persuade her I wasn't running a con. Even made me sign a waiver."

"Did she seem reluctant? Maybe for a reason?"

"Nah, just a legal secretary who thinks she's been at the job long enough to practice law herself."

I turned around the phone to show him a list. "I plugged in what we know, and this is what I get. Eight possible rituals, more if whatever she has in her hand isn't significant."

"Whoa, and I'm still working from paper files."

"Paige kludged together an app and hacked it into the proprietary software."

"Whatever that means . . ."

"No idea. To me it means we have database access on the road. Of course, I could just walk twenty feet and pull this up on a computer, but that wouldn't be nearly as impressive. Would you like the list texted to you, e-mailed, or sent to our printer?"

"Okay, now you're just showing off. Text it." He handed me a card with his cell number and I punched it in.

"So I'm guessing this is what you need from us—you supply the details and we'll access our resources to figure out which ritual you're dealing with. If we're lucky, what she has in her hand will answer all our questions. Well, except whodunit. That's your job."

"See, now this is why I asked to talk to Lucas," he said. "If I showed him this, he'd be all, 'Hmm, this bears investigation. I take it you're on the case?' And I'd be, like, 'Well, I will be, right after I finish a job.' Then he'd ask if I minded if he looked into it himself, and say he'd hate to take a job from me and I'd joke that it's not a paying one anyway and if he wants to take a look . . ."

"So you actually brought this to us hoping we'd investigate it for you?"

His cheeks colored. "Shit. Could you just channel Lucas for a minute? Please? Make me feel like a generous colleague?"

"If you were truly generous, you'd be passing us a paying case. Being the accountant for this place, I'm all about the bills."

As I picked up the photos, my heart beat a little faster. I could take this case. My first solo investigation. I'd been asking for one since I turned eighteen. By the time I reached twenty, I realized I had to stop bugging and start working my ass off to prove I could handle it.

I had a hell of a reputation to overcome, though. I'd made more mistakes as a teen than most people do in a lifetime. Paige and Lucas knew that better than anyone. They weren't just my bosses—they'd been my guardians. I'd been twelve when my mother died, and Paige had taken me in, and she'd gone through hell because of it.

So I didn't blame them for only letting me assist in investigations. Here, though, was a case I could handle, working under the supervision of a guy Lucas trusted.

So I said, as casually as I could, "My schedule is clear this week. I'll look into it."

Jesse looked over. Sizing me up. I knew that and I could feel my hackles rising, but I kept my mouth shut because I've come to understand that I can't blame people for underestimating me. Twenty-one might feel terribly grown up to me, but to others I'm still a kid, and insisting I can handle it would sound defensive, not mature.

"Lucas says you've been doing some investigative work," he finally said.

"I've been part of the team since we opened. I've done research and legwork for the past five years. I've assisted on investigations for three. I'd even done a few small local ones myself. Yes, triple homicide isn't small, but you're looking for someone to do some legwork, presumably under your supervision."

He nodded. "If you can help me, I'd appreciate that. Normally, I'd suggest you run it past Lucas and Paige but . . ."

"Under the circumstances, they're better off not worrying about me. I'll tell Adam."

"Okay. Thanks. I'm not dumping this case on you. I *will* jump back in as soon as I can. But this latest murder is already cooling. I hoped to get out there two days ago, but got sidetracked with this case I'm on. It's a guy I've been chasing for two years now and he finally turned up in Portland. It's just child support, but, well, the client really needs the money . . ."

"And if you wait, he might bolt again."

"Exactly."

Frankly, I didn't care what his motivation was. I just wanted the job.

If it was a ritual, it was magic, probably witch or sorcerer, and I was both. Add some demon blood on my mom's side, and I was a damned amazing spell-caster. More important for this case, I had contacts in the black market and dark arts.

So I told Jesse I'd take it. I made it clear, though, that although I'd welcome his help when he was ready, I wasn't doing the legwork and dropping the case. I was the primary on this. He agreed and left me with the file.

The moment Jesse was gone, I pulled up his photo file on the computer. Everything he'd said fit with what I'd heard about the guy, but double-checking is standard procedure around here, where we have to deal with everything from unstable clients to Cabal assassins. So I checked the photo. There was no question that the guy I'd talked to was Jesse Aanes.

Next I looked up the murders on the Internet and downloaded everything I could find, which wasn't much. Ditto for the victims. I got a few hits on the latest one—Claire Kennedy—but nothing on the first two, Ginny Thompson and Brandi Degas. Yep, Gin and Brandi. Call me crazy, but naming your daughters after alcoholic beverages is just asking for trouble.

Next I worked on identifying the ritual. I'd just finished plugging in ideas for the silver object in Claire's hand—coin, amulet, key—when I glanced at the clock. It was almost eleven. If I planned to get to Columbus today, I had to get going.

I grabbed my helmet from the back room and wheeled my bike into the alley. Not a bicycle, a motorcycle. I might live in the green belt, but I'd never quite embraced the lifestyle. I drove a 1950 Triumph Thunderbird that Lucas and I had restored together. It was a sweet ride, and a lot more fuel-efficient than a car, so I could feel virtuous without sacrificing the cool factor.

I zipped home, then called Adam. No answer. That was fine—I wasn't calling to get his approval, just to let him know. Adam wouldn't stop me anyway. He was my biggest supporter when I argued for getting out in the field more.

Paige had baked me cookies before she left, and I was filling a box to take when my cell rang. The Doors's "Light My Fire." Adam's picture popped up, a god-awful one of him snapped before his first coffee on a ski trip last winter.

I'd been in love with Adam since I was twelve. I'd grown up secure in the knowledge that while other girls dreamed about their ideal partner, I'd already found mine. I just needed to wait until I was old enough for him to realize I wasn't just his friends' ward; I was his soul mate.

Sixteen sounded about right. By the time I actually reached sixteen, though, I realized it was way too young. No decent twenty-seven-year-old should be interested in a kid that age. Eighteen then. When eighteen passed, I told myself the gap was still too wide. Twenty? Nope. Twenty-one. It had to be twenty-one.

We went out for my twenty-first birthday, just the two of us. That wasn't a sign of anything—we've always been good friends. When he asked where I wanted to go, I said the most expensive place in town, just to give him a hard time. Then I bought a knockout dress, got my hair done, even had a manicure. That night Adam would finally realize the smart-ass, irresponsible Savannah was gone for good. I was a woman now.

If he did notice, it didn't seem to make any difference. I *wasn't* his friends' ward anymore. I was his co-worker and pal, and that was all I was ever going to be. Take it or leave it. I'd decided to take it. That didn't mean, though, that my heart didn't flutter every time I heard his ringtone.

"Let me guess," he said when I answered. "You're bored and lonely already."

"Nope. Got a triple homicide with possible ritualistic overtones already."

I gave him a quick rundown.

"Jesse's a good guy," he said when I finished. "You could use the experience. As the senior employee in Paige and Lucas's absence, I'm making an executive decision."

"You like that, don't you?"

"Anything that gives me the upper hand. I promise not to lord it over you when I get there, though."

"You're at a conference. As boring as it might be, you're stuck."

"There are just a couple more seminars I want to sit in on, so I'll leave early and come give you a hand. Jesse's fine, but better to work with someone you know, right? We make a good team."

True. But as much as I loved working with Adam, I really wanted this to be my first solo case. As solo as I could make it, anyway. So I said we'd discuss it later. He was fine with that.

"Now, you're going to stay in Columbus, right? Not commute back and forth."

"It's only an hour's drive. I have to come back or Paige and Lucas will know something's up."

"I'll say I sent you out to do legwork for me."

"But the office—"

"—will run just fine without you. Yes, I know you'd rather come home every night, but if you really want field experience, you need to get out in the field and stay there. It's a small town. You have to meld in, become part of the community. It'll be good for you, getting out, mingling, trying to fit in . . ."

Mingling with *humans*. Trying to fit into *human* society. That's what he meant. Damn.

I reluctantly agreed. He made me promise to call him with an update tomorrow.

THREE

I TOOK THE BACK ROADS TO COLUMBUS. HIGHWAYS AND
motorcycles don't mix. Neither do motorcycles and the Pacific
Northwest. Like Lucas, though, I refuse to yield to the climate.
I ride when I can, and have a rainsuit in my saddlebags. I could
have taken Paige's Prius, but the forecast was clear for the next
week. So I was zooming along, enjoying the ride, when I passed
a service station warning "last gas for ten miles," which seemed
odd, considering Columbus was only a few miles away. Still, I
had under half a tank, so I stopped.

As I filled up, a couple of truckers stood outside a rig, the
younger one checking me out, the older one checking out my
ride.

"Marlon Brando," the older guy said, nodding at my ride.
"That's the bike he had in *The Wild Ones*."

The younger guy's gaze slithered over me. "So are you a wild
one, hon?"

The older one shut him up with a glare, then turned to me.
"Where you heading? There isn't much around out here."

I doubted these guys were from Columbus, but if they were
on this back road, they were probably familiar with the area.

Channeling Paige, I pasted on a big, friendly smile. "Columbus."

"Why?" the younger guy said. "Nothing there for a girl like you."

"And not the safest place either," the older one said. "They've had themselves a few murders in the past year. Young women."

This was easier than I thought. I only had to say, "Seriously?" and I got all the details. They didn't tell me anything I didn't read in Jesse's reports, though. Not until they'd finished, and the older man said, "If you ask me, there's something hinky going on in that town."

"Hinky?"

"Buddy of mine stopped there last fall, making a delivery. Went in the wrong building and found one of them satanic rituals."

"In progress?"

"Nah, from the night before, he figured. But it was all there. Pentacles. Black candles. Dead cat. He tore out of there like the Devil himself was after him. Won't stop in that town ever again."

Satanic rituals. I'd be a lot more excited about that if the ritualistic signs left near those bodies suggested anything like a black mass. Still, it was a start—a hint that something supernatural might be going on in Columbus. Which was good, because from the look of the place, I'd never have guessed it.

The articles on the murders had given me a good image of Columbus. Your typical small town struggling to survive, the kids shipping out to Seattle or Portland as soon as they could. There would be a subdivision for commuters, but mostly you'd see streets of small postwar homes fronted by tidy postage-stamp lawns. The downtown would be a patchwork of basic-service businesses that had been there for three generations.

As I drove into town, though, I joined every local kid in chomping at the bit to be someplace else, anyplace else. Ghost town was too fanciful a term for Columbus, conjuring up visions of porch swings creaking in the breeze and tattered vintage Coke signs flapping. This place was a zombie, rotting before my eyes, dead but still somehow functioning.

The population sign looked as if it had recently been reduced from four digits to three, even that estimate bearing an air of desperate optimism. I drove past three businesses on the outskirts of town—a boarded-up bowling alley, a used-car lot with three mud-mired clunkers, and a darkened gas station.

The residential streets came next, if one can still call them that when there's little sign of actual residents. Maybe a quarter of the lots bore the kind of tidy postwar homes I'd envisioned. Almost half, though, had For Sale signs, most faded or fallen, all hope abandoned. As for the others, it seemed the home-owners hadn't even been able to work up the confidence to put their house on the market, the yards overgrown, windows boarded up or broken, as if the residents were resigned to the fact they were stuck here, but resentfully, refusing even to do basic maintenance.

I didn't need magical powers to cast my mind's eye out to the other edge of town and see a closed sawmill or small factory along the rail tracks. Columbus was the kind of place that wouldn't have anything to recommend it *except* good-paying industrial jobs. It was an ugly town in a beautiful state. Portland was close enough for commuting, but so were lots of other, better places, with highway access.

As I rode down Main Street, I started wishing I'd rented a car—something old and rusty, something that would fit in. Normally, I'm all about the attention, but the heads turning my way, the eyes narrowing, the lips tightening, wasn't the kind of attention I needed if I was about to poke my nose into local murders. Everything about me screamed big city, proof that the world was chugging along in relative ease outside the town limits.

I rode down a quiet secondary road where the only business still operating was a pawnshop. Finally, I spotted the building where Brandi, Ginny, and Claire had died. According to my notes, it used to be an office. I couldn't tell—it looked like it'd been closed for a decade. It'd probably been the town eyesore for years. Now it fit right in.

I parked in the lot across the road. The only other car parked there was a BMW. An older model but in A1 shape. I wasn't surprised to see an out-of-state plate on it. Texas.

As I got off my bike, I could see the driver in my mirror, checking me out as he climbed from the car. Even though my back was to him, it was a discreet ogle, almost reluctant. I played to my audience, tugging my helmet free, giving my long dark hair a toss as it fell over my back. Yes, I'm an attention-whore. It didn't hurt that the guy was worth checking out himself.

He looked taller than me, which was always a bonus. A lean build. Wearing a suit that straddled the line between department store and designer. Short dark hair. Chiseled face. Glasses, maybe worn for effect; a guy who wanted to be taken seriously and hoped the glasses would help.

I considered introducing myself, making some wry comment about a fellow out-of-towner. I have no problem approaching guys. I figure if they're intimidated by a woman who makes the first move, then I'm not the girl for them. Before I made up my mind, though, he headed toward Main Street.

I left my bike secured with a perimeter spell. It sucked as a long-distance alarm, but nothing was better for close range.

In case anyone was watching me, I headed for the pawnshop, then zipped back to the old office under cover of a blur spell. Lucas and Paige always say never to use it in a public place during daylight. While seeing a blur might make someone rub his eyes, I figure it's safer than seeing a stranger breaking into a crime scene.

Another spell opened the locked front door, and I slipped inside. The place was cool and damp, reeking of mildew. I spell-locked the door behind me and cast a sensing spell. It came back negative. I recited another incantation and a ball of light appeared, hovering in my path.

Yep, that's a lot of spells in a short period of time, but that's what life is like for a witch. We can go days without exercising our powers, then we'll encounter a situation—usually involving the words *threat* and *danger*—and it's a regular paranormal power fest.

With the light ball illuminating my way, I searched for the basement stairs, weaving past the occasional piece of office furniture that people deemed too crappy to steal. I tried to picture what had happened here, with Ginny and Brandi and then Claire. Lucas would say trying to visualize what happened to a victim was yet another way to leap to unwarranted conclusions, and Paige would agree.

But they aren't me, and imagining the crime helps me see the victim as a person, not just a problem to be solved. For Paige and Lucas, empathy is never a problem—they're bursting with it. Me? Not so much.

The articles hadn't speculated whether the women had died here, but having seen the blood pools under them I was going to take the leap and say yes.

I tried to imagine what might draw me here. For Ginny and Brandi, the possibilities were endless—anything from a drug deal to a party to a hookup. If they were willing to trade a blow job for a hit, this would be a good place to do it.

The problem was Claire Kennedy. A college student on summer break, according to the paper. Honors student. Arts major. Wrote for the college paper. Quiet and straitlaced was the impression I got from the account. Looking around, I couldn't imagine anything that would bring *me* to this place—and straitlaced has never been an adjective applied to me. So what brought Claire?

That led to the bigger question. What brought a girl like Claire to Columbus at all? According to the article, she'd been here two weeks, coming right after her finals. Short of two broken legs, nothing would keep me here that long. Hell, with two broken legs I'd drag myself the twenty miles to the highway and hitch a ride.

I took out the crime-scene photos. Unlike the other two, Claire wasn't lying in her own blood. So shot-and-moved seemed a reasonable assumption for her. If she'd been killed else-where in the building, there would be blood traces—I couldn't imagine the owner had sprung for much in the way of cleaning afterward. I could search, but the cops would have already done that. I'd get the details from them.

When I finally located the basement door, I cast the sensing spell again. There was no sign the cops were still securing the scene. Jesse said they'd been here only yesterday, though.

My spell did detect small presences, but that was to be expected in a rat hotel like this. I searched for the big "ping" that said human and ignored the rest.

At the bottom of the stairs, I realized that finding the base-ment didn't mean finding the crime scene. I should have stopped at the police station first to let them know I was in town, so I could have sweet-talked some cop into telling me exactly where in this basement the bodies had been found.

I took out the photos. Concrete floor. Concrete wall. Yeah, that narrowed it down.

I started walking, light ball illuminating the photos as I

compared them to my surroundings, as if I was a TV detective, able to identify a speck of *Flora whateveris* on the photo and match it to one on the floor. I scanned the floor, searching for . . . oh, I don't know, matching dirt patterns? Then I caught sight of a torn piece of yellow plastic taped to a pillar.

"Or you could just look for crime-scene tape, stupid."

As I spoke, something scuttled to my left. I wheeled, hands poised to launch an energy bolt. I peered into the darkness, but couldn't see very far. I listened for the chattering of rats. Instead, I heard breathing.

I took a step. The breathing stopped. A long pause, then a gasp, like he couldn't hold his breath anymore. I murmured the sensing spell under my breath. It agreed something was there, but not a human-sized something.

I took another sliding step. The breathing came faster, as if in fear. I cast again, to be sure, and this time when I got the same result, I realized it *was* sensing a human, just a smaller one than I expected. I extinguished my light ball and walked toward the breathing sounds.

"Okay, kid," I said. "I know you're there, so—"

A flash blinded me.

"Don't move," said a girl's voice, squeaky with fear. A pale arm reached from the darkness, clutching a cell phone, finger over a button. "Take another step and I'll send your picture to the cops."

Smart kid. Bluffing, I was sure, but smart nonetheless.

"You've got a cell phone?" I rolled my eyes. "Kids these days. I wasn't allowed one until I was sixteen, and then I had to pay for my own plan."

The girl turned on a plastic flashlight, stepped out, and gave me a look that said she wasn't lowering her guard, no matter how friendly I seemed. Yep, smart kid.

Tiny kid, too, which explained the spell feedback. I'd put her around eight, maybe nine, probably the smallest in her class. She was skinny, with a thin face and twiglike arms, but not undernourished—her eyes were bright and her freckled face glowed. Her hair was her best feature, gleaming blond and tied back with a strip of pink lace that hung over one shoulder. She wore faded jeans and a sweatshirt with a worn decal. Hand-me-downs, but clean, the jeans patched with a rainbow on one knee and a skull and crossbones on the other. Interesting . . .

"So did you do it?" she asked, her gaze holding mine.

"Do what?"

She waved at the crime-scene photos clearly displayed in my hand.

"Shit! I mean . . ." A better choice of language escaped me and I flipped the photos over fast and tried to shove them back in the envelope.

"I read somewhere that killers sometimes come back to the scene," the girl said, matter-of-factly, like she was telling me that elephants are the largest land mammal.

I kept fumbling to get the pictures in the envelope.

"It's okay," she said. "I've seen them. Tim Bruyn from school showed me. His grandpa is the police chief. He's investigating the murders. Or he's supposed to be, but he's doing a lousy job."

"Is he?"

She nodded solemnly. "Everybody says so. Even Grandma. Not in front of me, of course, but I heard her say it on the phone, and she never says bad stuff about anyone."

"A good policy." I smiled, but she only stared at me, as if she could tell I didn't mean it.

"So that's your cell phone?" I said, pointing to it. "Pretty cool. Mine doesn't have a flash."

"It's my mom's."

"And she lets you use it? Very cool."

Again, she just stared at me with those appraising eyes. *Come on, kid. Help me out here.*

"Well, I'm not going to ask how you got in here," I said. "But it isn't the kind of place for kids to hang out, so I'll walk you upstairs—"

"I'm not hanging out. I'm investigating."

She tugged a backpack off her shoulder, reached in, and pulled out a pad of paper. She flipped to a page, then, pen poised, looked up at me. "Your name, please."

"Savannah Levine. Private investigator."

"License?"

I started pulling out my ID. She gave me a look that called me a moron.

"*Private investigator's* license?"

Damn, she was good. What did they teach kids in this town? Fortunately, I had one—two, actually, for both Oregon and Washington. I gave her both. She wasn't impressed; just jotted details down and handed them back.

"So you're an investigator, too," I said.

"No, I'm a kid."

"So how come you're here?"

"Because the police aren't."

"Ah. So you're investigating because you want to grow up to be a detective?"

"No." Her gaze lifted to mine. "I'm investigating because I want to know who killed my mother."

FOUR

IT WASN'T THAT I DIDN'T KNOW WHAT TO SAY—IT WAS THAT
I knew from experience that almost anything I did say would be
wrong. After my mom died, I wanted to plug my ears every time
someone found out . . . or zap them with an energy bolt before
they could speak.

It was always the same empty words. *I'm sorry for your loss*,
from people who didn't give a shit about me or my loss. *Deep
down, your mom was a good person*, from people who, deep
down, thought she was an evil bitch. *She's gone to a better
place.* That one killed me. Like any twelve-year-old gives a
damn where her dead mother went—all that matters is that
she's not with you.

The only thing I liked to hear was stories about her—something cool or funny she'd done. But I'd never met this girl's
mother, so I couldn't offer anything there. After fumbling
around, I said the obvious—you must be Ginny's daughter—
which *was* obvious because only Ginny Thompson had a child.

She nodded. "Her real name was Genevieve, but the newspapers didn't say that because the reporters were too lazy
to ask."

Stupid cops. Lazy reporters. A girl after my own heart.

"They didn't mention your name either."

"Kayla Thompson." She extended her hand.

I shook it. "Shouldn't you be in school?"

"I'm homeschooled. Grandma didn't like the way the other kids acted after my mom died." After what she'd said about the chief's grandson, I didn't blame her grandmother. I'd like to have a chat with the little ghoul's parents myself. "Grandma's at work today, so I'm staying with Aunt Rose. She thinks I'm at the library."

"Well, then, Kayla, since it seems we're both investigating this crime, we'd better get to work."

Kayla was not impressed by my lack of fingerprint powder and evidence bags. I tried to explain that wasn't how private investigators worked, but she clearly considered that a pathetic excuse. *She* had powder and plastic zip bags from her Junior Detective kit.

I did manage to redeem myself a bit by teaching her the proper way to use the powder. Then I left her to her work while I did mine. She was so quiet I'd almost forgotten she was there until she announced she had to go—her aunt was picking her up at the library and she needed to check out some books to show for her visit.

We went out the back door, then around the building together.

"Is he with you?" she asked, pointing. It was the guy from earlier, now standing in front of his BMW, hood open, scowling down as if he could shame the motor into turning over.

"Nope. Think I should offer to help?"

"You can fix cars?" Her look said she was mildly impressed.

"Cars, bikes . . . That's my motorcycle over there." I hoped to win some cool points for the bike, too, but she only glanced at it, then back to the guy with the BMW.

"I bet he can't fix it," she said. "I bet he can't even pump his own gas."

"You're probably right."

"You should see if you can help."

"Nah, I'll walk you to—"

"I've got a few minutes."

She started across the road and I hurried to catch up.

"Hey, there," I called. "Having trouble getting her running?"

He turned. He blinked, as if seeing a mirage, then turned back to glare at the misbehaving engine again.

"Transmission, I think," he said, with the air of a man who couldn't find the transmission on a dare, but wants to sound like he could reassemble one with his eyes shut.

"You're in luck. Transmissions are my specialty."

He eyed me, clearly torn between not really wanting to tell an attractive young woman to get lost, but not wanting her mucking about with his luxury car either.

"I'm going to call for a tow," he said.

Kayla snorted. "From where? Nearest tow truck is in Battle Ground." She gave him that same critical look I'd gotten earlier. "You don't think she can do it because she's a girl."

"Of course not. I just don't want to bother—"

"No bother," I said.

I walked over to my saddlebags and got out my tools. Then I set to work. It wasn't the transmission. I could have figured out what was wrong, but after a few minutes of hovering anxiously, the guy insisted I give up.

I wish I could say I was gracious about the blow-off. I wasn't. But he wasn't gracious either. All the more reason, I say, not to do favors, even for hot guys.

"Jerk," Kayla muttered as we walked away. "Real estate

vulture, I bet. They've been hovering, picking at the corpse of this town."

A line obviously picked up from eavesdropping on an adult conversation. I had a feeling Kayla did a lot of that. An only child, homeschooled, mother dead, no father in the picture, an off-kilter personality that would make most other kids steer clear. She'd spend a lot of time around adults. Probably, in some ways, thought of herself as one. A feeling I remembered well.

As I walked her to the library, there were a dozen questions I longed to ask—about her mother, about the investigation— but I suspected that if I started treating her as a witness, she'd shut down. Just another adult playing nice to get something in return. I'd see her around and maybe, if she decided I was up to the job, she'd share her thoughts on her own.

Before we parted, I asked where to find the police station and she directed me to a tiny house on Main Street, just past the downtown. When I walked in, two guys were standing in front of a huge desk, dwarfing an elderly receptionist. One man was in his early forties, his belly straining the buttons on his uniform. The other was in his twenties and would be a whole lot cuter if he cultivated a beard to hide a weak chin and golf-ball-size Adam's apple. The younger one was hamming it up for his fellow employees, telling them about a call from the night before.

"So Mel was cowering in the corner, Leslie waving around her big old frying pan, telling him if he's late again, she's gonna bash his damn brains in with it. He tried to explain—you know Mel, always got an excuse. So she swings that pan and he puts his arms up and, wham. He starts screaming about breaking his arm and you know what she says?"

The other officer answered in a falsetto. "Keep it up and I'll bust the other one."

The two guffawed, and the receptionist chimed in with creaky titters.

"You know what would make that story even funnier?" I said. "If it was the other way around, and ol' Mel was whaling on his wife with the frying pan."

The older cop scowled at me. "That wouldn't be funny at all."

"Kinda my point."

They all continued to stare. I reminded myself that ignorance is not idiocy. Or so I'm told.

"I don't get it," the younger cop finally said.

I was tempted to explain. Damn tempted. But mocking them probably wasn't the best way to make a good first impression. "I'd like to speak to Chief Bruyn."

"He's not here," the receptionist said.

"Do you know when he'll be back?"

"He went out."

"Can I make an appointment for later?"

"He's not here."

Sometimes you've got to figure that small-town people pull the rube routine just for us city folks, a passive-aggressive way of telling us to go fuck ourselves.

"Can you give him my card then?" I asked. "I'd like to speak to him as soon as he gets a chance."

The receptionist took it and laid it facedown on her desk, where I was sure it would accidentally slide into the trash the moment I left. The younger cop picked it up. He looked at me. Read it, lips moving, then pursing.

"Private investigator?"

"Yep." I flashed my license. "That's why I'd like to speak to Chief Bruyn. I've been hired to investigate Claire Kennedy's murder and I wanted to touch base with him first."

When no one said a word, I took that as a dismissal and left.

FIVE

MY FIRST BIG SOLO CASE AND I GOT REDNECK MORONS FOR law enforcement. Figured.

A tiny voice in my head—one that sounded a lot like Paige—said I should have kept my mouth shut about the frying pan incident. I doubted that would have helped, though.

I decided my next step would be to visit the diner I'd noticed downtown. As I walked, I tried to take in my surroundings, get a better sense of the town, but it was too damned depressing. Empty storefronts. Empty streets.

Even the few people I saw looked empty. Hopeless. A gaunt middle-aged woman standing in the window of a store festooned with Going Out of Business signs. Two boys no more than thirteen, kicking a can along the side of the road, skipping school and not caring who noticed. A pregnant teenage girl sitting on a dilapidated bench, as if hoping someone would drive by and whisk her off to a better life.

The diner looked like your stereotypical small-town eatery, right down to the vinyl seats and beehived waitress in a frilly dress better suited to someone half her age—and size. The patrons were all on the far side of fifty, most courting heart disease and diabetes, most wearing clothing bought in the last millennium.

I sat at the counter, ordered coffee and a slice of pie, then chatted with a couple of customers. Both were balding. Both wore button-down plaid shirts and jeans. Both seemed to have made the diner their new home after the sawmill shut down. The only way I could tell them apart was the accent—Bill's was local and Jacob's sounded like he'd come from the Southwest.

After some chitchat, I said, "I hear a young woman was murdered here about a week ago. I don't need to be worried, do I?"

"Not unless you plan to join that cult of wackos up on the hill," Jacob said.

The server rolled her eyes. "It's a *commune*."

"Same difference."

"There's a commune around here?" I asked.

"Cult."

"Commune," the server insisted.

I pushed my mug toward her for a refill. "Let me rephrase. There are people engaged in a group living arrangement that doesn't conform to social norms?"

The server—Lorraine by her name tag—laughed. "That's a good way of putting it. They aren't brainwashed cultists waiting for the aliens to come and take them away. Just nice young girls with a different way of living."

Jacob snorted. "Nice young girls living with one old guy doing who-knows-what."

"Oh, we know what they're doing," Bill said with a snicker.

"So what is that, if not a cult?" Jacob said.

"Heaven," Bill replied.

Laughter from the few patrons listening in.

"Was the girl who was killed last week from there?"

"Yeah," Jacob said. "And she seemed like such a nice kid."

Lorraine glowered. "She *was* a nice kid. They all are. It's not

Charles Manson up there. Just kids experimenting with a different way of life. I did some of that at their age."

"I heard there were two other girls killed last fall," I said. "Were they part of the, uh, group?"

"Ginny and Brandi?" Bill shook his head. "Those girls were into a whole other kind of trouble."

"Ginny and Brandi were lost souls," Lorraine said. "Those girls up at Alastair's place are lost, too, but they're getting back on track."

"Alastair? So he's the—?"

The door banged open. In strode a man of about sixty, rail-thin but walking like a man twice his weight. He wore a uniform and his gaze was fixed on me.

I slid off my stool, hand extended. "Chief Bruyn. I'm—"

"Savannah Levine," he said with a scowl. "Private investigator."

Heads whipped my way. Lorraine stepped back fast, distancing herself. Bill scowled at me. Jacob looked confused, like a dog getting a kick after a treat.

"That's right," I said. "I left my card at the station. I wanted to let you know I'm here before I started investigating."

"*If* you start investigating," Bruyn said.

Actually, there was nothing he could do to stop me, but I kept my mouth shut.

"Well, you're off to a hell of a start, Miss Levine, bothering these people."

"She wasn't bothering anyone, Chris," said Jacob. "Just asking about Claire."

"Oh, was she? Miss Levine? Come with me, please. You and I need to have a talk."

SIX

AS BRUYN MARCHED ME DOWN MAIN STREET, PEOPLE GAWKED through windows, some even stepping outside for a better look. I might as well have been in handcuffs—and I was sure, in more than a few recountings of this story, I would be.

Now, as for why the local police chief was involved in an investigation that should have been handled by the county sheriff's department, Jesse had said the county was officially investigating, but when the local leads went cold, they'd backed off and now the town looked to Bruyn for answers. Or something like that. It'd been a long explanation and I hadn't paid much attention. All that mattered to me was that Bruyn was the guy I needed to impress. And I was doing a bang-up job of it so far.

When we reached the station, Bruyn ushered me inside.

"Beth?" he said to the receptionist.

Her white head popped up from behind the desk and she smiled.

"Is anyone else here?" he asked.

"No, dear. I mean, sir."

"Good. I need you to walk up to the grocer and buy some coffee. We're low on cream, too. Take your time."

"But—"

He stepped up to the desk, lowering his voice. "We talked about this when I gave you the job, Mom."

Mom? He was kidding, right? I looked from him to the old woman. Nope. Not kidding.

"There are some things you can't be a part of," he said. "We discussed that."

She shot an anxious glance my way.

"I need you to leave," Bruyn said. "Can you do that?"

She nodded and scooped up her purse. As she passed, she gave me a look that was almost pitying.

A million stories about small-town cops ran through my mind, images of pistol-whippings and broken fingers. Granted, 99.9 percent of those images came from movies and TV, but still, every now and then I'd hear a story that suggested some of that shit happened in real life.

With a binding spell at the ready, I followed him into his office. He kicked out a chair. "Sit."

I did.

He walked to the window, looked out, and nodded as the tiny figure of his mother headed downtown. Then he filled two mugs from the pot on his desk.

"What do you take?"

"Um, black . . ."

"Tough girl, huh?"

I braced myself, but when he turned, he was smiling. He handed me the mug and started adding cream and sugar to his own.

"Little young to be a private eye, aren't you? I've got a grand-nephew at Everest about your age."

"I've been with my firm for five years."

"Firm?" He took my card from his pocket. "Cortez-Winterbourne Investigations. Out of Portland."

I nodded. "We have a staff of four investigators with over thirty years' experience among them. On this particular case we're working in conjunction with a Seattle firm. Their lead investigator will be joining me soon. My primary job here is information gathering."

He nodded, then perched on the edge of his desk. "So who hired you?"

"Claire Kennedy's mother."

"I can check that, you know."

"Please do. The lead investigator is Jesse Aanes, from the Seattle firm I mentioned. Here's his card." I passed it over.

He took it. "So Mrs. Kennedy doesn't think small-town cops are up to the job?"

I struggled to remember the line Lucas always used. "No, she just hoped a private investigator might be able to . . . cut corners." Not exactly what Lucas would say, but I was improvising. "Go where the law can't."

"Huh."

He held my gaze. I probably should have dropped it, acted deferential, but it took everything I had just to hold it, calmly, not challenging.

"Let's cut the bullshit, Miss Levine. Maybe you talked Mrs. Kennedy into hiring you, but I know who called you first. It was Paula, wasn't it?"

"Paula?"

His face darkened. "You really think I'm an idiot, don't you? Small-town cop doesn't know his elbow from his asshole. Paula Thompson called you because she doesn't think I give a shit about what happened to her druggie daughter. She can't afford to hire a PI, though, so she gets you to hit up Claire Kennedy's rich parents. Am I right?"

I looked him in the eye. "No."

He glowered at me, and held my gaze. Did Lucas and Paige have to go through this crap every time they spoke to local law enforcement? I was tempted to walk out and dare him to do anything about it. I was even more tempted to practice my new persuasion spell. Memory loss in the recipient was the most common side effect. I could live with that, but there was also the possibility of a three-day power outage for the caster. I'd have to be in serious shit to risk that.

"Look," I said. "Paula Thompson has nothing to do with me being here, but I can tell that you don't believe me. So let's cut to the chase. You think Paula hired me to embarrass you, correct?"

"Correct."

"To do that, presumably I'd need to solve the case and make an ass out of you."

His face darkened again, as if he was two seconds from telling me to watch my mouth.

"What if I told you I don't care who claims the arrest?" I said. "In fact, you're welcome to it."

"Exactly how stupid—"

You already asked that. And, trust me, you don't want an answer. "The collar doesn't do me any good. All I need is a recommendation from you to my employer, telling them I was instrumental in solving the case."

He chewed that over, eyes narrowing in speculation now. Either I was naïve or I was desperate to prove myself on this job. Neither actually—a collar meant media attention, which we avoided, but he didn't know that. Naïve or desperate, I could be useful on a case that had obviously stalled.

"I'm not here to take the case away from you," I said after a minute of silence. "My client wants me to help you find who did it."

"Oh, I know who did it. I'm just compiling the evidence."

"Then maybe I can help with that. Like I said, there are things I can do, places I can go. No matter how good a cop you are, you're still bound by cop rules. Those girls deserve the best and most complete investigation they can get."

He considered that. Or at least he pretended to. Truth was, he didn't give a shit about the victims; I could see that in his eyes. But he did care about his job.

"All right," he said. "But if you interfere in my investigation in any way . . ."

He blustered for a few more minutes as I struggled to pay attention.

Finally he ran out of steam and I assured him I'd be a good little PI. "But to do a proper job, I'll need full access to the files," I said. "Crime-scene photos. Lab findings. Coroner's report. Witness interviews. A copy of everything. I'd hate to waste time going over ground you've already covered."

"I'll give you the lab findings and the coroner's report. You come back to me with proof that you can handle more and I'll give you more."

In other words, he'd dole out tidbits as I fed him my findings. That was fine. This place looked easy enough to break into. I'd get the files myself. So I agreed, and he ran off a copy of the lab and coroner's findings, and as a bonus, threw in the name of the killer.

"Cody Radu. Ginny Thompson's boyfriend."

"But you don't have enough evidence yet to charge him."

Bruyn snorted. "No one in this town needs a scrap of evidence to tell us Cody's guilty." He cocked his head, then glanced to the window. "And speaking of that son of a bitch, I hear him now."

He walked to the front door and opened it just as a rusty pickup squealed past, muffler dragging and belching blue smoke, earning a glare from a guy getting out of his silver SUV across the road.

The pickup driver was a weasel-faced guy with hair that hadn't been washed since Christmas. He slowed to give me a skeevy once-over, mouthing something I was sure wasn't hello. Then he shot Bruyn the finger, gunned the engine, and roared off.

"Nice guy," I said.

"Oh, Cody's a sweetheart. Look at that bastard. Off playing golf, not a care in the world."

Stereotyping is bad. Living with Lucas and Paige, that's a lesson that's been drilled into my head. I can't say it always penetrated. However hard I tried to imagine the loser in the pickup swinging a nine iron at the country club, it just wasn't working.

A boom from across the road made me jump, and I looked to see the SUV owner standing at the back of his vehicle, hatch closed, golf bag in hand. He was in his midthirties, clean-shaven, blandly good-looking, dressed in a bright blue golf shirt and pressed trousers. I could see *him* at the country club. But with Ginny Thompson? No way.

He strolled up the walk to a house—a picture-perfect over-sized English cottage, with a swing on the porch, ivy climbing over every surface, and a cat napping in the garden. It was no McMansion, but it was the fanciest place I'd seen in town. Definitely the prettiest thing on Main Street.

The SUV now parked out front was a Lexus, as was the sedan in the drive, both gleaming so brightly I was sure if you opened the doors, you'd still get that new-car smell. An equally new powerboat took up most of the driveway. Behind it, a garage was under construction. Someone definitely wasn't feeling Columbus's economic pinch. Taking advantage of it, more like—from the construction, it looked as if they'd moved in recently, snatching up the best house in town.

The door opened to a pretty blond woman holding an infant. The guy bounced up the steps, gave his baby a kiss, put his arm around his wife, and ushered them back inside.

"Makes you want to puke, doesn't it?" Bruyn said.

I nodded. Domesticity has that effect on me. Then I looked at him.

"That's Cody Radu?" I said. "Ginny's boyfriend?"

"Yep."

Was Bruyn bullshitting me? Sending me on a wild-goose chase after the wrong guy? Easy enough to find out. Ask someone. Just not Bruyn.

As Bruyn was walking me out with my files, I promised to provide him with regular updates.

"Make sure you do or you won't find this town nearly so cooperative."

"Yes, sir."

We were at the door when it opened, and in walked the guy whose BMW I'd failed to fix earlier. He frowned at me, then turned to Bruyn.

"Chief Bruyn?"

"That's right."

The man flipped out a badge. "Detective Michael Kennedy. Dallas PD. I believe you're investigating the death of my sister, Claire. I'm here to help."

SEVEN

BRUYN LED KENNEDY INTO HIS OFFICE AND PERCHED ON the desk. Kennedy took the chair I'd sat in earlier. I stood inside the door, file folders in hand.

Kennedy explained that he'd come to offer his help solving his sister's murder. He'd already spoken to the sheriff's department and they said they didn't have a problem with it, but he'd have to clear things with Bruyn.

"I have resources and contacts. I know what it's like, everyone tightening their belts. A multiple-murder investigation must have your budget shot already."

Kennedy was playing it just right. Bruyn fairly rubbed his hands with glee at the prospect of getting a big-city detective, free of charge. The fact that the detective didn't look over thirty and was the victim's *brother* seemed lost on him.

He put the same deal to Kennedy that he had to me. Kennedy was welcome to investigate, provided he kept Bruyn abreast of his findings. Kennedy was fine with that.

"You don't call your mom nearly as often as you should," I finally said.

Kennedy jumped.

"Savannah Levine," I said, extending a hand. "The private

investigator whose partner your mother hired to investigate your sister's death."

"If you're referring to Annette Kennedy, that's Claire's mother, not mine. And, no, I don't speak to her any more than necessary. If she hired you, I'm sorry. Claim your time and move on. I'm here now."

"Does that one work for you a lot?"

"I'm a professional."

"Then I guess you win." I waved my license. "I got this out of a gumball machine. You may be a cop, but this isn't Dallas. I'm the professional here."

The look he gave me made me want to slap him with an energy bolt.

"Well now, this is a situation, isn't it?" Bruyn said. Then he smiled, and I knew what was coming next. "I'm sure, Detective, that you have resources and contacts that I don't. So does Miss Levine—different resources, different contacts, and a different set of playing rules. Between the two of you—"

"I don't work with private detectives," Kennedy said.

"I'm not suggesting you pool resources," Bruyn said. "But your sister deserves the best investigation possible, which means as many investigators as possible. You can both have a go."

I could tell Kennedy didn't like that. If he made Bruyn choose, I knew who'd lose.

"How's your car doing?" I said.

"What?" Kennedy said.

"Your car. Is it fixed?"

"No, but even if it doesn't get repaired, I can rent one, so if you're suggesting I'm lacking transportation—"

"Let me take another shot at it. If I can't fix your car in one hour, I'll leave."

He eyed me. He hated reducing this to a wager, but I hadn't

made much headway the last time. Finally he tossed me the keys.

"She needs the oil topped off," I said an hour later as the car purred beside me. "And the driver's side rear tire is a little low. Otherwise, you're good to go. And, apparently, I'm good to stay—on the case."

"Hold on."

He took the car for a spin around the lot. And I do mean a spin, driving like he was on a race circuit. I was impressed. I could say I was surprised, too, but I'd seen the modifications he'd had done. Michael Kennedy might act like a guy who'd never take a hairpin curve at sixty miles an hour, but his car said otherwise.

He stopped beside me and rolled down the window. "Funny, seems you had a lot more trouble with it earlier."

"Yes. I was faking you out. I'm psychic. I knew you were Claire's cop brother and I knew I'd need to make this bet to stay on the case. Impressing a hot guy is great, but keeping a case I really want is much better motivation."

He opened his mouth, closed it, frowning, as he replayed what I just said. He busied himself adjusting the mirror, then cleared his throat.

"I don't like this, Ms. Levine. Solving my sister's murder is not—"

"—a game to you. I know. And it's not to me either. It's a job. Yes, I'm young. Yes, I don't have your experience. But solving this will go a long way toward cementing my reputation, so I'm not going to screw it up. Now, if you'll excuse me, I have leads to pursue, as I'm sure you do. Let's just try not to trip over each other chasing them."

I made it to the sidewalk when my phone chirped, telling me I had a text.

It was from Adam. He'd sent it while I'd been busy with Kennedy's car.

No call. No txt. U alive?

I sent a text. *Sry. Working.*

The reply came back before I could even close my phone.

Can I help? Rsrch? Bkgrd chk?

I *could* use him for background checks on Bruyn, Kennedy, and Cody Radu, but I reminded myself that I had an official partner on this—Jesse. If I needed help, I should go to him. Better yet, I should do it myself when I got to the motel.

So I sent another text. *I'm good. Will call l8r.*

One word: *ok.* I closed the phone and headed back to the diner. I had no idea what kind of reception I'd get there. Probably be kicked out on my ass. But I needed information, and this was the best place to get it.

Turned out Bruyn had already called Lorraine to spread the word that he'd appreciate any help folks could give me and Kennedy, citing my line about the girls deserving the best investigation possible.

That was all the encouragement the diner patrons needed. This was the kind of town where detectives and private investigators are mythical beings found only on a TV screen. I haven't been cooler since my senior year, when I showed up at school on my motorcycle.

I regaled my new friends with tales of the dangerous and adventurous life of a PI. Yep, I lied. I've learned that no one's particularly impressed with my stories of long, treacherous days spent navigating the deadly waters of the Internet, conducting background searches.

Once I figured I'd done my duty, I demonstrated a real-life

application of those cool PI skills by questioning the patrons about the murders. I asked about the victims, but their answers boiled down to this: They didn't know Claire, and the other two had been addicted to everything, good for nothing.

"Now, just a second," Lorraine said after her customers had fallen silent. "Ginny could be decent enough if you got her alone. She was just weak, doing whatever Brandi wanted. It was like that from the time they were kids."

"Maybe so," Jacob said. "But let's face it—those girls ended up right where everyone expected them to, as much as we might have wished otherwise. If Chief Bruyn wasn't exactly twisting himself in knots to solve the murders, that's why."

"Oh, that's not why," Lorraine muttered.

"Is it something to do with Paula Thompson?" I said. "I got the feeling there was bad blood between her and Bruyn."

Lorraine shook her head, unwilling to answer. Jacob didn't share her qualms. "Paula worked for him," he said. "Until she got tired of running and quit."

"Running?"

"Around and around the desk. Chief Bruyn had a thing for her. But Paula? She runs fast."

A chorus of laughter from everyone within hearing distance.

"Paula's a smart cookie," Lorraine said. "After she had Ginny, she got a lot more careful about men."

"Another lesson Ginny never learned," Jacob said.

Lots of solemn nods on that one.

"You mean Ginny's boyfriend, right?" I said. "A local guy?"

"Cody Radu," Jacob said.

Mutters circled the room. Even Lorraine didn't jump in to his defense.

Jacob was the first to speak. "Cody's a rich brat who thinks he's a lot smarter, a lot better looking, and a lot richer than he is. Big fish, small pond. His daddy's a developer. Cody works for him. Not exactly the Vanderbilts, but around here, they're high society, which is why they stay."

"So it was *rumored* Cody was seeing Ginny?"

Lorraine snorted and muttered, "No rumor about it. He was and everyone knew it."

"Did Ginny threaten to tell his wife?"

Jacob shook his head. "Tiffany Radu knew all about Ginny. She married the local rich boy and isn't about to let him go, no matter what."

Which sounded like a motive for murder, if that rich boy decided he wanted to permanently relocate to greener pastures.

"Cody likes to wallow in the mud," Jacob said. "Tiffany's happy to let him, as long as he keeps the muck out of her pretty little life."

Lorraine shushed him, but only halfheartedly.

"Are we talking more muck than trashy girlfriends?" I asked.

"Sure are," Jacob said. "Dope, parties, hookers. Hell, I've even heard he runs a white slavery ring out of Seattle."

"Okay, that's enough," Lorraine said. She looked at me. "Folks around here don't have a lot of time for Cody Radu, but all that is just rumor."

"Like hell," Jacob said. "Chief Bruyn's been investigating him for years. Everyone knows he's up to a shitload of crap, but the cops can't pin a thing on him. That's how he figures Ginny and Brandi got killed. Maybe even Claire Kennedy."

"Blackmail or extortion," I said. "They threatened to give Bruyn the proof he needed."

"You got it. The way those girls were killed? Wasn't about sex. Wasn't about rage. It was execution, pure and simple."

EIGHT

NEXT STOP: THE COMMUNE.

Before leaving the diner, I'd grilled Lorraine and her patrons on the local cult/commune. They were very reluctant to talk about it, wanting to leave the group in peace. Yeah, right. Show me a town where no one jumps at the chance to gossip about the local religious sect, and I'll show you a town full of deaf-mutes.

The guy who ran the place was Alastair Koppel, a former Columbus resident who'd gone off to college and never came back. Or, at least, not until he wanted an isolated place to start a cult of nubile young women. According to the diner folk, he had at least a dozen of them living up there. Just him and the girls baking cookies.

Yep, cookies. That's apparently how they made their living. Like a cross between Moonies and Girl Scouts, I imagined, hanging out at airports, giving away world peace with every box of thin mints purchased.

The cult was on a farm. Otherwise, it wasn't what I had in mind at all. No guard-dogs. No security cameras. No booby traps. Not even an eight-foot fence to hide the orgies. Very disappointing.

As I was pulling off my helmet, an unearthly screech shattered the silence. The frantic clucking that followed didn't promise anything nearly as nefarious, but I was an optimist.

I followed the sound to the first building past the gate: a chicken coop. Outside it, a blond ponytailed woman was hacking the head off a chicken, the last victim still twitching, headless, by her feet.

I looked around for signs that I'd interrupted an animal sacrifice in progress. Unless cooking pots were the latest rage in occult rites, though, I was out of luck.

I waited until she was done decapitating the chicken before saying, "Got tired of the early morning wake-up calls?"

She turned. She was about my age, but with an air that said she hadn't acted my age in a long time. Tall, lanky, and beautiful in a way that could make her a model if she deigned to wear makeup, but with an expression that said "fat chance" to that. She wiped her bloodied hands on her apron and gave me the kind of assessment I haven't had since Paige brought me before the Coven. Considering how that turned out, this was not a good sign.

"Savannah Levine," I said, extending a hand.

She held her bloodied hands palms up. "You might not want to do that."

"I'm washable," I said.

She shook my hand.

I pointed at the dead chicken. "Did he crow at dawn one too many times?"

"No, *she* didn't crow at all. They're laying hens that reached the end of their laying days." The woman pointed at the pot. "Soup time."

Nice retirement package. I looked down at the headless chicken, now lying motionless on its side.

"Lorraine at the diner said to ask for Megan," I said. "I'm

guessing that's you." If this wasn't the woman in charge, I'd hate to be the one who tried to order her around.

"I am. You're here about the opening?"

"No, I'm investigating Claire Kennedy's death."

I braced myself for the stiffening back, the hardening face, but she actually seemed to relax.

"Well, then, you've come to the right place," she said. "Claire died here. The victim of an unspeakable sex act gone horribly awry. Isn't that what you heard?"

"Nope."

"Then it must be the satanic ritual. We ran out of babies, so we used her. Now we're down to these ladies." She held up a chicken. "Sure you don't want to apply for that opening?"

"The unspeakable sex acts might change my mind, but for now I'm happy with my current employment. The story I heard was that Claire wanted out, so Alastair killed her and dumped her body in town."

"Boring."

"I thought so, too."

She laid the chickens on an old wooden table. "Really, we don't need to kill anyone who wants to leave. The brainwashing works just fine. If that fails, there are always drugs. And, of course, chaining the girls to their beds drastically cuts back on the runaway rate."

She started plucking the first chicken. "Yes, Claire was one of ours. She joined two weeks before she was killed. We didn't know her well, but we'd like her killer caught, particularly since he seems to have a fondness for young women, and we don't like foxes in our henhouse."

"Understandable. Now, there were two other—"

"Ginny and Brandi. I saw them in town a few times." She registered her opinion in a single lip curl. "I wouldn't let them stay here if they asked, and they didn't ask. This is a place for women who want to straighten out their lives, and those girls liked theirs just fine."

"So they never had any contact with Alastair?"

"Outside of participating in a few bouts of wild group sex?" Megan set down the chicken. "Let's get this out of the way now. Yes, we have one man and a houseful of young women, but it's not what everyone thinks."

"No orgies? Damn. There goes my application."

She smiled. "Sorry to disappoint, but Alastair has realized there's another advantage to having a house filled with young women. A far more profitable one."

My brows shot up.

She laughed. "You have a dirty mind, you know that? What we sell here, as you may have heard, is cookies."

She motioned me away from the stink of the coop and I smelled something far sweeter wafting from an open side door up at the house.

"Ever heard of Taste of Heaven cookies?" Megan asked.

"Sorry. I bake my own." Close enough.

"I guarantee they aren't as good as ours. We aren't talking Mr. Christie or even Mrs. Fields. These are top-end gourmet cookies, twelve dollars a dozen, made from farm-fresh eggs and butter." She pointed to the chickens, then to a barn. "Fair-trade dark and milk chocolate. Microfarm macadamia nuts from Hawaii and pecans from Georgia. Organic, kosher, nut-free, you want it, we offer it. Even in today's economy, we can't keep up with the orders."

"Comfort food is recession-proof."

"So we're hoping." She walked back and picked the last few feathers from the chicken carcass. "If you're looking for lost and vulnerable souls brainwashed into slavery, you've come to the wrong place. Yes, we have a few recovering addicts and abuse victims. Alastair was a group-home counselor, and he's a licensed therapist. What you'll mostly find here, though, is young women overdosed on dreams. Like me. Fast-tracked through an MBA from Columbia, got a Wall Street job, nearly killed myself with uppers so I could make money that I didn't have time to spend."

"So you traded in your BlackBerry for . . ." I waved at the dead chickens.

"A life of eviscerating poultry?" A sardonic smile. "Not what you'd choose, I suspect. And not what any of the girls here would choose, which is why you don't see them helping me. I spent summers on my grandparents' farm. Mucking out cow barns might not be every MBA's dream job, but after a year on Wall Street, it started looking damned attractive."

"The simpler life," I said, trying to sound as if I understood the appeal. "Between the MBA and the farm experience, you must be a valuable part of the, uh, group here."

"I am. And I'm well compensated for it, too." She started plucking the other chicken. "But if I wanted to leave tomorrow, I could. No one would stop me. No one would stop any of the girls. Unhappy workers aren't productive, and we always have an applicant pool lined up to get in. Even if you wanted to join, you'd only get on the waiting list. We've filled Claire's spot already. Alastair is in a therapy session with the new girl right now."

"Can I speak to him when he's done?"

"Sorry. He's tied up until dinner."

Convenient. "Can I make an appointment?"

"You can try, but he's very busy."

"And the girls? Can I speak to any of them?"

"If you come back after dinner. We're running a business here."

I didn't push; didn't say I'd be back later either. As reassuring as her earlier spiel had been, it sounded like just that—public relations lines. By dinner, she'd have had time to tell the girls exactly what to say. That wouldn't do.

NINE

MEGAN WATCHED UNTIL I WALKED OUT THE GATE. THEN
I rolled my bike behind some trees, cast a blur spell, and
slipped around the side of the house, following my nose to an
open door around the rear. As I approached, I rubbed the back
of my neck. A headache was settling in. I don't get them often,
but my motorcycle helmet was new, and sat different from my
last one.

Once out of sight of the chicken coop, I ended the spell,
walked to the screen door, and rapped. A dark-haired girl, no
more than eighteen, glanced up, startled. I waved my PI license.
She opened the door.

I introduced myself and added that Megan said I could speak
to the girls, which was technically true. That put her at ease. She
gave me her name—Deirdre—and a cookie—chocolate-chunk,
still warm from the oven. After one bite I declared it delicious
and offered to buy a box. She got one off a shelf and set it on the
counter.

As the cookies cooled, we stepped outside and chatted, long
enough for me to realize this was the girl I wanted to talk to,
someone who liked a bit of gossip and wasn't quite smart
enough to know when to keep her mouth shut.

"I was hoping to talk to Alastair," I said. "But Megan says he's in a session. She really didn't seem to want me talking to him." I nibbled the cookie. "Seems suspicious . . ."

Deirdre laughed. "No. She just doesn't want you talking to Alastair."

"So Megan and Alastair are . . . a couple."

"Sometimes. When there's not a new girl sharing his bed."

"Is that a requirement? For new girls?"

"Oh, no. Some girls do, some don't. It's up to them. He's a nice guy. Not bad looking . . . for his age."

"And there aren't many guys up here to choose from."

She grinned. "Exactly."

Compulsory orgies are all well and fine, but it'd be a lot easier to sleep at night if you told yourself the girls were coming to you of their own free will. Easier on the ego, too.

"And Megan fills the void between girls," I said. "So how did she feel about Claire coming along, shoving her aside?"

"I can't say for sure that Claire was sleeping with him, but Megan figured it was only a matter of time." She leaned over. "Let's just say we're all really happy that the new girl isn't exactly gorgeous. When Megan's not getting any, we all pay the price."

"And Claire was one of those times."

"Oh, yeah. Alastair liked Claire. She wasn't as pretty as Megan, but she was just as smart, without the bitch-itude. Claire and Alastair had private sessions all the time. It was supposedly therapy but . . ." She waggled her brows. "It was a lot of sessions and—"

"Deirdre?" Megan called from the kitchen. "Where are you? These cookies are still baking on this hot sheet. I've told you to take them off—"

I backed up, but not fast enough to get around the corner.

Megan glared at me as Deirdre slipped inside. I caught the screen door and followed her in.

"Sorry," I said, lifting my half-eaten cookie. "I smelled them and couldn't resist. I was just buying a box." I waved at the one on the counter.

Megan handed me the box and pointed at the door. I pulled a twenty from my pocket. She shook her head and kept pointing.

"Now, let's grab a couple of cookies while they're warm . . ." a man's voice said.

Megan moved in for the block, swinging the kitchen door partially closed. I caught only a glimpse of a man with silvery hair and an angular, patrician face. I got a better look at the girl walking beside him. She was, as Deirdre put it, not gorgeous. Her broad face and pug nose would have been framed better by a short, bouncy haircut. Long, straight, dirty-blond hair didn't help. Neither did her frown as she looked at me, squinting slightly, like she'd left her glasses at home.

"I'm—" I began.

"We'll bring cookies for you and Amy into the dining room, Alastair," Megan said. "Deirdre has spilled some sugar and I don't want it tracked all over the house."

If Alastair noticed me, he gave no sign, just saying "all right," and leading the girl—Amy—away.

Megan turned to me and wordlessly pointed at the door. I left. She trailed until I was outside the gate, then stood on the lawn, watching.

As I was passing the gate, something caught my eye. A smear of dark blood on the wooden post.

I bent to fuss with my pant leg in order to get a better look. Someone had drawn what looked like a talisman. In blood. Sure it might have been red paint, but my money was on blood. When

I glanced back, Megan was still watching. I waved. As she turned away, I surreptitiously snapped a picture of the red mark with my phone. Then I got on my bike and rode back to town.

Next stop: that building where the trucker said his buddy had seen a satanic ritual. I doubted there'd be anything left after eight months, but it was worth a look.

As I walked, I was checking out Main Street, mentally constructing a map of Columbus. Maybe I was just in a more hopeful mood than I'd been earlier, but the town seemed brighter now.

I still saw the For Sale signs on the shops, but I also noticed optimistic Opening Soon! signs on a couple. A banner over Main Street announced the annual strawberry social. Another in front of the library congratulated "Steve and Dawn" on their wedding. A shopkeeper helped an elderly woman load groceries into her car. I saw the pregnant teenage girl again, too, this time coming out of the diner, smiling, hand-in-hand with a boy carrying a steel lunchbox, and realized she hadn't been waiting to leave, just waiting for someone to come home.

Columbus might be a dying town, but not everyone was willing to give up the fight so easily. I admired that, and I was still looking around when a silver SUV pulled up in front of the post office. Cody Radu. He ignored the No Stopping signs. Hell, he didn't even bother pulling to the curb. Just stopped, slammed her into park, and hopped out.

I swung my gaze away. I'd get around to Cody eventually. Until then, I'd take no interest in the guy. Make him wonder *why* I was taking no interest. Make him sweat.

From the corner of my eye, I could see him checking me out. It wasn't the furtive interest of Michael Kennedy or even the lascivious ogle of the knuckle-dragger in the pickup. This was a cold, hard once-over, like I was an item on a menu, his to order if he decided I looked tasty. I kept walking.

I found the store—an empty furniture shop, sign announcing all inventory at 20 percent off, then 50 percent, then in final, desperate handwritten red strokes, 75 percent off, final sale.

I went around back, presuming that was where the trucker entered, and found a huge double door for the furniture place, a sign with foot-high letters announcing Deliveries.

The delivery door was dented so badly I was surprised it still closed. Kicked in by someone looking for a private place to conduct rituals? That might explain the shiny big padlock on it now.

An unlock spell cleared the way. Inside, I cast a sensing spell that came back clean. There were two doors off the loading dock. One led to an empty room with enough electrical outlets and phone jacks to tell me it had once held desks. The other was a bathroom. At the end, the hall opened into the display gallery.

The place had been stripped bare and kept reasonably clean, the owner still apparently optimistic about its resale value. A thin layer of dust said that optimism was waning, but the unit was still tidy enough to be shown. Too tidy to be an ideal place for anyone to practice the dark arts.

As I walked into the gallery, though, I could see a circle of black on the floor. I knelt and ran my finger over the ring. Wax. A black candle had sat here, dripping, for hours. I looked at the front and frowned. Big display windows. Not even boarded up. Who would conduct a ritual when anyone walking past could see the candle burning?

Near the candle wax, I noticed red smears on the linoleum. I bent and touched them. Long dried and faint, as if someone had mopped them up. I licked my finger and smudged some. Definitely red. Too red to be blood?

I took a picture and compared it with the one from the commune gate. The resolution was crap, though. I needed to see both on a laptop screen and zoom in.

The trucker's buddy said he'd seen a dead cat, too. You couldn't have a black mass without a dead cat. Or so said common wisdom. The truth was that cats—or sacrifice of any kind—had nothing to do with a real satanic black mass.

I searched the room, but found no sign of cats. I did, however, find a pile of rags in the corner. Black rags.

I reached down and grabbed an edge. It wasn't rags, but a huge sheet of black fabric. Other pieces lay beneath it, some black, some white, one red. The piece in my hand seemed like some kind of cape.

Something dropped from the fabric as it unraveled, and landed with a dull thump. I glanced down and saw a hand. A human hand, pale in the dim light, the severed stump nestled in the fabric.

A creak sounded behind me. I wheeled as a shadow slunk from the hall. My fingers flew up in a knockback spell before I could think. A gasp as the figure flew back. Shoes scuffled, a door banged, and a man said, "In here!"

I backed up to the wall and cast a cover spell just as two men burst through the door. One was Cody Radu. The other was the younger officer.

The cop looked around. Cody passed him, circling the room. I shifted my gaze to the pile of cloth in the corner. When I'd dropped the cape, it had settled over the hand. Two curved fingers still peeked out.

Cody walked right past me, then planted himself in front of the pile.

"There's no one here, Mr. Radu," the cop said.

"Bill saw a girl sneak in the back," Cody said. "He flagged me down as I was leaving the post office . . . not five minutes after that private-eye chick walked by. And someone opened the lock on the door."

"Okay, but there's no one here now. I don't know what you expect me to do, sir."

"I expect you to earn what I pay you. I expect you to protect my interests, and as the owner of this building, this is one of my interests."

"Okay but . . ." The young officer turned, surveying the room. "There's nothing here to steal."

"It's my property. That's all that matters. I want a new lock on the door and drive-bys every two hours. If you see that lock broken again, you call me."

"Yes, sir."

They left. I cast my sensing spell. The building was empty.

So Cody Radu was paying off one of the local cops. That was definitely something to keep in mind, but right now, I was more interested in that severed hand.

I crouched and gingerly peeled back the cape covering the hand. The hand was fresh, no sign of decay. The skin shone unnaturally. Preserved?

I was betting preserved. In wax, it looked like. Which meant I knew what this was—the Hand of Glory. Years ago, one had been planted at our house . . . right after a black mass had been staged, complete with dead cats. That had been the work of a half-demon hired by my father, who'd been trying to get custody of me by spooking Paige with the threat of exposure.

I touched the severed hand. Cold, as I expected. Oddly smooth, too, even for wax. I lifted it, wrapped in cloth. From the severed end protruded a bone. A bone that looked . . . silver.

I squinted in the dim light. Not a bone, but a metal rod. And the severing cut? Perfectly even.

I was holding a mannequin's hand.

I grabbed the black cloth and shook it out. Definitely a cape. Under it was more clothing. A shapeless white shirt. A red velvet bustier. And, at the bottom of the pile, more mannequin parts— the other hand and the head. The "stumps" of both had been painted red.

"Props," I muttered. "They're props."

Someone had staged a fake black mass here, complete with fake body parts, probably designed to scare the crap out of someone. Maybe someone supernatural.

I took photos of the props, then put them back the way I'd found them, gave the room one last look, then got out of there.

I was halfway to my bike when my phone rang. "People Are Strange." My ringtone for anyone I don't know.

"Savannah Levine," I said.

"Hello, it's Michael Kennedy. We met earlier?"

"Detective Kennedy. How's it going? Solve the case yet?"

A small noise that could have been a laugh. "No. I just . . . I wanted to apologize for being a jerk at Bruyn's office."

"Okay."

Silence. I let it tick to ten seconds, then said, "If you're expecting me to say you weren't a jerk, this will be a very short call. I could point out that you'd already achieved jerk status before the chief's office, but that would be rude. Apology accepted."

This time I was sure he laughed. "Well, at least you're honest."

"I am nothing if not honest, Detective Kennedy. Now, if you'll excuse—"

"Do you have plans for dinner?"

Now it was my turn to hesitate. "It was the hot-guy comment, wasn't it?"

A chuckle. "Could be."

Liar, liar. I knew what drove this sudden interest.

"Sure," I said. "Pick me up at the Rose Haven Motel at seven. There doesn't seem to be anything decent in this town, so we'll have to go elsewhere. I like Italian and American."

"A woman who knows what she wants."

"Always. See you at seven."

TEN

I WAS GETTING ON MY BIKE WHEN "PEOPLE ARE STRANGE" played again.

It was Jesse.

"Looking for an update?" I asked.

"Yeah, I hate to bug you, so if I am, just tell me to go to hell."

"You're not." I gave him the rundown.

"The detective could be a problem. Is he giving you a rough time?"

"He asked me to dinner."

"Seriously? Did you zap him with an energy bolt?"

"Oh, he's not really asking me out. He wants to pick my brain and steal my leads. So I accepted. Should be fun."

"You've obviously got it under control. About those lab and coroner's reports, any chance I can take a look?"

"I'll fax them over."

I ended the call with Jesse only to find that I'd gotten a message in the meantime. If only I'd been this popular in high school, I might have shown up more often. Speaking of school, the message was from a retired history teacher, Mr. Mulligan. Lorraine at the diner had told him about me, and he was wondering if I'd gotten all the local information I'd needed. If not, he'd be happy to provide more background. He'd taught Paula, Ginny, Brandi, even coached Kayla with her homeschooling.

My first impulse was to call back and say "thanks but no thanks." I had plenty of leads to follow up and no time to waste sitting in some old guy's parlor, sipping instant coffee and listening to a lecture on town history. If the guy had been a friend of Ginny's and Brandi's, sure. But their teacher? Something told me that compared to those two, my attendance record would be exemplary.

And yet . . . Maybe I was a little more anxious about my first case than I was admitting. Maybe I couldn't help thinking *What if this is the guy with information that'll solve the case, and I blew him off*. Or maybe it was just those damned voices in my head, Paige and Lucas telling me never to ignore a potential source. I called back and asked if I could stop by in the next hour.

Next, I had files to fax to Jesse. Easier said than done. While I didn't expect a small-town motel to have a business center, I thought they'd at least have a fax machine in the office. They didn't. Nor did the town have a copy center.

I remembered the library, and arrived there to find it had closed at four and wouldn't reopen for two days. Someone was kind enough to suggest the real estate office—apparently they ran an unofficial copy shop on the side. But it had closed at four, too. In fact, except for the diner, the whole town seemed to have shut down.

When I called Jesse, he said that was fine—he'd pop by tomorrow on his way home from Portland. Next stop, Mr. Mulligan, retired teacher.

The address Mr. Mulligan gave led to a place outside town. The sign on the mailbox read J&C Hogs. I checked the address, but it seemed right, so I started up the lane to a sprawling ranch with a massive detached garage. The garage door was open. Through it I could see three gleaming black motorcycles. Harley Davidsons. Hogs.

I swung off my bike as a man walked out. His grease-stained short-sleeved shirt showed off an impressive set of muscles for a guy who had to be in his midsixties.

"Ms. Levine," he said, wiping a hand before extending it. "Chuck Mulligan."

I shook his hand. His gaze had already slid over to my bike, and our fingers hadn't fully disconnected before he was walking toward it.

"You didn't really call me out here to wax nostalgic on past students, did you," I said. "You heard what I was riding."

He smiled, face creasing. "Guilty."

"Only you realize I can't stay and chat," I said. "Not with a Harley man."

"Those are clients' bikes. Mine's a BMW."

"Even worse."

He laughed and crouched beside my bike, checking it out.

"So you must be the C in J&C Hogs. Who's the J?"

"Janice. My wife. She just put me on the sign so I'd feel special. It's her business." He paused. "*Was* her business, I should say. Still not used to that. She passed away last year. I took over after I retired."

He pushed to his feet. "Let's get inside. I'm sure you'll be more comfortable there."

"Actually, I'd be more comfortable there." I pointed to the garage. "If that's okay."

"Certainly."

We spent the next half hour looking at bikes and talking about them. His wife's business had been customizing Harleys—making them faster and fancier.

I'd have been tempted to move on to business a lot faster if I didn't see how much he was enjoying the opportunity to talk about his wife and her work. I understood that, so I let it keep going until he steered things on track by saying, "Have you met Paula Thompson yet?"

"No, just Kayla. Cool kid."

His gray eyes sparkled. "Cool. Yes, that's a good word to describe Kayla. One of those little characters who don't quite fit in, but you know, when they grow up, they'll do better in life than all the popular kids. Paula brings her up once a week to go over her lessons, make sure she's on track. I offer to help more, but Paula won't even take the supervision work for nothing— insists on cleaning my house while I'm working with Kayla."

"You taught her, too, didn't you? Paula Thompson?"

He nodded and led me to a couple of chairs in a makeshift office space. "She started high school the same year I started teaching. I taught her, then Genevieve, and now Kayla. Three generations of Thompson girls. And three more different girls you couldn't hope to find."

"Tell me about Ginny and Brandi."

He settled in his chair and took a moment, as if trying to decide how to start. "When I first started teaching, I was convinced every student could be helped. It's a spark of idealism that fades fast. Some can, and you learn to concentrate on them. The others . . . The others you can't help because they just aren't interested."

Sounded familiar. I'd never had much use for school myself.

"I had Ginny and Brandi in my class," he said, "when they *came* to class, which wasn't often. They spent most of the day in the woods behind the school, smoking with their boyfriends. Then Ginny got pregnant with Kayla."

"Did that help?"

He rubbed his chin and I could tell he wanted to say yes, but after a moment, gave a slow shake of his head. "Ginny was thrilled about Kayla, but only because it meant she could quit school. Otherwise, she was perfectly happy to dump the baby on Paula and go off getting drunk and high with Brandi."

"No father in the picture I take it?"

"Daddy was some loser Ginny hooked up with on a weekend in Portland. I'd be surprised if she even got a name. Paula has Kayla now, thank God. Should have had her from the start but . . ." He shrugged. "Paula had Ginny when she was a kid herself and it turned her life around, so she kept hoping having Kayla would do the same for Ginny. Paula would babysit Kayla, make sure she was fed, had clothing, play dates, all that, but she insisted Ginny step up and be a mother, get a job, get an apartment . . ."

"Did she?"

"The job? On and off, mostly off. She had a place, though, over one of the shops on Main Street. Kayla wasn't neglected— Paula made sure of that. But like I said, those Thompson girls were very different. Having Ginny might have been a life-changing experience for Paula, but her life didn't need as much changing as Ginny's. Even if Paula wasn't much of a student, she still showed up in class and did the work. Hung out with a rough crowd, but she was the best of the bunch. Polite and respectful even when she came to class stoned."

"And Ginny's dad? Was he part of that rough crowd?"

"I don't think so. Paula had a string of boyfriends in ninth and tenth grade. Then she seemed to stop dating. Next thing you know, she's pregnant."

"Meaning she *was* dating. Just not anyone she could be seen with in public. There were rumors, though, I bet."

"Plenty. Most of them involving married men, not surprisingly.

A couple of names floated around. I don't like spreading rumors, so I won't give them to you, but I will say that neither of them killed Ginny. One left for the East Coast years back, and the other's dead."

We talked about Ginny for a few more minutes, but he couldn't add any dimension to the picture I'd drawn of her. It was even worse when we got talking about Brandi.

"I barely remember the girl," Mulligan said. "I felt bad about that, but when I went to the funeral, I remembered why. There wasn't much to Brandi Degas. Nothing memorable. She was Ginny Thompson's shadow. I don't mean in regards to their friendship—Brandi was clearly the leader there. But Ginny was the one you noticed. The prettier one. The louder one."

"They'd been friends a long time, I heard."

"Since they were babies. Both had single moms and I think Paula and Carol went to the same support group."

"Were *they* friends? Paula and Carol?"

"Close acquaintances more like. Carol was an alcoholic even back then, and Paula didn't take with that. She helped out, though, looking after Brandi when she could."

"Is Carol Degas still in town?"

"She is. And you can try talking to her, but don't expect much. A lifetime of boozing has taken its toll. When Brandi died, Carol couldn't even sober up for the funeral. She's doing better, but her memory's shot."

"And Brandi's father?"

"A kid who died in a drunk-driving accident a year after Brandi was born."

"No dad in the picture for either. Those girls *did* have a lot in common."

"Pretty much everything. Never finished school. Were into drugs and booze. Couldn't hold a job. No kids for Brandi, though."

"What about boyfriends? Did she have anyone like Cody Radu?"

He shook his head. "Brandi didn't date. She hooked up with men at parties. Or so I hear. She . . . wasn't an attractive girl. She had a certain kind of smarts, though. Feral cunning, I'd call it. She kept a tight hold on Ginny, wouldn't let her make other friends."

"Was she envious of Ginny's relationship with Cody? Maybe tried to break them up?"

"No. Like I said, she had a certain kind of smarts, and she knew a good thing when she saw it. To her, Cody was a good thing. He had money and, from what I hear, kept Ginny well supplied with alcohol and drugs, which she shared with Brandi."

"So Brandi relied on Ginny."

"And vice versa. You never saw the two of them apart."

Not even in death.

I finished up with Mulligan and left with a business card, as he jokingly promised to set me up with a "real bike" if I ever got tired of the Triumph. I had about an hour before my dinner with Michael Kennedy, so I retreated to the motel to do some research. I started with a call to Jaime, my necromancer contact, to see whether this ritual sounded like anything she knew.

Jaime Vegas was a celebrity spiritualist. She mainly did live shows these days, where she contacted the dead to reassure the living. Great gig for a necromancer . . . except most times, Jaime faked it. She had to. The messages that the living need aren't necessarily the ones the dead want to impart.

There's one ghost whose messages Jaime does occasionally pass on. My mother's. Some necromancers have spirit guides, and my mother is Jaime's. She's not supposed to convey messages to Mom's loved ones—it's considered disruptive to both the living and the dead—but we bend the rules . . . just not often enough to get Mom reassigned.

I consider Jaime a friend, even if she's over twice my age and I've known her since I was a kid. That's how it is with most of my really good friends. I grew up with these people. I sat backstage at Jaime's shows. I went to art galleries with Cassandra DuCharme, a three-hundred-year-old vampire. I spent summers with the werewolf Pack—Elena and Clay and Jeremy. It's a strange way to grow up, but I wouldn't have traded it for anything.

Jaime answered on the fourth ring. She sounded out of breath. I waited, not too worried that she was fleeing mortal danger or anything. If Jaime's out of breath, it's from overdoing it on the treadmill.

"I've been trying to get in touch with Paige," she said. "Has she already left for Hawaii?"

"Yep. Anything I can help with?"

"No, just council business. Hold on." I heard her muffled voice talking to someone. She came back with, "Sorry about that. So are you holding down the fort alone?"

"Actually not holding it down at all. I'm off on a case."

"Really? That's great. Where?"

"About an hour from Portland."

"Oh." She sounded disappointed, like she'd been hoping I was close enough to visit. "So you're going home at night, then?"

"No, staying in a motel. Getting some experience living on the road."

"That's a good idea. A *great* idea," she said, with more enthusiasm than it warranted. "With everyone else gone, you might as well have some fun. Take your time, too. You deserve a break."

"Uh, okay. Speaking of breaks, we're still on for New York later this month, right?"

"Absolutely."

"Great, now if you have a second, I've got a question for you."

"Sure."

I described the chalk marks and the silver object, and she said there were a few rituals that came to mind, and asked me to send the pictures for a better look.

Then we talked about our trip for a few minutes. Summer was almost here, and I needed a new wardrobe, which meant a trip to New York with my favorite shopping buddy.

Going to New York to buy clothes is my one real indulgence. I'm independently wealthy—a phrase I've come to love, to Adam's unending annoyance.

My dad, being the scion of the Nast Cabal, left a fortune to his kids. Or to his sons, at least. My half brother Sean is sure our father had rewritten his will to add me when he discovered he had a daughter. Kristof Nast might have been a cold-blooded bastard, but he'd loved my mother and he loved his children. After his death, though, only the original will was found—the one dividing his estate between his two sons. My grandfather refuses to acknowledge me, so if there was a new will, I'm sure he got rid of it.

If Sean thought I should have been included, though, he was going to make sure I got my share. So he'd set up a trust fund for me with part of his own inheritance. Until I was twenty-five, it only paid an allowance—five thousand a month—but I re-invested most of that. My salary covered my daily expenses, and it didn't feel right, blowing my inheritance when it had come out of Sean's money.

I supposed when I got access to the funds, I'd buy a condo or something. I didn't have any firm plans. That applied to most of my life right now. I liked where I was. Occasionally, I got the feeling I should be leaving home and setting out on my own, but it never happened. I'd go when I was ready, I guess.

After saying good-bye to Jaime, I read the reports, which could be summed up as "three young women were murdered."

The coroner's report did mention the object in Claire's hand. A pewter bead. A note on the file speculated it came from something she'd been wearing, but no one had found a necklace or bracelet. Had it been yanked off her killer? That was a possibility. A plain piece of pewter, though, was more likely symbolic.

I searched the reports for Ginny and Brandi. No mention of anything found in their hands or of any pewter in the vicinity. I could ask Bruyn, but if it was supernatural in origin, I didn't want him to know it might be significant.

I moved on to Internet searches. As I expected by now, the motel didn't offer Internet service. Luckily, Paige showed me how to tether my laptop to my iPhone, which was a relief, because as cool as that little browser app is, it's a bitch for doing serious Web work.

The first person I looked up was Michael Kennedy. With a name like that, can you imagine how many hits I got? Even knowing he was from Texas didn't help.

Eventually, I found a newspaper article about a case he'd worked. Being a photogenic guy, his picture was included— one of him turning away, unimpressed with the prospect of being captured on film. It was clearly him, though, so his story was legit.

Next on my list: Cody Radu, a name that was much easier to search. The first hit I got was Facebook. One look at the picture and I had my guy, and a read through his profile gave me more information on him than I cared to know. That alone suggested the diner folks were right about Cody. He was one of those people who pretends to be an open book, putting every bit of minutiae about himself into the public domain, as if to say "See, I'm not holding anything back," which tells you that he is.

I tried pairing up Cody with search terms like "drugs," "sex," "gambling," everything I could think of that might link to illegal activity. Nothing. If it were that easy, though, Bruyn would have nabbed him by now.

So I switched to Alastair Koppel. Plenty of hits for him. There was a Facebook group and a website run by the parents of girls who'd joined his commune. Neither were exactly flattering to the old guy.

He wasn't that old, though. Midforties. Decent enough looking. Dignified. The kind of guy whom lost little girls would flock to.

Flock they did. Megan hadn't been lying about that. I found a dozen message boards with young women asking how to get into the commune, and more from young women agonizing over why they hadn't been accepted.

Megan hadn't been lying about the cookies either. The small business had been written up in a handful of magazines as a model of entrepreneurship. Of course, they glossed over the commune part, preferring to praise the company's "unique and philanthropic" model, which combined rehabilitation with enterprise.

As Megan had said, Alastair was a therapist, though the sites run by the girls' parents were quick to point out he had a bachelor's degree, not a doctorate. They also noted his work history, which showed that the guy liked to move around. And he changed wives as fast as he did jobs. Four ex-wives, the dates of the weddings running close enough to the divorce decrees that you knew he hadn't finished with one before starting on the next. Each divorce petition charged infidelity. Alastair liked variety. Surprise, surprise.

That was all very interesting, but nothing more than I'd have expected. A guy who had made a very nice life for himself, surrounded by girls half his age, who when they weren't fighting to share his bed, were raking in some serious cookie dough for his coffers.

What interested me was that talisman painted on the gate. It looked like a simple protective symbol, though I couldn't identify it. Maybe one of the girls was a practicing Wiccan. Nothing wrong with that, but considering I was investigating possible occult-linked killings, it was a lot more interesting than Alastair's ex-wives.

I ran a bunch of searches on his name and the company name, combining them with everything from "satanic" to "occult" to "ritual." The closest thing to a hit I got was a deeply buried post on a message board where someone joked that Taste of Heaven cookies had more than just organic flour in them, explaining their popularity.

I was pretty sure you couldn't get drug-laced cookies past the FDA, but was it possible to enchant them? I always said that Paige did something with her cookies—they never turned out the same for me—but she just rolled her eyes and said that the only "magic" was that she actually followed the recipe and measured the ingredients.

There are hundreds, if not thousands, of "lost" spells and rituals floating around. Most likely, though, they were simply good cookies.

My alarm rang then, reminding me of my non-date with Michael. I showered and dressed, grateful that Paige always insisted we pack an outfit for every undercover eventuality, including cocktail parties.

As I got ready, I racked my brain for more things to research. I was doing my makeup when an idea hit. I returned to my laptop and combined the occult keywords with Cody's name. Bingo. On Facebook no less, in a frat buddy's photo album. A picture of Cody Radu conducting an occult ritual.

It was tucked into a section from rush week—old photos of guys making jackasses of themselves and, ten years later, thinking it was cool to post evidence of their youthful stupidity online for the world to see.

There were two pictures conveniently labeled "Awesome Occult Ritual." The first showed a bunch of guys standing around a young Cody, who was kneeling, drawing with chalk on the floor. The caption read "Cody shows us how it's done." The second was too dark to make out, but was obviously the ritual in progress, captioned "Cody leads the way."

While I couldn't make out details, there was enough to suggest Cody knew what he was doing. Had he seen it in a movie? Researched it for rush week? Or was it something more sinister?

A honk outside my motel room made me jump. I bookmarked the site, disconnected, and hurried to the door. I waved at Michael, motioning that I'd be just a couple of minutes. I was putting on lipstick when he rapped at the door.

"Come in."

The door clicked. "No rush. I'm early—"

He stopped. I turned. He gawked, then blushed, clearing his throat and saying, "That's a good color for you," before looking away so fast you'd think I was naked.

It wasn't even a very revealing dress. I don't have a lot to reveal. My legs are my best feature so, yes, the skirt was short. Damned short, actually. Other than that, it was just your basic little black cocktail dress, only it wasn't black—it was peacock blue, like my eyes. I know, bringing out your eye color is such a cliché, but if I have a second-best feature, my eyes are it, and I always play to my strengths.

Obviously it worked for Michael, who continued to gaze around the room as if committing the wallpaper to memory.

"Research?" he said, pointing at my laptop. "Have you found—?" He cut himself short with a wry smile. "Sorry. Occupational hazard. Tonight isn't about the case, and I won't say another word about it."

"Is that a promise?"

"Er, more of an intention. But a strong intention."

I laughed, closed up my laptop, and tucked it under the mattress. Then we left.

ELEVEN

FOR THE FIRST PART OF THE DRIVE, MICHAEL STRUGGLED TO make conversation, but without the case, we didn't have anything to discuss, and he was playing up his determination to avoid that. I tried asking about Claire but he only gave short answers, clearly uncomfortable discussing his sister with a stranger. Finally, I asked about his job, and that got him talking. Yes, he did use it to veer toward the case a few times, checking to see if I'd nibble. I didn't. No sense making this easy for him . . . or risk losing out on a free meal.

And it wasn't a meal I'd have cared to miss. Michael had gone all out, making reservations in the nearest city— Vancouver, Washington, just across the state border from Portland. He'd picked one of the best restaurants there. Upscale continental. The kind of place that made me really glad I'd packed the dress.

I ordered what I wanted. I never get the most expensive thing on the menu, but I don't stress about the cost. Michael didn't bat an eye, even suggested an appetizer. Added a very nice bottle of wine, too. I don't know my wines, but it was good.

Michael kept my glass filled. Being a considerate guy, though, meant keeping his filled as well. Being nervous meant that he drank *his* a lot faster, and didn't seem to notice that I was barely on my second when he was starting his third. It hit him a lot harder, too, and by the middle of the entrée, the granite-jawed cop was gone and I was getting a very nice look at the guy underneath, the one who drove a modified BMW and blushed at being caught eyeing a pretty girl.

"—so at this point, the guy finally notices the video camera," he was saying. "He stares at it for a minute. Just stares, like he's never imagined such a thing in a liquor store. Then you see him mouth two words."

"Oh, shit."

"Exactly. He's standing there, a hole in the ceiling behind him, broken bottles from his crash everywhere, blood dripping down his face. Then he sees the flashing lights. He could still run. But, no, he figures he can salvage this. Cops walk in two minutes later, and find the guy leaving a twenty at the till with a note. *Store was closed. Keep the change.*"

"Big of him."

"I thought so."

He took another sip of wine. The server stopped by to ask about dessert. I took a menu, and Michael followed suit. As we read them, I could see him doing a mental "oh, shit" of his own, his fuzzy brain realizing the meal was almost over and he hadn't gotten anything out of me.

We ordered. After the server left, he said, "Speaking of dumb criminals, how about that Cody Radu? Everyone in town is sure he at least killed the first two girls. Maybe Claire, too."

"But no one can prove it, which doesn't make him very dumb."

"No, of course not." It was cute, watching his brain skidding on the wine. "He's the *opposite* of a dumb criminal. That's what I meant."

The coffee arrived. He took a big gulp, gasping as it burned his throat. I decided to help him out. If he wanted leads, I'd give him some . . . just not real ones.

"From what I hear, there's a good reason Bruyn can't pin Ginny and Brandi's murders on Radu," I said. "He didn't kill them himself. He hired someone."

"What?"

"I don't know if it was the same for Claire. I'm still trying to find a link between her and Radu . . ." I trailed off, but he didn't bite. "Word is that Radu hired this guy who lives over near Cougar. You know where that is?"

"I think so."

"Guy's name is Brody Manchester. Claims to be an Iraq vet, but I can't find a record of him serving. I suspect the only serving he did was in a penitentiary. Sounds like a real whack-job."

"And he lives in Cougar?"

"Near it. He has a camper and moves around outside town staying ahead of the cops. I figured I'd swing by tomorrow afternoon and hunt him down."

"Good idea."

"Do you want me to call you if I find anything? I might need backup."

"Sure. Absolutely. Manchester, you said?"

"Like the soccer team."

He took out his BlackBerry. "I'll do some digging myself."

"Thanks. I'd appreciate that."

Two cups of coffee and an espresso crème brûlée had not made Michael any steadier on his feet.

When we reached his car, I held out my hand. "Keys?"

"I'm good."

"Please tell me you're not one of those cops who thinks the laws don't apply to him."

"No, course not. I . . ." He looked around, blinking, then nodded. "You're right. One glass too many. But you had—"

"One and a half, the last sip an hour ago, and I'm fine." I walked along a yellow line dividing parking spots. "Want me to do it backwards?"

"Sure."

I did, making him laugh . . . and hand over the keys.

As I pulled out of the parking space, he said, "Watch out. She's got a lot of—"

I hit the gas, smacking him back in his seat. At the street, I braked, sending him snapping forward.

"Sweet," I said.

"Just be careful. You may not be impaired, but your reflexes could be a little—"

I tore off, accelerating, then hitting the corner fast and hard. Three blocks later I idled at a stop sign.

"Reflexes okay?" I said.

"Carry on."

I turned left.

"Actually, the highway is—" he began.

"Too many cars. Don't worry. I have an excellent sense of direction." I took the first left onto a back road. "Columbus is this way. Roughly."

I hit the gas.

I parked beside my motorcycle.

"Good thing we took the back roads," he said. "One cop and you'd have been out of a license."

"Not too worried about that," I said as I got out.

He eyed me over the roof. "You do have your license, don't you?"

"Sure. I've got one."

"One?" He looked at my bike. "Please don't tell me—"

"Then don't ask. I'm honest, remember? Not necessarily law-abiding, but unrelentingly honest." I walked around and held out the keys. "And I do believe you're ready for these."

As I handed them over, he caught my hand.

"I had a good time tonight," he said.

"So did I. You aren't nearly as boring as you look."

His laugh rang through the empty lot. "God, you *are* honest." His hand slid around my waist, pulling me to him. I back-pedaled away.

"Kissing? On a first date?" I said. "What kind of girl do you think I am?"

He grinned and tried again, but I danced out of his reach.

"Second date," I said. "And only if you let me drive your car again."

"Without a license?"

"Ah, such a moral dilemma." I unlocked my motel room door. "Call me tomorrow night if you've made up your mind."

"I don't think it'll take that long."

"Mmm, it might. Better wait until then. See if you're still interested."

I slid inside and closed the door before he could say more.

I stood there, fingers on the chain. I'd had a good time, too. Not a rock-my-world date, but a really nice one.

As I got older, I dated less, and I'd thought I was just slowing down, getting ready for that big moment when Adam would notice me, but after I realized that wasn't happening, I just kept slowing down.

In some ways, it was like mourning after a bad breakup.

I needed to get back in the game, and Michael would have been a nice place to start. Too bad he'd never call for that second date.

"Now that's a dress," said a voice behind me. "He let you get away that easily? What's wrong with the guy?"

I spun to see Jesse stretched out in the armchair, file on his lap.

"Good thing I *didn't* invite him in," I said.

"Why would you do that? It was business, wasn't it?"

"I can multitask."

He laughed.

"You seem to have a talent for getting into places you aren't supposed to be," I said, kicking off my heels.

"You did read my record, right?"

"It's juvie. Sealed."

He arched his brows. "What kind of detective are you? Break and enter, as you probably guessed. Two years in juvenile detention, where the only thing I learned was how *not* to get caught next time."

"Shocking." I sat on the edge of the bed. "And you'll give me pointers, right?"

"Anything you want to know." He set the file on the side table. "I apologize for breaking in. Kind of. But I was sitting in my truck and the manager kept looking at me like he was five seconds from calling the cops."

"That's your pickup? The blue one? Or, presumably, used to be blue, at some point?"

"Yes, which explains the manager's interest."

"So, to avoid being suspected of breaking in, you broke in."

"Exactly. If it bothers you, though, I won't do it again."

He said it like he was offering not to smoke in front of me.

"Call me next time," I said. "So I know you're inside and don't blast you with an energy bolt."

"Hadn't thought of that. Consider it noted."

He reached for an open Coke bottle on the table. When he couldn't quite get it, he flexed his right hand slightly and the bottle slid to him.

"Show-off," I said.

"Hey, I have to use my powers for something. They aren't good for much else. Not like I'm a supercharged Volo."

"And good thing, too."

He frowned, then snapped his fingers. "Right. Lucas mentioned that you guys knew one. Quite the character, I hear."

"Crazy psycho bitch, more like. Left me trapped in a research lab, tried to kill Paige and Lucas, and probably had something to do with my mom's death. Let's just say I fondly recall the day Paige sent her home to hell."

"Don't blame you." He took a swig of Coke. "So, as you can tell, I'm swinging by earlier than expected. I figured I'd read the files, and make copies of some pages." He held up a camera. "I also figured I'd take you for a beer and discuss the case if it's not too late."

"It's only ten o'clock."

"I'm giving you an out, in case you're still pissed off at me for dumping the case on you."

"I was never—"

"Annoyed, then. So you'll join me for a beer?"

"Or two."

"Good."

I grabbed my shoes. My cell phone chirped on the night table.

"You forgot this," Jesse said, grabbing it for me. "It's been going off all night."

Not so much *forgotten* as left behind so I couldn't get a call from Adam when I was out with another guy.

I checked it. Three text messages. One missed call. All from Adam, looking for that promised update. Damn.

"Just a sec," I said to Jesse. Then I popped off a quick text, saying I was still working and I'd call in the morning.

TWELVE

THERE WAS NO CHANCE OF FINDING A BAR OPEN IN Columbus—I wasn't even sure there was one. So we headed over to Battle Ground. Jesse bought the beer, then announced he had reason to celebrate. He'd found the deadbeat dad he'd been hunting.

"Bet your client is happy," I said.

"Thrilled. I just hope it means they'll get the guy to pay up. You should see this woman. Juggles two part-time jobs so she can be there when her four kids go to school and back when they get home. Lives in a dump and takes in typing work so she can pay for paint to spruce the place up. And the bitch of it? Once, when she was ready to crack, she admitted that she hadn't wanted four kids. She didn't think they could afford so many, but her husband came from a big family. He wouldn't let her go on the pill and would keep 'forgetting' to use protection, knocking her around if she complained."

"Bastard."

"Yeah." He took a gulp of beer. "I mean, my family life wasn't the best. I think my dad had a suspicion I wasn't his kid—the whole half-demon thing—so he didn't want much to do with me, but then I see people like this family, and I realize

I had it okay. Anyway, I'm really hoping this guy gives up and pays. And if not, let's just say that my next visit won't be so friendly."

"If you need backup, I'm a phone call away."

"Or closer. At least for a few days. My case is done, meaning I'm now at your disposal. I just need to head to Seattle and grab clean clothes, and I'll be back tomorrow."

I must not have looked as happy about that as he'd hoped, because he said, "Or not . . ."

That had been the plan, right? That he'd join in as soon as he could. Only I'd been doing pretty good so far. I'd made a few mistakes, but I'd learned from them. That was the point of going solo.

I didn't want to offend Jesse by refusing his help, though, so I fell back on my best strategy: honesty. I really wanted to do as much of this job as I could. If things got ugly, I'd call him in a heartbeat. For now, though . . .

"You want to try it on your own. I think it's a good idea, actually. Lucas should have had you running solo long ago. If it's okay with you, though, I'd like to keep my hand in. Research, sounding board, backup, whatever you might need. That okay?"

"Definitely."

"Good."

Jesse dropped me off at the motel. I waited until he'd left, then hopped on my bike and headed for the police station. I hadn't told him what I was planning. There are lines you shouldn't cross as a private investigator. Breaking into a cop shop is one of them.

After twenty minutes outside the building, I was beginning to think I wouldn't be crossing this line tonight either. The station wasn't empty.

Earlier that day, at the diner, I'd asked about nighttime law enforcement. It was obviously a very small department and I'd hate to need police backup at night and be unable to contact anyone. They said there hadn't been a night dispatcher since the last budget cuts. Any calls after midnight went straight to the chief's house. The officers did patrol sporadically, but on a schedule known only to the department. That, though, should have left the station empty, and it was—empty of cops, at least. After hours, though, was cleaning time.

Cleaning a place the size of a bachelor flat shouldn't have taken long. But apparently Bruyn didn't know that, and paid by the hour. When I'd cast a blur spell and slipped in, the woman was lounging in Bruyn's office, doing a crossword, her work not yet begun. I went back outside to wait.

After another twenty minutes, I began running through my repertoire of disarming spells. I had a sleep one that seemed promising. It was a "Mom spell"—one of hers I'd gotten through her contacts.

Mom had been a teacher of the dark arts, but she'd always kept me sheltered from that part of her life. Her contacts knew of me, though, and once I hit teen-hood, they'd started reaching out, hoping there was enough of my mother in me that I was chafing under the guardianship of two do-gooders.

That just proved they didn't know my mother as well as they thought. She was hardly an upright citizen, but she didn't embrace the dark side because she was evil. It simply made good economic sense. She used those contacts—as I did—with extreme caution. I gave them useless tidbits about the council and the Cabals, and in return, I could call on them with questions I couldn't ask Lucas and Paige.

Part of the wooing process is gifts. That's where the spells come in. They give them to me, saying stuff like "your mom would have wanted you to have this." I collect the spells. I practice them. I store them away in my secret safe deposit box and, when they fit the bill, I use them.

As for why a sleeping spell would be a secret dark magic spell, it was—like most of the spells I kept in my box—not the result that caused concern, but either the materials needed to cast it or the spell's potential side effects. In this case, the side effect was narcolepsy.

Like my less savory contacts, these spells have a place in my toolbox, and if inducing a few weeks of narcolepsy in an innocent woman would help me stop someone who's *killing* innocent women, then I didn't see a problem with that. Trouble was, the spell, like most dark magic, required dark ingredients. Only grave dirt in this case, but I hadn't brought any with me.

I was debating a search for the local cemetery when the cleaning woman came out for a smoke. That didn't give me time to ransack the station, but I had another idea.

I hid in the shadows as she pulled out her lighter. Then I launched a teeny, tiny energy bolt. The lighter exploded. The woman dropped it, shaking her hand and staring down at the remains.

Muttering, she kicked the lighter into the grass, reached into her pocket, and pulled out a matchbook. As she opened it, I launched a drizzle spell. As water trickled down, she scowled up at the rain gutter and cursed Bruyn for not fixing the apparent holes. When she went to light her cigarette, her matches were damp and useless.

More curses as she stuffed the cigarettes back into her bag. Now came the big test. How badly did she need that smoke? I held my breath until she yanked out her car keys and stomped off to her vehicle.

When she was gone, I slipped into the station. I knew from my diner small talk that there was a security alarm, installed a few years ago after evidence—small amounts of drugs and money, then a gun—disappeared from lockup. I knew how to disarm most systems, but didn't need to—the cleaner hadn't turned it on.

I found the case file easily enough. I knew I had a limited amount of time before the woman returned, so I took only what I needed, bypassing the files Bruyn gave me and the crime-scene photos I got from Jesse. I copied the rest as fast as I could, then hurried out and was gone before the cleaning woman came back.

When I got back to the motel, it was almost two. As tired as I was, I couldn't sleep. I wasn't used to being alone at night except at home.

There was a time when I couldn't wait to leave home, but when I was finally old enough to move out, I didn't. We had a big enough house. Paige and Lucas didn't mind me being there. I pulled my weight with chores and I paid rent. I liked where I was. Liked it too much maybe.

My phone chirped. Paige, sending a text to call her in the morning. I read it a few times, hearing her voice in my head and relaxing.

It helped. But not enough. I hit speed dial. It rang three times. Then Adam's drowsy voice came on, yawning a hello.

"You said to call you later," I said. "Is this late enough?"

He swore.

I smiled. "Couldn't resist. Go on back to sleep. I'll call in the morning."

Another yawn. "No, I'd better take the update while I can." A squeak of the bed, as if he was sitting up. "So what's happening?"

I told him. He didn't laugh at my fake black mass lead, just said, "Those mannequin props don't sound like anything from a black mass, real or fake. What time of year did you say that guy stumbled on the stuff?"

"Last fall." I thumped back onto the pillow. "And something tells me it was late October."

"Yeah. I'm betting it was on display because it was *supposed* to be on display."

"A haunted house for Halloween."

"It's a possibility. Ask around."

We talked until I was the one yawning. He chuckled and said, "Now it's my turn to keep you awake."

"I can just hang up."

"That would be rude."

"Yep."

"Okay, I'll let you go. And I won't pester you with a dozen texts tomorrow, but call, okay? I know you don't want me holding your hand. But toss me a bone. I just spent two days listening to lectures on research techniques. I'm dying here."

"And who signed you up for the conference?"

"Don't remind me."

"Aren't you done anyway? I thought your last thingy was canceled."

"Thingy? Glad you take such an interest. Someone asked me to sub on a panel tomorrow afternoon, and since you don't want me around . . ."

"There's a hot chick on the panel, isn't there?"

He snorted. "Just an old colleague of Dad's that I couldn't say no to. Meaning I'm stuck here another day at least, so you're stuck amusing me. Got it?"

I smiled. "Got it." I yawned some more.

"Okay, okay, I'm hanging up. Call tomorrow, though. Preferably before three A.M."

A rap at the door woke me. I groaned, rolled over, and squinted at the bedside clock. 7:12. Another rap, louder now.

"Miss Levine?" A woman's voice.

I rolled out of bed, grabbed jeans and a T-shirt, and yanked them on as I called, "Just a sec!"

I opened the door to a smiling middle-aged woman holding a take-out cup of coffee and a bag. I was pretty sure this place didn't have room service . . .

"I work at the coffee shop around the corner," she said before I could ask. "I was asked to deliver this to you at seven o'clock."

"Okay . . ." I took the bag and coffee.

"There's a message, too." She took a sheet from her pocket and read it. "If I had to wake up at an ungodly hour, so do you. Get to work, and don't forget to call me."

Adam.

"We don't usually do delivery, but I figured I could make an exception," she smiled. "Especially when he tacked a ten-dollar tip onto the bill."

I thanked her, then said, "Before you go, I've got a crazy question for you. I was talking to a friend of mine in Portland last night, and she swears she was here last fall. Said some service group was running a haunted house in the old furniture store. I think she's got it mixed up with another Columbus, but now we've got a bet on it. You don't remember anything like that, do you?"

"Sure do. Our high school put it on. The kids were raising money for a family whose place burned down. They couldn't afford house insurance after losing their jobs at the sawmill. The kids even got Manny Radu to let them use the empty fur-niture store, which, believe me, was an accomplishment in itself. His grandkids were all for it, though, so the old man couldn't say no."

Manny Radu—I'd heard the name around town. Cody's father, who must own the empty building, which would explain why Cody had been there. The rest explained what I'd found at the empty shop—everything teens need for a makeshift house o' horrors. As someone not far past her teens, I really should have seen that. My brain was too rooted in the supernatural world. That's what I saw, even when a simpler explanation was right in front of my nose. I had to remember that.

After the woman left, I set my coffee down and opened the bag. Two muffins—double-chocolate and blueberry bran.

I texted Adam a thank-you. I'd just started eating the chocolate muffin when he texted back *Put that one down and eat the bran. It's better for you.*

I laughed and carried the case file and my coffee and muffins outside, ignoring the cold concrete under my feet. There were weathered plastic patio chairs along the front walk and I pulled two of them over—one to sit in, one as a footrest. I stretched out, sipping my coffee, nibbling my muffin, and reading the interview reports.

I was almost done when a room door opened and a little girl of no more than seven came out. Her hair wasn't brushed. Her face was smeared with spaghetti or pizza sauce from the night before. As she started across the parking lot, someone shouted for her to close the door. The girl picked her way across the lot to a soda machine and got a Coke. Breakfast.

Seeing her made me think of Kayla, and what the folks at the diner had said—how her grandmother had kept her from a life like that. I needed to speak to Paula Thompson today. If she wasn't pleased with Bruyn's investigation, I could probably win her support.

I made a to-do list. Lucas would be so proud of me. Thinking of them, I checked my watch, but it was still too early to call their hotel, so I e-mailed Paige, saying I'd phone later.

I was sending the message when the hairs on my neck prickled so strongly that I looked up. The parking lot was empty.

I cast a sensing spell, but there were too many people in the motel rooms. I pretended to return my attention to the phone, while sneaking glances around. Nothing. Still, I had the distinct feeling of being watched.

Um, yeah, it's a motel. Could be the manager. Could be the perv in unit fourteen or the nosy lady in unit six . . .

True. I tore a chunk off my muffin. As I was popping it into my mouth, a figure passed between two tractor-trailers parked at the edge of the motel lot.

I got to my feet and stretched. As I worked out a kink in my shoulder and feigned a yawn, a dark figure emerged from behind one of the trailers, then quickly pulled back.

I opened the door to my room, walked in, then cast a blur spell and slid out again. I made it halfway to the trucks when my phone rang. A Hawaii area code popped up. Paige. I ducked behind the nearest car and hit ignore. Footsteps scrambled over pavement. I peeked out and caught a flash of movement as someone ducked behind the motel office.

I took off after it, but by the time I reached the building, there was no one around. I cast my sensing spell. It picked up two people.

The chimes jangled as I went inside. The manager and his wife sat behind the counter, eating bagels and doing paperwork.

"Did anyone just come in?" I asked.

Twin head shakes.

"Did you see anyone run past?"

Twin head shakes. Twin blank expressions.

I glanced around. There was no other way in, but also no way for them to see someone passing by.

I went back outside, walked around the building, and found a recessed doorway—the perfect place for someone to hide, then take off while I went into the office.

I took one last look around, then retreated to my room to call Paige.

It was an ungodly hour in Hawaii, but naturally they were already up. Paige put me on speaker phone so I could talk to both of them. They'd already spoken to Adam, so my story was in place. I was doing out-of-town legwork for Adam and staying in situ to get experience mingling with humans—an idea they both heartily endorsed.

When I got off the phone, I had a message.

"Ms. Levine? This is Paula Thompson, Ginny's mother. Kayla tells me you spoke to her yesterday." A pause, as if she was biting her tongue to keep from blasting me. Shit. When she continued, her voice was polite, but cool. "I heard you're investigating Ginny's death. I'm sure you'd like to speak to me. I'm home this morning until noon. I'll be expecting you."

As nicely as that was worded, it wasn't an offer—it was an appointment. A private investigator had talked to her granddaughter without her knowledge. It had been innocent enough, but it sounded bad, and I didn't blame her for being pissed. Paula Thompson had just moved to the top of my to-do list.

I left as soon as I was ready. I'd gone about a block when an SUV pulled in behind me—*right* behind me, practically clipping my back tire. One problem with a motorcycle is that you're light infantry on a battlefield of tanks. I wear all my gear, but one driver yapping on his cell phone could be the end of me. All I could see through my mirror was the grill . . . and the Lexus emblem.

Cody Radu.

I turned the corner. He turned the corner. I made an unnecessary turn. He followed. Another turn, taking me back the way I'd come. He swung in behind me, revving up again before backing off.

Is that supposed to scare me, asshole? Send the detective girl running back to Portland? Now I had a pretty good idea who'd been staking out my motel room.

I continued on at the speed limit, took the next turn, and headed up to Main Street. There was a stop sign at the intersection. I obeyed it. He stayed a respectful distance behind. I put on my signal, and pulled forward.

An engine squeal. Then a bump that nearly sent me flying over my handlebars. I slammed my feet down before the bike toppled. Then I looked back to see Cody getting out of his SUV, his face the perfect mask of concern.

"God, I'm sorry," he said as I pulled off my helmet. "I saw you start forward and I tapped the gas and bang. I have no idea what happened."

"Could be a sticky pedal." I swung off the bike. "Want me to take a look?"

"I hit you and you're offering to fix my car? That's forgiving. I'll get it into the shop later, thanks. You're okay?"

"It's not me I'm worried about."

I checked the back of the bike. Cody admired it, asking questions and acting like he'd know the difference between a Triumph and a Honda . . . or that he'd care.

"Looks okay," I said. "The alignment could be screwed up, though."

He handed me his card. "Send the bill to me."

"I will."

I started pulling my helmet on.

"You're the PI working on the murders, aren't you?" He said

this as if it had just dawned on him.

"Savannah Levine." I extended a hand.

"Pretty name. Suits you."

He smiled, but there was nothing in it. Forced flirtation with a girl he'd decided wasn't his type.

"So, Savannah, you've been in town a few days and still haven't gotten around to me? I'm shocked."

"Actually, I just arrived yesterday."

"Ah." A nod. A look that said I was full of shit and he knew it. Was there another six-foot-tall motorcycle-driving young woman in town? Somehow I doubted it, but I let the point pass. From what I'd heard yesterday, the guy was more than a little paranoid, probably figured I'd been stalking him for days now.

"You will want to talk to me, I assume, considering that I top Bruyn's list of suspects." He checked his watch. "I have time for breakfast if it won't take long."

"I've already eaten. Let's make it lunch."

His full lips pressed thin. After a second, he managed a smile, but it looked painful. "No can do, I'm afraid. I'm a busy man. It's breakfast or nothing."

I put on my helmet. "Nothing then. If you'll excuse me, I need to make a trip into the city, check on something I found last night." I got on my bike, then looked back at him. "You really should be more careful where you spend your money, Mr. Radu. And on what. Even when you think it doesn't leave a trail, it does. Not one the cops can find legally but . . ." I smiled. "That's what I'm for."

He froze, trying to figure out what I meant.

"Fine. Lunch," he said, spitting the words. "One o'clock. There's a McDonald's off the highway. Meet me there."

THIRTEEN

NOT SURPRISINGLY, CODY FOLLOWED ME A LITTLE LONGER as he tried to see which "city" I was heading for. I turned onto the same back road I'd traveled with Michael, crested a hill, then hit the gas, slamming through a half-mile of hills like they were ski jumps. Cody's SUV couldn't keep up. Once he was out of sight, I veered down the first side road and made my way back to town.

Paula Thompson lived in a mobile home. A very nice mobile home, I might add, on a piece of land I presumed she owned or rented, miles from any trailer park. The lawn was thick, and freshly cut, and the trailer had been painted in the last couple of years. An ancient sedan sat in the drive.

I rapped on the front door. Kayla answered.

"Did you find the killer yet?" she asked.

"I've only been on the job a day."

She waited for a better excuse.

"I did fix that guy's car, though."

She tilted her head, then after some thought, nodded, this apparently being an acceptable sign of competence.

"Is your grandma home?" I asked.

"Yes."

"Can I speak to her?"

"I don't know, can you?" She giggled.

"*May* I speak to her?"

"Stop giving Ms. Levine a hard time, Kayla."

A woman stepped from the next room. There was no question who she was—she looked like a forty-something clone of her granddaughter—small and wiry, with graying blond hair and quick blue eyes.

"Off with you, miss," she said, pointing to the front door. "Go outside, but stay—"

"—off the road and on the property." Kayla rolled her eyes. "But what if Savannah has questions for me? She needs to interview everyone. I'm someone."

Her grandmother's face softened and she bent to kiss the top of Kayla's head. "You are indeed, but for now, I'd like you to play outside."

When Kayla was out of earshot, I said, "About yesterday, it was an accident. Kayla found me checking out some things in the library and we started talking. When I realized who she was, I shut up. I apologize if I upset her in any way. If I'd known she was Ginny's daughter, I wouldn't have spoken to her."

"I'd like to believe you, Ms. Levine, but it'll be easier if you tell me the whole truth. She wasn't at the library, was she?"

"Well, she was *supposed* to be."

She gave a small laugh and finally stepped aside, unblocking the entrance to the family home.

She offered me a chair in the living room. "She was in the building where Genevieve was found, wasn't she? With her detective kit."

I said nothing.

"I'll take that as a yes." She sighed, still standing, as if she hadn't quite committed herself to talking to me yet. "I suppose buying her that kit wasn't my best parenting idea ever. She just . . . she wanted it so much. I thought it might help. Empower her." A wry smile. "Yes, I've read too many books on helping children cope with grief."

"I don't think it's a bad idea. I . . ." I hesitated. I wasn't the sharing type, but this seemed as good a time as any to work on that. "My mother died when I was a little older than Kayla. Murdered. It was just the two of us. If I could have found out who killed my mother—or thought I could—it would have helped me deal. Trying to solve the crime doesn't seem to upset her, and that's the main thing."

Paula turned away slightly at that, and her expression made me kick myself. I'd meant that it was a good thing Kayla wasn't traumatized, but I guess it was troubling, too. I saw that in Paula's face, the relief mingled with regret and sadness that her daughter had raised a child who didn't particularly mourn her passing.

"Can I get you a coffee? Tea? Cold drink?" she asked.

I could tell she wanted a minute to herself, so I said sure, whatever was easiest.

I'd been too direct. Not enough empathy and compassion. How would Paige handle this?

I looked around the room. There were pictures of Kayla and Ginny. Exactly equal numbers of each, as if Paula had been careful not to favor one. Even as a child, Ginny hadn't looked happy. Sullen, like the world owed her something and wasn't paying up. The shots of Kayla were mixed. If her mom was in the picture, she looked uncomfortable. Alone, she looked solemn, but content. It was in the two pictures with Paula that she shone. I could say the same for Paula.

She came back, and I struggled for a way to ease into the case. I noticed papers and textbooks on the table and waved at them. "Kayla told me she's homeschooled. She said you pulled her out after Bruyn's grandson had taken crime-scene photos to school."

"Yes. They made him very popular apparently, so he couldn't understand why I'd object. Neither could his parents."

"Seriously?"

"They understood that it upset Kayla, naturally, but they couldn't see why I'd bring the matter to *them*. The boy got hold of them himself. They didn't tell him he could take them to school. Therefore, it clearly wasn't their fault."

"Typical," I muttered.

She nodded and sipped her coffee, both hands wrapped around the mug, gaze dropping into its depths as she murmured, "A child turns out the way we raise her, and if she fails, we've failed."

Shit. I'd stumbled right into that one. I shook my head. "If a kid's waving around crime-scene photos and his parents do nothing about it, then it's their fault if he grows up to be an insensitive ass. If they punish him and explain what he did wrong, and he still grows up to be an insensitive ass . . ." I shrugged.

Paula nodded, but woodenly. She lowered her mug, hands still folded around it.

"Are you happy with the investigation?" I asked after a minute of silence.

It seemed like the right lead-in. But Paula's hands tightened around her mug and she said, very carefully, "The sheriff's department knows its job, and Chief Bruyn is doing his best to support them."

In other words, despite the antagonism between them, she wasn't going to question his competence. Not with a stranger, at least.

"You're very young, Ms. Levine," she said after another moment. "Yes, I know, you're obviously an adult, old enough to be done college, working. Twenty-three? Twenty-four?"

I didn't correct her, just gave something that could pass for a nod.

"When I was your age, Ginny was in school already, I was working two jobs and I had this house, and I wouldn't have appreciated someone saying how young I was. But from where I sit now, you *are* young, Ms. Levine. Young means inexperienced. I'm not unhappy to get extra help with my daughter's case, but I will admit I'm much happier to hear that a Dallas detective is also working it."

I bit my tongue—hard. How would she react when she realized Michael Kennedy wasn't much older than me?

"When he comes to me for an interview, I'll gladly grant it," she said. "So, to be fair, I'll do the same for you. I want my daughter's killer found, and I suppose more people investigating can't hurt."

"Thank you." I wasn't sure it was the kind of statement that expected thanks, but I appreciated it.

I took out my notebook. "Chief Bruyn is convinced he knows who killed Ginny."

"Cody Radu."

"And you think . . . ?"

She hesitated, her reluctance to disparage a local warring with other feelings. After a moment, her shoulders dropped, as if conceding the battle.

"I think he's a bastard," she said. "A lying, scheming bully. Is he capable of murder, though? No. I doubt he'd dirty his hands like that."

I thought of the lie I'd spun for Michael. "Would he hire someone?"

That gave her pause. "Yes, if Cody wanted someone dead, I suppose that's how he'd do it."

I asked her about Cody and Ginny's relationship. She didn't

tell me anything I wouldn't have already guessed. Cody's relationship with Ginny had been nothing short of toxic, and Paula had hated him for it.

Cody hadn't even done the typical wealthy-guy seduction and wooed Ginny with a better life. The only thing he gave her was booze and drugs. And black eyes. A lot of black eyes. Look at another man, get a black eye. Couldn't find someone to babysit Kayla when he wanted sex, get a black eye. Didn't get him a beer fast enough. Wouldn't entertain his friends. Complained about anything. All earned her a beating.

"But she loved him," Paula said. "Isn't that how it always is? The one guy who treats you worse than all the rest, that's the one you can't live without."

I thought of Adam. *Not always*. But I nodded. "What about Kayla? Did he ever hurt her?" Paula's face fairly crumpled with relief. "No, thank God. He wanted nothing to do with Kayla. Wouldn't have her around."

"He didn't like the reminder that his girlfriend was a mother."

"Maybe that was it. I was still careful, though. I started helping Kayla in the bath again, to look for signs . . . I had to be sure. I couldn't say anything about how he treated Ginny—she wouldn't listen. But if he'd ever touched Kayla . . ."

"Did Ginny or Brandi have any contact with Alastair Koppel?"

"Favorite suspect number two. I don't know anything about that commune or cult or whatever he has going up there. Neither did Ginny. He takes in young women, and Ginny and Brandi *were* young women, but that's the only connection. Mr. Koppel has never recruited in town. Never even approached one of our local girls. He's not stupid. Some people want him gone and he won't give them any excuse."

"What about Ginny's father?" I asked.

She started at that, coffee sloshing. "Pardon me?"

"Ginny's father. Is he a local? Did she have any contact with him?"

"Oh." She laughed. "Sometimes I forget she *had* a father. Certainly never felt like it. He left town before she was born. She was, for all intents and purposes, my daughter. Mine alone."

My responsibility. I heard that, even if she didn't say it.

"What about Claire Kennedy? I know she arrived after Ginny's death, but was there any way Ginny might have known her? Did Ginny ever move away from Columbus? Work outside it? Socialize outside it?"

"The only time Ginny left Columbus was to party, and even then, no farther than Portland. I encouraged her to take a job in the city. I thought it would help if she got away from Brandi. She just accused me of trying to get rid of her. The truth, I'm sure, is that she was afraid to leave. This was all she knew. Could she have met Claire at one of those parties in the city? I suppose it's possible, but from what I've heard of Ms. Kennedy, she didn't seem the type to have gone to them."

"Did Cody know Claire? Any rumors? A chance meeting, maybe?"

She shook her head. "Nothing I ever heard of."

"I did," said a voice from the hall.

We turned to see Kayla. She stood there, notepad clutched to her chest.

"Dorothy told Aunt Rose that she saw Cody talking to Claire the day before she died. They were fighting." She pursed her lips. "Arguing, I think she meant, not really fighting."

"I never heard this," Paula said.

"Neither has Bruyn," I said. "He'd have been all over it."

"Dorothy didn't tell the chief," Kayla said. "She doesn't like him. He egged her house at Halloween when he was a kid. She didn't say that—just that if he was a good cop, then he didn't need her giving him clues. She doesn't like Cody either. He let his dog poop on her lawn a few times." She looked at me. "Dorothy's really old, but she never forgets anything."

"Especially an insult," Paula murmured.

"Aunt Rose said Dorothy was just trying to stir up trouble because she was still mad at Cody. Dorothy said, no, she saw Claire arguing with him behind Martin's Hardware. The women from the cookie place were buying stuff in the store, and Cody came in, and Claire snuck out back with him, and no one saw but Dorothy. She followed them. They were arguing."

"Did she say what it was about?"

"Aunt Rose wouldn't let her. She said she was sick of rumors and that if Dorothy knew something that would help find Mom's killer, then she'd damned well better tell Chief Bruyn."

"Kayla . . ." Paula said.

"*She* said damned." Kayla held up her notepad. "I wrote it right here. Then Dorothy said maybe she was wrong, and that's when they saw me and started talking about something else. But I don't think Dorothy made it up. I'm sure she saw Cody arguing with Claire."

FOURTEEN

I LEFT WITH DOROTHY'S ADDRESS, THOUGH PAULA WARNED me that she probably wouldn't speak to me.

I went straight to Dorothy's house. Walked, not rode, in case she had something against motorcycles. The lights were on and a car was in the drive. I figured it was a bad idea to cut across the lawn, so I took the walkway to the porch, rang the bell, and waited very patiently for at least a minute before knocking. No one answered.

I left a card in the door, asking to meet for coffee—my treat—at her convenience. You couldn't get any more considerate and respectful than that. At least, I couldn't.

Next stop: the real estate agency to fax the crime-scene photos to Adam, who'd offered to check out the ritual for me. The agency operated not only as a copy shop, but as a typing, résumé-writing, and speech-writing service. They did website development, too. When times are tough, the weak bail and the tough get creative.

Tough definitely described the local real estate agent. While I was faxing my files, she tried to sell me on three rental properties—leased by the week, she promised. As for the murders, she said Cody was clearly the killer. If not him, then Alastair Koppel. She didn't have any evidence to support her claims, simply that Cody was a "useless little snot" and Alastair a "dirty old perv," which wasn't news on either count.

As I left the real estate agency, I was plotting my next move. When I saw a baby carriage blocking the sidewalk, I stopped so quickly I nearly fell into it. The woman behind it was in her early thirties with artfully streaked blond hair and the kind of designer blouse, slacks, and pumps ensemble you couldn't find within fifty miles of Columbus.

"My husband didn't kill Ginny Thompson," she said.

It took a moment before I recognized her as the distant figure I'd seen in a doorway yesterday: Tiffany Radu.

I offered my hand and said, "Savannah Levine. Pleased to meet you, Mrs. Radu."

She gripped the carriage tighter. "He's not a killer."

"I'm an independent investigator. I have nothing to gain by sending your husband to jail if he's innocent."

"I don't want you coming around the house."

"I don't intend to."

"You already have."

"Um, no. The closest I've been to your house is the police station, which is across the road. The only time I've spoken to your husband is this morning, when he bumped my bike with his SUV. Even then, I didn't question him, let alone accuse him—"

"You'd better not. I won't have my children hearing people say their father is a murderer."

"They won't hear it from me." Given that I'd heard the older two were school age, I was pretty sure they'd heard already. "If you'll excuse me . . ."

I tried to sidestep, but she used her carriage as a roadblock. Now, normally, no one gets in my way like that, but I drew the line at shoving sleeping babies.

She scowled up at me. "I want you to—"

"—stay away from your house, your husband, your kids. I get it. But you know what? If you really want to protect your kids, tell your husband to stop screwing around or, if he has to and you're okay with that, to be discreet. Because your kids are going to find out about *that*, and when they do, they'll hate him for treating you like garbage, and they'll hate you for putting up with it."

"Who are you to be giving marital advice?" She pointedly stared at my ring-free left hand.

"Well, if you're going to stand in my way, I have to talk about something. So you're okay with Cody screwing his way through every girl who's too drunk or doped up to notice what a sleaze he is?"

Her eyes narrowed, mouth opening, but nothing coming out.

"I bet you *are* okay with it," I said. "At least if it means he's knocking them around instead of you. It's not like you'd feel threatened by women like Ginny Thompson."

Across the road, Megan appeared, leading eight girls, the mother hen with her chicks, waving at the new girl dawdling at the back. The new girl was watching Tiffany and me, squinting nearsightedly, as if she recognized us, but couldn't remember from where.

"But Claire was different," I continued as the girls trooped into a store. "Claire was young, pretty, educated. *She* was competition."

"My husband never even met Claire Kennedy."

"I heard otherwise. If Claire was at that commune, she must have been as vulnerable as Ginny. Cody likes them vulnerable. Makes him feel like a man, apparently. More than you do."

Her hand flew up to slap me. I caught her by the wrist. She yanked away, twisting to claw the underside of my arm.

"*Ow*," I said, frowning at the scratches. "Are your nails clean? Because if I get infected—"

"Stay away from my family or you'll be sorry."

"Did you threaten Ginny like this, too? Guess I'll have to check those autopsy photos for claw marks. Now, if you'll excuse me . . ."

I put out a hand to block the stroller, and walked past.

The gossips of Columbus might be an old-fashioned bunch, pointing fingers at the guys when they had a killer on the loose. But between Tiffany and Megan, I was kinda liking the ladies for this one.

Tiffany didn't let me get away that easily. She tried to follow as fast as her short legs would carry her. I just sauntered along, letting my stride eat up the sidewalk. Then my cell rang. "Light My Fire."

"My Jeep needs a new top," Adam said in greeting.

"Uh-huh. I thought I mentioned this after I was rained on all the way to Seattle."

I took a seat on a bench outside the post office. Tiffany stopped ten feet away from me, glowering over her stroller.

"I can't afford one," Adam said.

"Oh, right, because you had to replace the brakes two months ago, and the transmission the month before that."

Tiffany finally moved on. I waved good-bye and turned my attention back to Adam.

"You know what you really need?" I said. "A new car, a grown-up vehicle that won't break down every few months. Time to lose the surfer-boy-mobile."

"*Off-road*-mobile, which I need for lugging around rock-climbing gear and spelunking gear and horseback-riding gear for a certain someone. Love to see you carrying your saddle on that motorcycle."

"Um, you're the one who got me into rock-climbing and spelunking because you wanted someone else to drag along. And you love horseback riding. You just hate to admit it because it's girly. Is this really why you called? Or are you just unbelievably bored?"

"I need an excuse to phone you now? But yes, the point of this call is that I need a new top for my Jeep. I'm thinking beige this time. Easier to keep clean."

"Uh-huh. Well, save your pennies and—"

"I'm thinking you'll buy it for me."

"Excuse me?"

"Payback," he said. "For a huge favor."

"Uh-huh."

"Not going to ask me what it is?"

"I'm afraid to."

"Come on."

"Fine, but requesting the information in no way obligates me to—"

"I surrender. No more Lucas-speak. That ritual Cody was conducting in the Facebook photos? It's a bastardized version of a very old home-security ritual. It's complicated, and witches and sorcerers have developed better and faster spells since. It's not something you'd learn unless your family was out of the supernatural loop, still using the old stuff."

"It's real magic, then?"

"Based on real magic, which means Cody Radu is a sorcerer, which is why I called you right away. Stay away from him if you can and if you can't, dark sunglasses are a fashion must."

"We've already met."

A pause. "Face to face?"

"Eye to eye. He's not a sorcerer." Witches recognize sorcerers on sight, and vice-versa. "He could be a magician"—a minor form of sorcerer—"or a shaman, druid, Vodoun priest, necromancer, something with magic juice, maybe learned the spell from a sorcerer buddy, remembered the basics for frat night."

"The important thing, though—"

"—is that we're dealing with a supernatural, which means we're probably dealing with the killer. Damn. I hate the obvious choice."

"Don't jump to conclusions. Just because he's a supernatural, doesn't mean someone else isn't. Oh, and that symbol on the gate? It's Santeria. A bastardized form. I found it online at a site selling amulets. They claim they're Santeria, but look like a mix of voodoo and Santeria, which means you probably don't have a real practitioner."

"Just the kind of wannabe that keeps occult shops in business."

"Yep. So, do I get a new top?"

"Better invest in duct tape. Now, I need to run so—"

"Call me later."

I gave an evil laugh.

"Let me rephrase that," he said. "Call me sometime later than now, but before midnight."

"We'll see."

FIFTEEN

I STILL HAD ALMOST TWO HOURS TO KILL BEFORE MEETING Cody. I called Jesse to let him know I'd sent the files. He was on the other line and said he'd phone back. I wandered into the first shop I came to—the hardware store where Dorothy claimed Cody and Claire had argued. I was browsing, trying to attract the clerk's attention so I could ask about it, when a voice behind my shoulder said, "I thought PIs were supposed to be unobtrusive."

I turned to see Megan. The rest of her group was outside, milling about.

"Getting in a catfight with the main suspect's wife?" she said. "On Main Street?"

"She started it."

Megan smiled. "I don't doubt that. Tiffany Radu is one of those women who believes it's easier to scare away the competition than to tell her husband to respect his wedding vows. You should have seen her when we first moved here—practically hissing every time we came to town."

"Did you ever see her facing off with Claire?"

Her eyes sparkled. "Is that the direction you're looking? Interesting. I can't say I did, but I'll ask the girls. Or you can ask them yourself. We're heading to the diner for an early lunch, if you want to join us."

"So I'm forgiven for yesterday?"

"You were just doing your job. And I was doing mine. Protecting the business."

I noticed she said the *business*, not the girls.

"I might take you up on that. And Alastair? Is he—?"

"Away today, I'm afraid. But we can set up an appointment."

I glanced out the window. "The new girl seems nervous. Still bracing for the orgies, I bet."

Megan laughed. "Is that all you think about?"

"I like sex. And from what I hear, so do you." I turned to go. "Or is it power?"

A good parting line, but I didn't get more than two steps before she said, "Power," and I spun back to face her.

"You didn't expect me to admit it?" she said. "Sure, the sex is a nice bonus, but sex is power, at least when you've got a houseful of girls and one man."

"That's honest."

"I thought you'd appreciate it."

Megan was clearly playing me, having decided I made a better ally than enemy. That was fine. I thought the same about her.

"So you're sleeping with Alastair?"

"I'd rather *not* admit it, because that's exactly what everyone expects, but I know you already got the scoop from Deirdre, so yes, Alastair doesn't spend a lot of nights alone. Under the circumstances, he'd have to be a saint or a eunuch if he did. I'm sure Deirdre also told you that I'm insanely jealous of every girl he takes to bed."

"And you're not."

"They like to think I am. They're like little girls, giggling because they put one over on the teacher. But I'm not Tiffany Radu. I encourage Alastair to take the new girls up on their offers. What matters isn't that he strays; it's that he comes back."

When I looked doubtful, she said, "Think about it. All those girls. All that temptation. He gives in—he's only human. But he always returns to me. To the girls, that means something."

"That you're the queen bee."

She smiled. "Every hive needs one."

I did join them for lunch, though I just got a coffee. But no one was about to say anything in front of Megan. When I asked about Claire and Cody, I noticed a girl with blue-streaked hair shifting in her seat, like she had something to add. She didn't speak, though. I needed to get her when the boss wasn't around.

The girls had barely ordered when my cell rang. Jesse. I excused myself to take it, and thanked them for their time, leaving a five to cover my coffee—and win brownie points with Lorraine.

I rubbed my neck as I headed outside to call Jesse back. The headache again. Definitely time for a different helmet . . . something I'm sure the hardware store didn't stock. I made a mental note to grab aspirin later.

Jesse had run a background check on Megan. She was twenty-six, older than I thought. Her story checked out— MBA from Columbia, worked on Wall Street for a while, then bailed.

"Burnout," Jesse said. "She doesn't strike me as the type to run off to a commune, but I guess you can never tell."

"Oh, you can usually tell. I don't think Megan burned out. She just realized she could make more working in a start-up company where she was in charge. That's what the commune is to her. A business. Those girls aren't working for much more than room and board, I'm sure of it. And they're pulling their own weight there, too—cooking and cleaning."

"So cynical, so young."

"You think I'm wrong?"

"No, I'm just kicking myself for not seeing the con first. I'm supposed to be the expert on the workings of the criminal mind. I'll make up for it now and dig into the financials."

"Please. Everyone here really likes the sexy angles—the philandering husband and the weird cult leader—but it may come down to money."

"It usually does. I'll get on that, then."

With the girls eating lunch in town and Alastair away, it was the perfect time to take a closer look at the commune. I parked my bike in a wooded area nearby, then headed in the back way. Once I was sure that the drive was empty and the lights all off, I approached the front gate, to get a better look at the symbol. It was there—and had been repainted.

I licked my finger and smudged a line. Yep, blood. Likely chicken blood, if someone was practicing Santeria.

I eyed the house wistfully. As rustic as it appeared, I was sure it had a burglar alarm. Disarming it wouldn't leave me much time for searching before Megan came back. And I figured I had just as good a chance of finding evidence of rituals out here.

I went through the outbuildings. Met some chickens, a couple of cows, even a pig. No horses, though, which seemed a complete waste of barn space. I did manage to make friends with a barn cat. Or it made friends with me.

I'm not a pet person—even with horses, I've never seriously considered owning one—but you have to give cats kudos for attitude. If you stop to pet them, they can't be bothered with you. Ignore them, and they rise to the challenge. By the time

I was done searching the outbuildings, the cat had brought me a gift—a still-twitching rat. I was impressed. I rewarded it with an ear scratch, and it took off, mission accomplished.

That was the only reward I got, though. A half hour of searching, and all I had to show for it was shit on my boots.

There was one other outbuilding behind the barns. It was locked, which seemed promising, until I opened it and found tools and a lawn tractor. I checked out the yard next. Vegetable garden, herb garden, even a couple of beehives behind the tool-shed. So very *Little House on the Prairie*. Why anyone would choose to live like this is beyond me.

I was checking out the hives when I noticed the boarded-up window above them. That made me realize I hadn't seen a boarded-up window from the inside . . . and that the toolshed looked a lot bigger from out here.

I went back in. Sure enough, there was a false wall. And behind it? A sacrificial altar. Not for human sacrifice—Santerians don't practice that. I've been well schooled in basic respect for religions, courtesy of Paige. Not that she always practices what she preaches—I recall a certain incident with naked Wiccans in our backyard—but she handled it more respectfully than I would have, and she would point out it'd been a small sect, not indicative of the religion as a whole.

Santeria is a Caribbean religion melding African, Catholic, and Native American traditions. Its rituals include the sacrifice of animals. There was evidence of that here—a small ornate axe and bloodstains on the floor. There were also coins, oils, flowers, herbs, colored cloth, stones, beads, even a set of dominos, for rituals of a less bloody sort.

A lamp burned on a table. It was a clay pot of oil with stuff floating in it and a wick on top. I could make out ashes and metal in the oil. Beside it lay a dead scorpion coated in oil.

I took pictures, sent them to Adam, then called.

"Now that you actually need my help, I can't get rid of you," he said when he answered.

"I just sent you—"

"Photos. I'm looking at them now. With the scorpion, we seem to have another home-protection ritual, this one specifically to keep away enemies. The oil has to burn for a few days, and most of it's still there. You were up at the house yesterday, weren't you?"

"So this ritual is to protect them from *me*? Cool. Doesn't work, though."

"I can't imagine anything that would. So we definitely have someone practicing Santeria. Presumably someone high on the group's food chain. One of the girls isn't going to construct a hidden room in the toolshed."

"I know Santeria doesn't condone human sacrifice, but if we're dealing with a wannabe, maybe they're bending the rules. If chickens don't work, try dead girls. Any link with the crime-scene stuff?"

"That bead Claire was clutching could be significant for the pewter or from the symbolism. Could even be a cheap stand-in for silver. I'll keep looking. Anything else?"

"No, Jesse's doing the background checks."

"Got the guys doing the grunt work, huh?"

"After years of doing it for you, Paige, and Lucas, I'm liking this a whole lot better."

"Just don't get used to it."

Evidence of Santeria did not mean we'd found our killer, any more than if I'd found evidence of a Catholic mass. But these ritualistic religions did attract fringe types who misunderstood the beliefs and focused on the occultlike aspects.

Now I needed to figure out *who* was the practitioner. The best place to find evidence of that would be in the house. If there was an alarm, I'd be out of luck, but I could always hope they were the sort who left without turning it on.

Even better—the back door was latched but not locked. I eased it open, bracing for the squeal of an alarm. Silence. I slipped in and looked around. I found a security panel, but it was green. Unarmed.

As I crept into the hall, a phone rang. On the third ring, it stopped. I paused, expecting an answering machine.

"Hello?" A man's voice. Alastair. Shit. That's why the door was open and the alarm off.

The voice came from the front of the house. I cast a blur spell, and began a slow retreat to the kitchen door. That sleep spell would have been really handy right about now. Damn. I needed to find a cemetery.

"Ice cream, huh?" He laughed. "No, that's fine. They could use the break and I could use the peace and quiet to finish this ledger. Take as long as you want, Meg."

Okay, he was busy in his office and the girls were enjoying after-lunch ice cream.

I took off my boots, cast another blur spell, and zipped up the stairs, boots in hand. Padding around in socks, I searched all six bedrooms. The closest thing to talismans I found were a four-leaf clover pendant on a dresser and a dream catcher hanging in a window. For drugs, I found only a stash of pot and a cache of diet pills. Whoever was practicing Santeria was keeping it out of the house.

I headed back downstairs. As I passed the living room, the doorbell rang. I darted into the living room, dove behind an armchair, and cast a cover spell. As long as I didn't move, I'd be okay.

When Alastair opened the door, I recognized the visitor's voice. Tiffany Radu.

"I met your new girl in town," she said. "She gave me a coupon for a dozen cookies. Getting a little bold, aren't you? It would be much easier to call."

Alastair laughed. "I wish I could take the credit, but no, Megan must have given Amy those to hand out. A nice way to introduce herself. Come in, please."

Tiffany pushed the baby buggy into the living room and returned to the hall.

"So, do you want those cookies?" he asked.

"Is that the only thing on the menu?"

A chuckle. Then a crash, like a body hitting a wall. I jumped, startling the baby, who stared at me, her blue eyes wide. From the hall came a grunt, then the whir of a zipper. A groan. A sucking noise. Another groan.

Okay, no one was getting killed. And I would have been less surprised if someone was.

The baby craned her head, trying to see her mother. I really hoped she couldn't. Seeing Mom blowing a guy who isn't your dad really isn't an experience any kid needs imprinted on her young memory.

I slid from behind the chair and tugged the buggy toward me until I was certain the baby couldn't see Tiffany. It's a sad day when I'm more concerned for a child than her mother is.

The baby started whimpering now. There was no way Tiffany could hear her—Alastair was too vocal in his appreciation. When a baby isn't heard, though, a baby gets louder, and I didn't want them coming in here.

I murmured an incantation. A light ball appeared on my fingertips. The baby's eyes rounded. I tossed it to hover over her buggy and she giggled and crowed.

"Mama, Mama!" she said, bouncing as I made the light ball dance.

Tiffany really needed to work on her parenting skills if her kid adopted the first stranger who paid attention to her.

I went through a repertoire of simple tricks—lights, sparks, fog, all the ones kids love. I'd learned all the ways to keep Elena and Clay's twins amused when I babysat. Now that they're school age, they want to learn the tricks . . . and get royally pissed off when they can't.

So I entertained the baby as Mom and the local cult dude moved to full-on screwing. When they started banging against the walls, the baby got concerned again. I did, too. The house was old and they were really going at it.

I picked up an ugly stuffed toy from the buggy and made it dance. The baby grabbed it and threw it. I knew this game. I picked it up and gave it back. She threw it, then chortled when the stupid grown-up fell for it again.

The toy looked homemade. Tiffany didn't seem the type to lovingly sew toys for her baby. It was definitely an amateur job, with weird stitching along the seams. An older sibling? Whatever they'd stuffed it with, it wasn't exactly soft and cuddly. It felt like . . . dried herbs.

I caught a whiff of something that made my eyes fly open. I lifted the toy to my nose.

It was stuffed with blessed thistle. Most witches don't use herbs outside of rituals, but blessed thistle used to be stuffed into sachets for protection and health. I think Wiccans still used it. I glanced toward the front hall. Was Tiffany Wiccan?

I looked closer at the toy and noticed the stitching wasn't actually messy. It was symbolic. Special stitching for protection. Not Wiccan. Witch.

Now I knew why the baby had been calling me Mama when she saw the spells. Cody Radu wasn't the spell-caster in the family. Tiffany was.

SIXTEEN

TIFFANY WASN'T THE CUDDLES AND COOING TYPE. SHE GOT what she wanted and left with a box of cookies to excuse her visit. I suspected the Radu household ate a lot of cookies.

Was Tiffany punishing her husband for screwing around with girls like Ginny? Maybe. But whatever Cody's hang-ups, I bet there was a touch of the Madonna/whore complex going on. Ginny and her ilk were for wall-shaking sex and Tiffany was for making babies and adorning his arm at company dinners. Only it turned out that Tiffany liked her share of wall-shaking, too. Alastair was a safe outlet—an outsider who was unlikely to ask for any commitment while he had a houseful of young women offering the same goodies.

It was all a little too soap-opera confusing for my brain right now, so I zeroed in on the part that really piqued my interest— finding out that I wasn't the only witch in town.

Back at my bike, I called Jesse to see if he had a maiden name for Tiffany. He did. Baker. Not exactly as uncommon as I hoped. I asked him to dig a little deeper and see where she was from, maybe get some family details.

"So you've got one witch," he said when I explained.

"Presumably married to another supernatural if she's been showing him rituals. You've also got Santeria. Sounds like there's more to this town than it seems."

My next call was to Paige. I still wasn't telling her about the case, of course, but she'd be my best source of background on Tiffany.

"I have a local witch," I said. "But she's using outdated magic."

"Which suggests she's from a family that has slipped outside the network. Well, whatever network still exists for witches."

I could hear the regret in her voice. Paige works hard to get that network running again, but after the witch hunts, most witches took a "never again" attitude and disassociated themselves from their magic.

"Maybe," I said. "But if it's nearly useless magic, that screams Coven."

Paige sighed. She'd grown up a Coven witch herself. She didn't argue, though. The Coven was the worst offender when it came to keeping witches in the Dark Ages of magic, only allowing its members to use old and simplistic spells, like the light ball.

"Her name was Baker," I said. "Tiffany Baker. She's a few years older than you, so even if her family left the Coven, you should remember her."

"I don't. I'll check the records, though."

If Paige didn't recognize the name, the Bakers hadn't been part of the Coven, so I told her not to bother. I could handle this one.

I arrived at the McDonald's twenty minutes late for my appointment. Cutting through the parking lot, I saw Cody Radu stalking out of the restaurant, another man hurrying along at his side, trying to talk to him.

Cody's SUV was nearby, so I cast a blur spell, zipped around it, then cast a cover one.

"Every shred of evidence was supposed to be concealed," Cody was saying as they approached. "That's your job, Tommy."

"Yes, and I've covered it. If this PI has dug up something, then we've got a leak. But that's why I'm here—to throw her off the trail."

"Then you'd better work fast. I can handle the bitch. She's going after Tiff, though, and I won't take that."

Had Tiffany told him I'd confronted her? I remembered what Cody had said about me being in town a few days. Only hours later, Tiffany had accused me of coming to her house. Was somebody stalking them? Or had Cody and Tiffany just been under Bruyn's magnifying glass too long?

"It'll end," Tommy said. "As your friend, I promise you it will. As your lawyer, I strongly suggest you get your ass back in that restaurant and wait for her."

"She's late."

"She's testing you. She's trying to make you sweat, and it's working."

Cody snarled something I couldn't hear.

"Christ, buddy, cool it, okay? I know you're worried about the shipment tonight, but it's all under control. Just go back in that restaurant, and when we're done here, we'll hit Lula's place for a couple of hours." A chuckle. "That'll get your mind off things."

"I'm not going back in the restaurant," Cody said. "I do not give any smart-ass piece of pussy—"

"Hey, guys," I said walking around the front of the SUV. "Sorry I'm late. I didn't have a cell number to call." I held my hand out to Tommy, whom I recognized as the frat brother who'd posted the occult ritual pics on Facebook. "Savannah Levine."

He didn't respond right away, too busy ogling to notice my outstretched hand. Then he took it in a firm shake. "Thompson Harris. Cody's lawyer."

I grinned. "So I'm already lawyer-worthy? Cool. Let's go inside then. I'm starving."

"Have you ever done any modeling?" Tommy asked as I bit into my Big Mac.

It was a line I got a lot. I think every tall, thin, reasonably attractive woman does.

"Not eating like that, she doesn't," Cody muttered, waving a hand at my fries, burger, and milk shake.

"I eat this way because I still can," I said. "After a certain age, my metabolism will hit the brakes and I'll be stuck with that shit." I waved at Cody's salad.

Tommy laughed. "Cody was right. You are feisty."

"*Feisty* wasn't the word I heard him use. As for modeling, let's just say not in the traditional sense." I flashed a wicked grin. "But a girl's gotta pay the rent somehow."

I bullshitted like a pro, giving Tommy enough hints to send him looking for booty shots online when he should be doing a standard background check. I'm sure he'd tell himself it was business, digging up something to discredit me. Probably even bill Cody for the time he spent porn surfing.

Flirting also kept him distracted enough not to jump in with objections when I questioned Cody. Not that it helped much. Cody knew better than to incriminate himself and I didn't have enough details yet to ask about the fight with Claire. Instead we spent the time circling, each trying to get a peek at the other's cards.

Finally Cody got fed up and went to sulk in the bathroom. He was gone a while, doubtless hoping I'd give up and leave. I flirted some more with Tommy, which seemed to convince him

I wasn't anything more than a pretty face. Screwing potential: high. Threat potential: zilch.

I'll admit to being a little nervous when we left. Maybe nervous isn't the right word. Cautious. The back road from here to Columbus was long and empty, and if Cody pulled out right behind me, I'd be tempted to take the highway, rather than play road warrior again with his SUV. But apparently he was taking Tommy up on his offer to visit Lula's. They left in separate vehicles, and headed for the highway.

I was zooming down the empty back road, the wind whistling past, when my bike did a little *bump-bump*. I glanced in my rearview mirror, thinking I'd hit a pothole. Another bump. Then the rear tire wobbled. I barely had time to think *Oh, shit!* and the tire blew with a deafening bang.

SEVENTEEN

THE BIKE STARTED VEERING TOWARD THE CENTER LINE. I wrenched it the other way, desperately steering for the side of the road, hitting it, dust and gravel flying up. The bike went into a slide. I held on as tight as I could, bracing myself for that final bone-jarring topple.

I lay in the gravel at the side of the road, bike pinning my leg down, panic arcing through me. Then, slowly, I heaved the bike off me. I braced for a wave of pain, but it didn't come. I felt like I'd been thrown out of a van. Nothing screamed "I'm broken," though.

A clean lay-down, which is the most you can hope for. Still holding the bike up, I slid out from under it and rose, stretching and patting myself down. My leather jacket was scratched to shit. My jeans were studded with pebbles. I was okay, though, which is more than I could say for my bike.

I assessed the damage—dings and scrapes and twisted handlebars—and decided we'd both gotten away pretty damned good. Which wouldn't keep me from kicking Cody Radu's ass when I got hold of him. Sulking in the bathroom? No, he'd been sabotaging my bike and—

A silver vehicle crested the hill. I froze, but it was only a car.

I let out a sigh of relief, then a string of curses as the stupid bitches in the front seat gawked at me, not even slowing to see if I needed help.

That made me realize Cody might have more in mind than just sabotaging my ride. I was now stranded on a very empty stretch of road.

I took out my cell phone. It had survived the fall, but it didn't matter. No service.

The back tire was blown, meaning the motorcycle was useless, and I was still two or three miles from town. I started pushing. My left leg seized up. Okay, not as uninjured as I'd thought. Shit.

Another vehicle came over the hill. A pickup this time. I took off my helmet, making it clear I was female, and waved at the wrecked bike. Too late I heard the scrape of the muffler. It was the skeevy guy who'd driven past the police station yesterday.

He stopped beside me. "Laid her down, huh?" He grinned. "That's why little girls shouldn't play with big-boy toys. I suppose you want a lift now."

"No, I'm good. I could use the exercise. Build up my muscles so I can handle her next time."

His grin faltered. "It's about five miles."

"Thanks, but I'm fine."

He hesitated, then sped off, steering into the gravel to dust me. I answered with an energy bolt to his back tire. Just a little one. A slow leak that would, if I was lucky, strand him on an empty road of his own in a day or two.

I looked at the hill, then at the truck speeding away. Five miles to town? I was sure he was exaggerating, but even half of that was too far to push a motorcycle.

I headed off the road. I set her down in the brush, too far from the road to be seen, then went back and cleaned up the signs of my lay-down. I was barely done when the top of another silver vehicle came over the hill.

Hiding in those bushes was one of the hardest things I'd ever done. Everything in me screamed that I should stand at the side of the road and wait for the bastard.

But I had a pretty good idea what Cody had in mind. This wasn't a guy who let women stand up to him. He had to bring me down and if I wasn't lying on the side of the road, he'd put me there.

I thought I could take him in a fight, even if I wasn't sure what kind of supernatural he was. But I was on a case. As tempting as it was to show up assholes like Cody Radu, I'd deal with him later, in a way that wouldn't run me any risk of being hauled off to jail for assault.

I hadn't done as good a job as I thought of disguising where I went off the road. He slowed there, put down his window, and squinted into the brush beyond. He didn't stop, though, just rolled along slowly, scanning the roadside for me.

Once he was gone, I set out again. I kept a watch on the horizon, in case he doubled back. He didn't. I'd gotten as far as the spot where I hid my bike when I heard the purr of a performance engine behind me. I turned to see a black BMW.

Michael Kennedy. My day was now complete.

I continued walking, expecting, hoping, he'd drive past with a honk and a wave, happy to see me suffering after I'd sent him on a wild-goose chase. Instead, he slowed and drove beside me in silence for a minute.

Finally he rolled down the window. "Are you okay?"

"Better than my bike," I said, gesturing to where I'd hidden it.

"One could say this is karma."

"Yeah, yeah. So how was your visit to Cougar?"

"A wasted morning, which I completely deserved. I promised I wouldn't fish for leads, and that's exactly what I did."

"Because that's exactly why you asked me out."

"What? No. I wouldn't—"

He met my gaze and the denial dried up. He swore, blushing, and pulled ahead onto the shoulder and got out.

"I'm sorry," he said. "I was a jerk and my only excuse—"

"—is that you want to find your sister's killer. I get that. But I'm not competing with you, Detective Kennedy. If you'd asked what I'd found, I would have told you. I just don't like being played."

He nodded, walked over, and handed me the keys. "Drive her back. I'll walk the bike and meet you at the garage. There's one just off Main."

I'd seen it—the former town gas station, now just a garage. I took the keys, got in his car, and waited for his reaction. Offering to take my bike was a nice gesture, but it was just that—a gesture. He didn't expect me to take him up on it.

I started the engine. He retrieved my bike and began walking. I rolled the car up beside him.

"You're okay with this?"

"I offered, didn't I? Just be careful. Driving without a license . . . I hate to sound like a cop, but you could get in a lot of trouble."

I stopped the car. "You're right. You should—"

"No, I was just saying to take it easy." When I hesitated, he waved me on. "Go. You're slowing me down."

I reached into my pocket and held up a card. My driver's license.

"I thought you said—"

"Implied, never said."

He laughed and waved me on again. I drove a quarter-mile, then circled back and came up beside him again.

"You're serious, aren't you?" I said.

"Uh, yeah. I'm serious about the apology, too. I was a jerk."

"You're a cop. You're supposed to be a jerk."

"I don't think that's in the code."

"Read the fine print. It's there." I parked and got out. "I'm not leaving you to walk my bike two miles."

We argued for a minute. Then he gave me my bike and started walking . . . south away from his car.

"Hey!" I called. "Where—?"

He flagged down an approaching pickup. The old guy stopped, which probably had something to do with the badge Michael was waving. He explained that we needed a lift. The guy assumed it was police business and grumbled, but didn't argue. Michael and I loaded the bike into the back, then he waved me to his car.

"I'll go with him." He held up a hand against my protest. "I'm protecting the old guy, not you. Pretty girl in the passenger seat, he might not be able to help himself, and I don't think he wants to spend the rest of the day in the hospital." He walked to the truck. "See you in town."

Not surprisingly, the garage didn't carry my tires. There wasn't even a mechanic on duty, just a kid fresh out of high school who "knew a lot about cars." He liked my bike, though. Liked Michael's car even better, and declared that he was definitely moving to Portland or Seattle next year, as if life in a big city came with keys to a sweet ride.

He called two other garages trying to get me a tire. Neither had one, but they recommended a bike shop in Vancouver. He called and they had one in stock and would hold it for me until they closed at seven.

"I'll give you a lift," Michael said as we drove off, leaving my bike behind the shop.

"You really are sorry, aren't you? No. We both have a case to work and you've already spent most of the day on a wild-goose chase."

"You can't investigate without wheels, Savannah, and the nearest car rental is in Vancouver. I checked when mine was acting up."

"All right then. Pick me up at my motel at five-thirty. We'll grab the tire, then I'll take you out. I promise to feed you only dinner—no more false leads." I glanced out the window. "Oh, can you drop me off here? I've got some legwork to do."

He parked on Main Street. "So, are you going to tell me what happened with the bike?"

"Tire blew."

"I saw that. If there was an ongoing problem with it, though, you would have noticed. And if you'd run over something, you would have stopped."

I told him what happened. When he finished cursing out Cody, I said, "I could be wrong. Maybe I did just run over a nail or something."

"And he just happened to drive past slowly to admire the scenery?"

"I'm trying not to be paranoid."

"I'd say you have a right to be. You—" He noticed the hardware store clerk staring at us through the store window.

"We look like we're on a stakeout," I said. "We're making the townies nervous."

He opened the door. We got out and stood on the sidewalk.

"You need to be careful, Savannah."

"Um, no, I need to teach this control-freak scumbag that he can't mess with me."

Michael's mouth opened, then closed.

"What?" I said.

"I'm just asking you not to egg him on. You did the right thing today, not confronting him."

"I'm glad you approve."

He leaned against his car. "Okay, I've overstepped, obviously. I should mind my own business. Let you goad him into another strike."

"What better way to catch him if he's the killer?"

"You're right." His gaze frosted over, and his words were sharp. "Go right ahead. See if he'll go after you again. Make sure he does some damage, too—it's far more convincing if we have hospital records. Better yet, morgue records."

"I'm not stupid—"

"No, but maybe you are just a little bit reckless."

I shook my head.

"What?" he said.

"You sound like a guy I know."

"Well, he's a smart guy, then, and maybe you should listen. Cody Radu could have killed you out there. I'm not saying to back down. Stand firm, just don't goad him."

Adam would tell me the same thing—he was always the last person to stop me from standing up for myself, but the first to tear a strip off me when I got reckless.

"All right," I said. "I should ease off him for a while anyway. I'm not getting anywhere."

"I've got my own appointment with him tomorrow morning. I'll give him a shake. See if anything comes loose. Maybe some of those pearly whites, if we're lucky."

I hesitated. The problem with my job is that the two priorities—solving the case and uncovering any supernatural involvement—sometimes clashed. I wanted to find Claire's killer. Yet I needed to keep Michael from finding any supernatural angles. I weighed the threat potential of what I was about to say and decided to go for it.

"I have a lead that might link Claire and Cody," I offered.

"What?"

"Legit this time. I won't play you anymore. I don't want to tip him off until I have details, but there's a good chance he had a conversation with Claire the day before she died. Also, he's definitely up to something illegal." I told him about the conversation I'd overheard with his lawyer friend. "A delivery. That's all I know."

"I can use that. Thanks. A lot." He stepped closer, gaze holding mine. "Really, I appreciate—"

"Are you guys done arguing?" a voice asked.

We looked over to see Kayla. Michael stepped back.

"Hey," I said.

"I saw you arguing earlier and I didn't want to get in the way."

"We weren't arguing," Michael said. "Just debating strategy."

She looked disappointed.

"I know we met, Kayla, but not officially." Michael held out his hand. "Michael Kennedy, I'm Claire's brother and I'm—"

"A police detective. I've heard." She lifted her chin, as if to say others might be impressed by his credentials, but she wasn't.

"I'm just heading over to see your grandma," Michael said. "Will I see you there?"

"Probably not." She turned to me. "Are you busy? I need to talk to you." A look Michael's way. "It's private."

"Okay," he said. Then to me, "Pick you up at five-thirty?"

I nodded. Kayla waited until he was gone, then turned, expression unreadable.

"You're going out with him?" she said.

"A good private investigator uses every method at her disposal." I winked as the BMW roared from the curb. "Plus he's cute and drives a really hot car."

She rolled her eyes so high they threatened to disappear.

"Okay," I said. "You wanted to talk. I heard this town has ice cream—"

"Later. Did you see Dorothy?"

"She wouldn't answer the door."

"I'll get you in. Come on."

EIGHTEEN

I KNOCKED. WHEN NO ONE ANSWERED, KAYLA OPENED THE door.

"Hey, Dorothy! It's me. Aunt Rose sent some of that peppermint tea you like."

A wizened old woman with fire-engine-red hair peeked around the corner. Spotting me, she scowled. "Kayla Thompson, you're a lying little—"

Kayla held up a bag. "Here's the tea. Oh, and this is Savannah Levine. She's investigating my mom's murder. I told her you saw Cody and Claire arguing, but she needs to hear it from you."

Kayla marched past her into the kitchen. "I'll make your tea while you tell her."

Dorothy followed. "I'm not telling her anything, Miss Kayla. I don't know what you heard—"

"You saw Claire and Cody arguing behind the hardware store."

"Who told you—?"

"You did. I heard you at Aunt Rose's."

"So you were eavesdropping."

"Yep." She filled the kettle.

Dorothy turned to me. "Kayla heard wrong. I never saw—"

"Yes, you did." Kayla plunked the kettle on the stove, flicked the burner, then parked herself on a kitchen chair. "You don't want to tell Chief Bruyn because you're still mad at him for egging your house when he was twelve."

"And thirteen. And fourteen."

"So you don't want to help him. That's okay. You're telling *Savannah*. You don't have anything against her, do you?"

Dorothy's look said just give her time and she'd find something.

"If she solves the case, it'll make Chief Bruyn look bad," Kayla pointed out.

Dorothy's eyes glittered, but after a moment, she shook her head. "I don't want to get involved."

"That's up to you," Kayla said. "Just as long as you don't mind having a killer in your town. One who might have *seen* you spying on him that day."

Dorothy scowled at her, then finally waved me to a chair.

She settled across the table, looked me over again, then said, "It was the day before that girl died."

Dorothy had been in the hardware store, trying to return a frying pan she'd left on the stove too long. Cody had been in line behind her, getting impatient as she argued with the clerk, which I'm sure only made Dorothy all the more determined not to step aside.

That's when Claire came in. She'd walked past Cody and smiled.

"The hussy," Dorothy sniffed. "Don't you ever behave like that, Kayla. That's how your mom got into trouble."

"If my mom hadn't gotten into trouble, I wouldn't be here," Kayla said.

Dorothy harrumphed and resumed her story. Claire had smiled at Cody. Then she'd walked out the back door, tossing another smile over her shoulder. Cody—"being a man, and you know how men are"—forgot whatever he'd been there to buy and followed Claire out.

That's when the clerk gave up and agreed to exchange Dorothy's frying pan, so she didn't notice what was transpiring outside until she was about to leave, and caught a glimpse of Cody and Claire out the back door.

"That girl wasn't smiling anymore. She was saying something and Cody didn't like it one bit. He caught her by the wrist. She shook him off and tried walking back into the hardware store, but he stepped in front of her. Grabbed her arm. I headed for them. That girl was stupid, flirting with a boy like Cody Radu, but I wasn't going to stand by and let him hurt her. Cody saw me and let her go real fast. She came inside. He took off down the alley, I bet. Coward."

"Did Claire say anything to you?" I asked.

"I told her she ought to be more careful, and she agreed. Looked real shook up, too. Felt kinda sorry for her."

Not sorry enough to tell Bruyn about the fight. Claire had flirted to lure Cody outside, meaning they hadn't been lovers. What had she said to him? And, more important, was it worth killing her for?

As we left Dorothy's, Kayla reminded me of my ice cream offer. We'd just turned onto Main Street when a familiar silver SUV roared past.

When Cody saw me, he braked and squinted out the window, like he was hoping for a limp, a broken nose . . . I waved. He sped off.

"I hate him," Kayla said, almost too softly to be heard. "Even if he didn't kill my mom, I hate him."

She led me into the diner. We got ice cream and went back outside.

"Grandma decided I should talk to you," Kayla said. "On my own, without her there. That's why I came over when I saw you with that cop. I think she figures I'll tell you things I wouldn't with her there. She's still worried that Cody might have hit me."

"Did he?"

She hesitated, and my heart slid up to my throat. Shit. I wasn't prepared for this. I had no idea what to do and I was sure that whatever I did would be the wrong thing and it would be so important to do exactly the right thing—

"Would he go to jail if I said he did?" she asked.

"If he did hit you, then yes, that would help." I noticed her expression was studiously blank and said, slowly, "But if you lie about it, that could make things worse."

She sighed, shoulders slumping. "He never did. When they started dating, it was good. I mean, Cody didn't want anything to do with me, but I didn't care because Mom was happy." She looked up at me. "Really happy. Like I'd never seen her before. She said she'd finally found the right guy and he was going to be my dad one day. I didn't want him to be, but if she wanted it . . ."

"Then you were okay with that."

She nodded. "She said she was going to clean up, so she could be a good wife for him. She gave all her dope to Brandi, and she hardly drank at all. She showed me how to paint my nails, and one day we went into Battle Ground and got our hair done at a real beauty parlor—Grandma usually cuts mine—and Mom had the lady do our hair the same way and it was cool." Her gaze dropped. "It was really cool."

I waited for her to go on. After a moment, she did.

"Only Cody didn't want her to clean up. He'd bring her stuff—dope and booze—and if she didn't take it, he'd hit her. Brandi said that was okay, he liked her just the way she was and she should be happy."

"Was she?"

"For a while. One day, when she was high, she took me to Cody's house. His family was away for the weekend. She found the key and took me in, and she said it was going to be our house one day. She had me pick out a bedroom and everything." She watched ice cream drip down her fingers. "I didn't like that. Taryn—Cody's oldest daughter—was in my Girl Scout group before it closed down, and she was nice. That was her house. Her bedroom. I . . . I didn't like it. But it made Mom happy."

Again I waited, and she went on.

"Then Cody got worse. He brought my mom more drugs, and she was worse than ever, but he wouldn't let her stop. He started telling her what to wear—sexy clothes and more makeup. Once, he came over after I was in bed, and he brought this friend. I heard Mom saying she didn't want to do something and I heard him hitting her, and I snuck into the living room to make sure she was okay and she was . . . doing stuff. With the friend."

Oh, shit. "Do you want to talk about that? What you saw?"

"I know what it was." Her cheeks reddened. "I just . . . I never saw it before."

A girl her age *shouldn't*. Especially not when the one demonstrating is her mother.

I asked Kayla how she felt about what she'd seen, which seemed the right thing to do, but she squirmed and blushed, and I decided just to tell Paula, so she could deal with it.

"After a while, when Cody didn't leave his wife, Brandi told Mom she should at least ask for a better place to live. A good place, so Brandi could move out of her mom's house and live with us. There were lots of empty apartments around and Brandi figured that Cody could get us a good place super cheap."

"Did she ask?"

"I think so. I came back from school one day and she was drunk. She said we weren't moving—not into Cody's house or anyplace else—and it was all my fault." Kayla's voice went monotone, like she was reciting the times table. "She said she wished I'd never been born. She said Grandma was a selfish bitch for not taking me so she could be happy and marry Cody."

"You know that wouldn't have made a difference, right? Cody was just looking for an excuse and he blamed you. He wasn't going to leave his family. If your grandma took you, he'd have found another reason."

"I know." She got up and walked away, and I thought *Shit, I've said something wrong,* but she only dumped her half-eaten cone in the trash, then came back.

"After that, things got really bad," she said. "Mom was crying all the time, and she wasn't taking care of herself, having showers or anything, which only made Cody madder and made him hit her more. Brandi didn't help at all. She never did. Grandma told Mom not to listen to Brandi—that she only wanted the booze and dope Cody brought—and Mom should leave him. She wouldn't. Grandma tried getting Mom to talk to Dr. Graham about it, but that only made Mom get mad . . ." She looked out across the street. "It was bad."

"You know your grandma was trying to help, right?"

Kayla nodded. "That's when she told Mom she'd take me, but Mom said it didn't matter because I'd still be around. She'd still *have* a kid."

If I'd worked up any empathy for Ginny Thompson, it died at that moment. Hearing that your mother wanted you not just out of the house, but out of her life . . .

There were some parallels between me and Kayla—never knew our dads, mothers who weren't exactly PTA material. But whatever my mother's faults, I'd been the center of her universe.

Even when I'd gone to live with Paige, as overwhelmed as Paige had been, she'd loved and protected me. She'd risked and lost everything to keep me. I could not even begin to fathom Kayla's experience. I only thanked God she had her own Paige now in Paula.

"Then Mom and Cody broke up."

That startled me out of my thoughts. According to everything I'd heard, they'd still been dating at the time of Ginny's death.

"When did that happen?" I asked.

"About a week before she died."

"But they got back together?"

She shook her head. "Cody hadn't come over to our place all week and I heard Mom telling Brandi that he wasn't answering her text messages. Brandi gave Mom all these ideas for getting him back. She said Mom *had* to get Cody back."

"Did you tell Chief Bruyn this after the murders?"

"I did, but Cody said I was lying, and Grandma said maybe I misunderstood. But I didn't. Cody was the liar."

If Cody had dumped Ginny and she'd desperately wanted him back, she might have threatened his family. Or threatened to expose his underground business. Either was a motive for murder.

NINETEEN

KAYLA AND I TALKED A BIT MORE AFTER THAT. I ASKED HER if she had anything to share on the case—any tidbits she'd picked up in her detective work. She liked that, and gave me information that offered a fascinating glimpse into Columbus and what a child can hear when no one's paying attention to her.

I learned that the grocer, Mrs. Dean, was planning to leave her husband when their last child, Rob, went off to college. I learned that Mr. Martin told his wife he was looking for work, when really, he was just driving around, knowing there were no jobs for a fifty-year-old mill worker. I learned that Emily Rossi was sneaking into empty buildings to meet Rob Dean, though her parents told her she wasn't supposed to see him anymore, and they were planning to run away after they graduated high school. All very interesting, even if it didn't add anything to my investigation.

When we got back to Kayla's place, Michael was still talking with Paula. That made Kayla decide to play outside. I went inside and asked Michael if I could speak to Paula alone. He was cool with that. I sat her down at the kitchen table and told her that Kayla overheard Ginny say she didn't want Kayla around—at all. Then I told her how Kayla had seen Ginny with Cody's friend.

That last part was tough. I'm not sure what was worse, explaining it or seeing Paula's reaction. She was horrified . . . and guilt-stricken that she hadn't known. Kayla had gone to a therapist after her mom died, she said, and she was going to get in touch with the woman again.

I walked back to the motel after that, and on my way, I called Jesse with a rundown of my progress. I mentioned the tire blowout, but downplayed it. I told him I was going out with Michael and, no, it wasn't to trick him into giving away leads. I was hoping that after the tips I'd given him, he'd willingly offer some of his own.

Jesse was a little nervous about bringing Michael into the investigation. Typical ex-con—wary of cops and their motivations. I assured him we weren't teaming up. Nor, though, was I going to turn down the opportunity to share information with him.

I called Adam, too, in case I didn't get a chance later. No, I wasn't planning to bring Michael to my room, however well the evening went. Been there, done that. In my late teens I'd gone through a phase where I'd decided relationships, even short-term, weren't my thing. Sex was, though. Ergo, I had sex without the relationship. Which was fine at the time, but the appeal wore off. These days I took my time.

I updated Adam on the case, then we chatted until I reached the motel, and I realized Michael would be picking me up in about ten minutes.

"I'll call you tomorrow afternoon," I said.

"With any luck, I'll already be on my way there."

"Here?"

"Um, yeah. That's what I said, right? That I'd swing by after the conference? Help you out?" When I didn't answer, he said, "I won't get in the way, Savannah. I'm just coming to help. And wake up after this conference. I'm in *serious* need of an adventure fix."

I laughed. "I can believe that. All right then. Just don't rush, okay?" I paused. "That didn't come out right. What I mean is—"

"—that you're handling it just fine and you don't need me breathing down your neck. I won't."

"Thank you."

I'd told Michael to dress casual. I only had the one dress and he'd seen it. For tonight, I went with a nice blouse, then waited until Michael got out of his car, saw he was wearing chinos, and decided I could get away with jeans.

I stuck to boots with low heels, though. I used to strap on three inches and didn't care if it made me taller than the guy. It was a test. Most failed. I'd learned to tone it down. The high heels still came out, just a little later.

When Michael handed me his keys again, I knew I could have worn the heels. A guy who was cool with me being in the driver's seat wouldn't have minded me being an inch taller.

"Did you get a chance to talk to Kayla?" I asked.

"I tried, but she's decided I'm an asshole, and she's not budging. Paula was great, though, and I'm not really comfortable interviewing a kid." He glanced over at me. "Thanks, too, for the tips. I really appreciated that. In return I should tell you that I might know why Claire was talking to Cody. She didn't come here to join the commune. She came here to investigate it."

"I thought she was a student."

"She was. But she had a friend—Tamara—who joined the commune, and left after Ginny and Brandi died. Something had happened, Claire was sure of it, but she couldn't get anything out of her. Then Tamara took off and Claire couldn't find her. No one could."

"She disappeared?"

He nodded. "Claire was afraid whatever happened to her was connected to the commune. I helped Tamara's family file a missing person's report but . . . let's just say they weren't the most engaged parents in the world. They as much as told the police they figured Claire was overreacting and Tamara just took off, which meant there wasn't much hope of an actual investigation."

"So she launched her own. And you knew about it?"

"No. Claire and I . . ." He took a deep breath. "We're half siblings. Her mom married my dad after she was born, which was the soonest he could get a divorce from my mom."

"Ouch."

"Yeah. It's an old story. Dad knocks up his secretary and has to choose a family. He picked them. Mom tried to keep that from me, but I figured it out pretty fast. I didn't want to have anything to do with his new family, and he was fine with that. He wanted a complete do-over. I saw Claire maybe five times growing up. Then, the week she started college, she called, wanting to see me. I wasn't really looking for a baby sister, but if she wanted to make contact, that was fine."

He eased back in his seat. "That first lunch was hellishly awkward. But . . . there was something there. Enough for me to look her up when I had a seminar near her college the next month. We eventually got to the whole brother and sister thing. Calls every few weeks, e-mails, visits when we were nearby, Christmas and birthday presents.

"When Tamara joined Alastair Koppel's group, Claire called me. Tamara and Claire had been friends forever. Grew up together, double-dated, planned to go to college together. Tamara didn't get in the same one as Claire, though, so they drifted apart over the next couple of years. Still kept in touch, just . . . drifted. Claire blamed herself for that. She got caught up in school and made new friends. Tamara was struggling, and Claire knew it, and kept telling herself they'd spend this summer together and everything would be fine."

"Then Tamara joined the commune."

Michael nodded. "Claire freaked. She was sure her friend was mixed up in a cult. She wanted me to check it out. I pulled some strings, got the file, and found the FBI had looked into Alastair's operation after some parents complained. But they'd concluded it was nothing more than a New Age commune. After Tamara disappeared, I forwarded Claire's concerns to the local FBI. That was all I could do. I didn't know she was in Columbus until . . . well, until she wasn't."

Michael went quiet for a few minutes after that. Then he reached into the backseat and grabbed a folder.

"This is for you," he said. "Notes on Claire. I thought . . ." He shrugged. "It might help. You can read them later. Or, if you want to read them now, ask me questions . . ."

I pulled over and gave him the keys.

The file was a mix of the personal and the professional, the brother vying with the investigator. For most of it, the brother prevailed.

There were photos of Claire, including some from her childhood that he must have gotten from his father. Tamara was in three of them—a small, freckled girl with earnest eyes, staring at the camera, with Claire beside her, arm thrown around her shoulders, grinning as if to say "cheer up, life's not so bad." Life *had* been bad for Tamara. The sketchy biography Michael included told the story of a child caught between divorced parents, neither of whom seemed to want her. A girl who'd grown into a young woman probably desperate for approval, for acceptance, for family. A young woman custom-made for Alastair's commune.

Claire, on the other hand, would have needed to work hard to convince Megan and Alastair that she'd fit in. A passion for acting—she'd played leads in every high school production— had probably helped. Claire didn't need approval, acceptance, or family. She got all that at home. In high school, she was the kind of girl I'd have wanted to hate, but couldn't. Pretty, smart, and athletic, she'd have had every right to be a stuck-up bitch, but had spent her spare time organizing fund-raisers instead of partying with the football team. She'd been completing a social work degree when she died.

Claire Kennedy was a girl who had cared. One who had taken the lead when no one else would. One who'd felt incredibly guilty when her friend disappeared. And one whose guilt made her fear the worst—that Alastair had killed Tamara for leaving them, or at least kidnapped her until she was properly brainwashed. Was it any wonder she'd decided to spend her summer term undercover at the commune? No. It was risky and naïve, but it was exactly the kind of thing Claire Kennedy would have done.

Why did Michael let me see this file? I could say he was a canny investigator. He knew it was important for me to see his sister as a person, not as an anonymous victim. But there was more to it than that. Giving me this said "I'm going to trust you, as hard as that might be for me." I hoped to repay that trust by finding his sister's killer.

After getting the tire, we went for Mexican and wore out our welcome with the staff, who kept coming by our table and casting looks at the growing line outside the door. We ignored them, and it was almost ten by the time we left.

We'd each had only one drink, hours ago, so driving wasn't an issue. Michael offered me the keys again, but I let him take the wheel this time.

We were passing a scenic outlook trail when Michael slowed, squinting at the sign.

"I'm up for a walk if you are," I said. Something I'd had for dinner hadn't combined well with the ride. Fresh air would help.

"It's closed after five," he said.

"Which means it'll be empty."

He parked. The sun was long gone, but a full moon lit the way. The trail wasn't that long. Nor was the outlook all that scenic.

It was just a walking bridge over a river with banks maybe twenty feet high. A wooden railing kept people from stumbling off the high banks. I ducked under it and sat on the rocky edge, legs dangling. Michael hesitated, then followed.

We sat in comfortable silence before he said, "Tell me about yourself."

"Um, I did that for three hours at the restaurant. You talked about you. I talked about me . . ."

"No, we talked about our jobs and about my car and your bike. I want to know more about Savannah. You've heard my sordid childhood. Now it's your turn."

Not an easy request to fulfill. As supernaturals we're taught to tread the line between cautious and cagey. It's worse to look as if we're holding something back. That went double with a cop.

So I gave him the basic Savannah bio, leaving out names and places. I'd lived with my mom until I was twelve. Then she died and I'd been taken in by a friend of the family. Our twosome soon expanded to three. My guardian's husband was a lawyer and investigator, and they'd opened their own firm. I'd worked there in school, then stayed on after.

I mentioned getting Lucas's help fixing the dents in my bike, and Michael said, "So you still live close, I guess?"

"Um, very close. Yes, I'm twenty-one and I still live at home."

He blinked. "Twenty-one?"

"Didn't you do your basic background check? What kind of cop are you?"

"I did one, but only to confirm your employment. I didn't dig up personal info." He looked at me. "Why? Did you?"

"I just made sure you were who you said you were. So how old did you think I was?"

"Twenty-three, twenty-four. You act older."

I laughed. "I do believe that's the first time anyone has said that about me. So, is it too young for you?"

He leaned over, lips coming to mine, arms pulling me into a kiss, soft at first, tentative, then . . . wow. The guy could kiss. I finally had to pull back to catch my breath.

"Good answer?" he said.

"Yep. You like them young."

He flushed. "That was *not* the message."

"Are you sure? Because it certainly seems—"

He cut me off with another oxygen-depriving kiss. When I teetered a bit on the edge, he grabbed me like I'd been about to go over, one arm around my waist, the other clutching the rail.

"I think we'd better back up," he said.

"Mmm." I glanced over the embankment. "It's not that far down. Not fatal unless you land wrong."

He hauled me back under the railing.

"Chicken," I said.

He snorted. "If I didn't move, you would have. You play a good game, Savannah, but you're not nearly as reckless as you seem."

"Wanna bet?"

I yanked off my boots and got up on the railing, balancing on it.

"I rest my case," he said, pointing at the discarded boots.

I stuck out my tongue.

"I take back that 'seem older' part."

"As well you should." I took a few steps along the railing, then hopped off. "So, are you going to tell me how old you are?"

"Twenty-seven."

"Relatively youthful. You might have to act more immature, though, so I don't feel bad."

"I can probably manage that."

He pulled me into another kiss and I was up against a tree pretty damned fast. He stuck to kissing, though. Like a high school make-out session. Only without the wandering hands, and with a guy who kissed a helluva lot better than anyone I'd dated in high school.

When things inevitably got a little too steamy, he backed off me, saying, "Okay, time out, or I'm going to try something I really shouldn't on a public path."

"You're right," I said. "We should cool it."

"Damn."

I laughed. "Sorry, but it's only our second date."

"So there's a schedule?"

"What if there is?"

"Then I should know it."

"To keep you from making any premature moves?"

"No, so I can decide if it's worth it."

I only laughed. We kissed a while longer, until I put on the brakes, and we sat down on the grass, looking up at the stars.

When I snuck a look at him, I felt my pulse quicken. That surprised me. I couldn't remember the last time I'd been this happy on a date. This comfortable. This hopeful. It wasn't the racing heart I got when Adam was around, but it was something. It was definitely something.

We sat there quietly for another minute, then Michael said, "So you said you worked through school. Which college?" When I didn't answer, he reddened. "Okay, that was presumptuous of me."

"Nah. It's cool. No college. Maybe someday. I wasn't ready. I'd planned to go through for art, then realized it wasn't what I wanted to do with my life. You know how some kids deal by writing angsty poetry? That's what art was for me. I still enjoy it, but the older I get, the less I do. Good thing I realized that before I blew a bundle on tuition."

"Smart move. I wish I'd taken a few years off. At eighteen, I barely knew what I wanted to do with my weekend, let alone my life."

"You don't like being a cop?"

He shrugged. "Don't love it, don't hate it. I won't stay in the job forever."

"What do you want to do?"

"I have no idea. I'm not exactly the most impulsive guy in the world. It takes me awhile to make a decision." He paused. "I do know one thing I want, though."

"What's that?"

"A third date." He put his arms around me and kissed me again.

TWENTY

WE DROPPED OFF THE TIRE BEHIND THE GARAGE AND GOT back to the motel around eleven. As tempted as I was to invite Michael in, I settled for making out at the door. He made it easier by saying he had a few things to check out before he headed back to his motel. He promised to call me in the morning.

I stood outside and watched him go. Was this something? It felt like something.

Yet again, I'd been dropped off for the night, but had no intention of staying in. Days were for interviewing witnesses and following leads; nights were for breaking into places. I wanted to get into Cody's office and, if I could, exact a little revenge for this afternoon.

One problem with this plan? Cody's office, according to my map of Columbus, was on the outskirts, near the sawmill. He had another in Vancouver, but I suspected I stood a better chance of finding something damning here. There had to be plenty of buildings in Columbus that would make nicer—and more convenient—offices. So why keep a place out there? Only if you had business you didn't want to conduct in town.

First, then, I needed my bike. The garage was a couple of blocks away. Columbus wasn't exactly a dangerous place to wander at night, so I headed over.

My bike was inside a side bay, which the resident mechanic kid had either forgotten to lock or never bothered to. I rolled out my bike, got my tire, took my tool kit, and set to work.

In the half hour I was there, two cars passed the Main Street intersection. The lack of activity only made me extra cautious. I'd cast a perimeter spell around the lot so I could concentrate on changing the tire. When I was finishing up, someone breached the spell, setting off a mental alarm.

I looked up sharply. I stood. Even called out a "Hello?" just to let the intruder know I'd noticed him. Silence answered.

I cast a sensing spell. Yep, definitely a presence. A human-sized one.

There was only one streetlamp near the garage, and my bike was under it. The full moon vanished behind clouds. When I stepped past the circle of light, I had to squint into the shadows. A flashlight would have helped. But I had a spell-powered one, so why would I weigh down my saddlebags with that? Well, maybe if I was being stalked by a human who shouldn't see me tossing a ball of light into the air.

I cupped my hand and cast the light ball inside it, to look like a flashlight. Kind of. Then I strode toward the garage, the light leading the way.

Metal tinkled across asphalt, like someone had kicked a screw. It came from the west side of the shop. I extinguished the light and ran that way just in time to see the heels of someone darting around the corner. White soles. Sneakers.

Knockback spell at the ready, I rounded the rear of the garage. Empty. There was, however, a convenient Dumpster. I slid off my boots and crept along the wall until I was beside the bin.

I listened and flexed my fingers, ready to cast at the first squeak of a shoe. When all stayed silent, I whispered a sensing spell. It came back positive.

Cardboard boxes were scattered around the base. I found the sturdiest, grabbed the edge of the bin, and swung up onto the box. It started to collapse just as I lifted off it.

The top of the bin was dented and filled with what I prayed was rainwater, not garbage sludge. I pushed to my feet and took one slow step across, knockback spell prepped to send my stalker reeling back the moment he noticed—

A sharp intake of breath. *Above me.* I wheeled to catch only a glimpse of someone dressed in black before he plummeted off the other side of the roof. Footsteps pounded pavement. I jumped down and tore off, but by the time I reached the street, it was empty.

I stood on the sidewalk. Looked left. Looked right. Nothing. Shit!

I cast my sensing spell. Someone was still nearby. I turned as a dark figure stepped from the shadows. My hands flew up in a knockback, cut short when I saw the scowling face of Bruyn's older officer.

I glanced down at his shoes. Loafers. Dark soles. Damn.

"Breaking and entering is a crime, Miss Levine," he said as he strode over to me.

I looked around at the shops, mostly vacant. "Breaking in . . . where? And if I was, I wouldn't park my bike under a streetlamp."

His scowl deepened.

"I'm fixing it," I waved at the tools still scattered around the bike. "The tire blew and they were keeping my bike here while I grabbed a new one from Vancouver. *My* bike. *My* tire. *My* tools. I didn't break in anywhere." Well, technically, I did enter, to get my bike, but I didn't see the need to mention that.

"You shouldn't be wandering around alone at night," he said. "We've got a killer on the loose, who likes 'em young and pretty." He smiled, as if imagining me lying inside a ring of crime-scene tape.

"I didn't realize how late it'd gotten," I said. "Thanks."

I started back to my bike, then turned.

"Did you see anyone else out here?" I asked. "I could have sworn I heard footsteps just a minute ago. That's why I was looking around."

"Nobody but me. That's the way it should be, this time of night."

He stood watch while I packed up my gear. I thanked him for that, though I knew he was just doing it to make sure I left. And I did. With this cop on the lookout, I couldn't exactly take off for Cody's office on the far side of town. And my bruised body was telling me it was ready for bed.

Back at the motel, I grabbed a couple of cookies—one of Paige's and one from the cult. Paige's were better, but the others were decent enough. I was pulling off my clothes when my cell phone rang. "Break on Through," which I'd set as Jesse's ringtone.

"Yes, I know, it's late," he said when I answered. "Did I wake you up?"

"Nope. Just getting ready to turn in."

"Good. I probably should have just texted, but I found something." A pause. "Not that you can do anything about it tonight. Never mind. It can wait."

"Oh, no you don't. If it's exciting enough to call me after midnight, I want to hear it."

He paused. "Okay, so I was going through the files again, making notes, trying to find connections. You know that Alastair Koppel used to live in Columbus, right?"

"He went to high school here, but he never came back after college. His parents moved away ten years ago, when they retired. No other family in town."

"You've done your homework then. Did you notice when he left?"

"Before—no, during college. He was going to college in Portland, so he commuted. That must not have worked out too well. In his third year, he moved out of his parents' place. Or second year. People weren't clear on that."

"It was 1983."

"Okay, 1983."

"Anything else happen in 1983?"

"No idea. I wasn't born."

"But someone else was. And it seems someone on this investigation is a *CSI* fan."

"What?"

"They went a little crazy gathering DNA. They got DNA profiles on Ginny, Brandi, Claire, and just about everyone questioned. Except Cody and his wife, who knew their rights and refused. When I was writing up the file, looking for connections, I saw one, and I faxed the profiles to a buddy to confirm. He just got back to me."

He stopped. I could feel his excitement buzzing down the line.

"DNA . . . 1983 . . ." I said. "Shit . . . 1983. The year both Ginny and Brandi were born. Our cult leader is Brandi's father, isn't he?"

"Not Brandi's."

"Ginny's?"

"Yep. Seems Paula Thompson wasn't exactly being honest when she said there was no connection between her daughter and Koppel. The cops never noticed it because, obviously, they were only holding the DNA profiles to compare to a potential suspect's, not cross-referencing—"

My phone blipped, telling me I had an incoming text. It was from Michael.

Lne bsy. Fnd s/t. Cody. Imp. Any way u can come? 384 SW 3rd Ave. B careful.

"Michael just texted me," I said to Jesse. "He found something and he'd like me over there. I'm guessing it's that delivery Cody had scheduled for tonight."

"Right. You go, then."

I hung up, called Michael, and got a message that the line was busy—probably as he tried to call me again. When it went to voice mail, I left a message, then I grabbed my jacket and sneakers and hurried out.

TWENTY-ONE

SOUTHWEST 3RD AVENUE. I KNEW EXACTLY WHERE THE street was, because I'd wanted to go there tonight. Cody's office was on that road, in a generic office block, with a medical and dental clinic on the first floor. Built to service the sawmill, I bet. Give workers a convenient place for daytime appointments and give contract and auxiliary companies a convenient place for their offices. Now, though, every entry on the communal front sign was taped over, every decal sign on the windows partly scratched away.

Just past that lone office building, there were a couple of abandoned warehouses. The address Michael had sent led to one.

I killed the engine three buildings back and coasted to a stop. Nothing says "company" like the roar of a motorcycle on an empty road. All was quiet, though. I sat there, helmet off, listening. I cast a sensing spell. Nothing.

I rolled the bike alongside the other warehouse and parked it in the shadows. Then I called Michael again. The phone went straight to voice mail. I switched to text and messaged him a simple *I'm here.*

No answer.

I crept along the building, then stopped. More listening. More looking. More casting. All negative. I double-checked the address.

Had he even meant Columbus? In this part of the country 3rd Avenue was a common street name. Maybe it was Battle Ground or Vancouver.

But we knew Cody was expecting a delivery. Could it be a coincidence that Michael's address led me to abandoned warehouses only doors away from Cody's office? I doubted it. Besides, Michael thought I didn't have my bike back. It would be tough enough for me to get out here, let alone to another town.

Still . . . Abandoned warehouse. Deserted road. Urgent late-night text message. Can't contact the sender. Yep, paranoia was warranted.

I cast a blur spell and zipped to the rear of the warehouse. The door was unlocked. With my back to the wall, I eased it open and cast a fast sensing spell. Only the faint pulse of small heartbeats came back. Rats, cats, or other furry squatters.

Had Michael come and gone? If he had, why not text me again?

I cast a blur spell and slid inside. The windows were filthy and when the door closed behind me, the light went out. Damn it, I needed a flashlight. Everyone said I relied too much on my spells. They might have a point. I used the light ball. It was easy enough to extinguish in a hurry, and safer than stumbling in the dark.

As I stepped past the entrance, I caught a whiff of smoke. There was the acrid scent of burned paper, but something sweeter, too. My shoe sent a white tube rolling silently across the floor. Cigarette? I bent. No, a joint. Was that what I smelled? Yes, I know what pot smells like—never tried it, knowing drugs could do funky things with my powers. But the scent seemed sweeter. Spicier. Cloves?

I walked a few more steps and picked up another burning scent. Candles. I found one on the floor, as if it had been dropped. I picked it up. Still warm. The sides were rough. I brought the light ball down lower and saw faint scratches. Symbols.

The hair on my neck prickled. A ritual? Was this what Michael found? Or, worse, stumbled on?

I walked slower as I scanned the floor for chalk marks. I found disturbances in a thick layer of dust that seemed to serve the same purpose. Ritual markings. Like the chalk mark in the crime-scene photos, they were faint. Easily overlooked.

Someone had definitely conducted a ritual here tonight.

I cast the sensing spell again. Still negative for people. I had my cell on vibrate, but I checked it anyway. No calls. No texts.

As I made my way deeper into the building, the dust on the floor thickened and I could make out footprints; lots of scuff marks at first, then clear impressions in spots where no one had ventured in a while. Men's loafers. Like Michael's.

The tracks led to a set of wooden stairs going up to an observation deck. I could see a couple of desks up there, and more boxes. Extra storage and a place for a security guard to work, looking out over the floor below. The perfect place to get a good view of the whole warehouse.

Michael's were the only prints leading up. As I started to climb, I noticed something dart between boxes below. Glowing green eyes flashed. A hiss. Then a waving tail as a cat tore off.

I seemed to be attracting cats these days. I shook my head, glanced back up the stairs, and cast my sensing spell. Nothing. I cast again, to be sure. Nothing. Michael must have gone down a set of stairs I couldn't see. I'd find those, then maybe climb up and get a look from above.

The cat moved alongside me, hopping over the boxes, turning

every few seconds to spit at me, pissed off, it seemed, because I insisted on traveling in the same direction.

I sent a few sparks flying its way and it gave me one last hiss, then tore off ahead, still keeping to the same path. *Determined* to head in this direction, however nervous I made it. I followed.

It had slid between two rows of boxes. A tight squeeze, but I made it. When I shone the light ball ahead, another cat turned, hissing, orange fur puffing. I stopped and it lowered its head to the floor again. A rasping sound. It was licking the floor. I tossed the light ball over it. Tendrils of blood snaked across the concrete.

I raced forward, elbows knocking the boxes on either side. Ahead, I saw a leg stretched out. Light chinos. Brown loafers. I pictured Michael from earlier, his tan pants and darker shoes.

I shoved my way through, sending boxes crashing. Michael was draped over the remains of a smashed wooden crate. On his back, face turned the other way, head at an angle that was wrong, just wrong. Blood dripped from his fingertips, slow and steady, a pool growing on the concrete floor beneath him.

I stood there, brain stuttering, telling myself it was someone else wearing clothing like Michael's. It wasn't him. Couldn't be him.

Then I thought I saw him breathe and I dropped beside him, slipping in the blood and not caring. My fingers went to his neck. No pulse. His skin was chilled, clammy.

I turned his face toward me. His head moved easily. Too easily. His neck was broken.

His eyes were open. Open and empty.

No, I'd seen him move. Goddamn it, I'd seen him move. How could he break his neck? What could—?

I looked up. The ledge of the observation deck was twenty feet above me.

He stepped back too far. Went over the edge. Hit the crates. Hit the cement. Broke his neck.

No! Goddamn it, no! Not Michael. He'd never be that careless.

My phone vibrated. It was like an electric shock and I jumped. I fumbled and pulled it out. Jesse. I answered.

"Hey, just wanted to make sure everything's—"

"Michael. He's— I found Michael. He fell. He's—" I squeezed my eyes shut. "He's dead."

When Jesse didn't answer, I said, "He's dead. Michael's dead."

"Shit . . ." He floundered, then came back, firm. "Are you still at the scene? Have you called 911?"

"N-no. I should. I will."

"Do that. I'm on my way." A pause. "Where are you?"

I gave him the address.

"Call 911 and hang tight. I'll be there as fast as I can. Don't move anything. Don't touch anything. Got it?"

I said I did. Then I hung up. I pressed 9, and crouched there, finger poised over the one.

This was no accident. I was sure of that. *Sure.* He'd been murdered.

Dead.

Oh, God.

Dial the numbers, damn it.

A squeak behind me. I turned to a flashlight shining in my eyes. Beside it, the barrel of a gun. The phone fell. My hands shot up. Sparks sizzled from my fingertips.

"Drop it!" a voice barked.

The flashlight swung out of my face and I saw Chief Bruyn. The younger officer stood behind him.

"Hands up," Bruyn said.

They already were, but I hoisted them higher, palms out. My fingers had stopped sparking.

"She had something," Bruyn said to his officer. "Find it, then take her out to the car."

"I had my phone," I said, my voice eerily calm. "I dropped it when you startled me. I was dialing 911. It's Michael Kennedy. He . . . he fell. From up there." I pointed. "He's dead."

The officer patted me down as I spoke. Bruyn checked Michael, then called the sheriff's department and doctor, then phoned the other officer, telling him to get over there. When he hung up, he walked back to Michael.

"He called me here," I said. "I found him."

"Sit her down over there," Bruyn said, pointing. "And stand guard."

"Stand guard? You think I killed—?"

I didn't finish. Stupid question. I'd been found over a dead body.

"Michael sent me a text. It's still on my phone." I pointed to it on the ground. "Just check—"

"Get her away from here," Bruyn said.

"You want her in the cruiser?"

"No, just over there." He pointed. "In case the doc has questions."

The other officer arrived, then the doctor. He didn't ask me anything. I don't think he even knew I was there. Having me sitting twenty feet away as they discussed the case wasn't exactly smart policing. After the doctor left, Bruyn seemed to figure that out, and had the young officer take me to the cruiser as the sheriff's department arrived.

"Someone called 911 before me, didn't they?" I said to Bruyn as I left. "Reported a disturbance? Just in time for you to find me with the body."

He said nothing, but I could tell by his expression that I was right.

"That would be your killer," I said. "He saw me arrive and is probably out there, right now, watching us."

"There's no one else for a mile."

"We're on a street with a bunch of empty buildings. Any one of those would be the perfect place—"

"We didn't see anything."

"Do you think the killer parked his car out front and left the lights on?"

He glared and swung open the back door of a king cab pickup marked "Columbus Police Dept."

With a roar of tires and a cloud of dust, another pickup swung into the lot. Jesse jammed it into park so fast the brakes hiccupped.

"Is she okay?" he called, running over as the officer prodded me into the back.

"I'm fine," I said. "The prime suspect, it seems, but otherwise fine."

"Suspect?" He wheeled on the cop. "Are you serious? She called it in."

"No, someone else beat me to it," I said.

"This is stupid. She got a text—"

I held up my hand as I climbed in. "It's okay. I'll answer their questions and we'll get this straightened out."

The officer tried to shut the door, but it wouldn't budge. He glared down at my feet—which were well within the cab confines—then at Jesse, who stood three feet away. He tried again. The door wouldn't shut, held by Jesse's telekinetic powers.

"Do you want me to call anyone?" Jesse asked.

"Not yet. I should be able to sort this out on my own."

He nodded. "That's what I thought you'd say. I'm here now, I can help, and if we need Lucas, he's only a call away."

"That's enough," the officer said.

He gave the door a sharp wrench and Jesse's telekinetic control over it snapped as it slammed shut. Jesse stood there, watching me, looking anxious.

"I'm okay," I mouthed.

He headed into the warehouse. The officer shouted at him to stay out of there. Jesse ignored him. The cop glanced from me to Jesse, and decided to remain at his post. A few minutes later, Jesse came out, escorted by the older cop.

"Look, just *talk* to her," I heard Jesse saying. "She was here because she was lured here. Set up."

I didn't catch the officer's answer, but Jesse's face darkened. He said something back, too low to hear. The cop stiffened, then pointed to Jesse's truck.

"Fucking rednecks," Jesse called back as he stormed off.

The cop's flashlight went flying. A parting shot from Jesse. As the officer chased after it, Jesse mouthed "I'll fix this" to me. Then he climbed in his truck and peeled out.

It got very, very quiet then, left alone with a silent cop standing guard.

Michael was dead.

The guy I'd just gone out to dinner with. Just laughed with. Talked with. Kissed and thought "this could be something."

I kept seeing him. Hearing his voice. Smelling the faint scent of his cologne. Then smelling blood, jerking out of the daydream, shivering, eyes prickling. I didn't cry. I don't cry. I wished I could. But all I could do was keep playing those memory loops. Michael alive. Michael dead.

The chief finally came out. He didn't say a word to me, just motioned for the officer guarding me to follow. Leaving the other cop guarding the scene, he got into his car. We followed him back to the station.

TWENTY-TWO

THE OFFICER TOOK ME THROUGH A NARROW DOOR BESIDE the front desk that led into a makeshift cell. I dug in my heels, about to say I wasn't going in there without being charged. Then I saw Bruyn was already inside, seated at a table. An interrogation room, apparently.

Still, I hesitated at the door. "I'll come in here to talk to you, but you're not locking that door without laying a charge."

"Oh, I expect to lay a charge, Ms. Levine."

Bullshit. The only way he was doing that is if I confessed. I sat. No one Miranda-ized me, which could mean Bruyn considered this just an interview. Otherwise, I'd be at the sheriff's office, not here.

Still, if there's one bit of legal advice Lucas drilled into my head growing up, it's this: If held by the police, for any reason, lawyer up. Don't say a word without him there.

I'd always rolled my eyes, wondering how stupid Lucas thought I was. I sure as hell wasn't going to be one of those morons you see on crime shows, who waives her rights straight into self-incrimination. You have the right to a lawyer, so get one, especially if he is also one of your best friends.

But I didn't ask for my phone call. Didn't mention my lawyer.

Lucas was more than a thousand miles away. All my phone call would do was get him on the next plane home, and I'd be free before he got here.

If I was transferred to the sheriff's department, I'd call. Otherwise, I'd deal with it . . . and deal with the lectures when Lucas found out.

Bruyn asked for my side of the story. I gave it, and when I was done, he just sat there.

"That's it," I said. "I found Michael. You found me. End of story."

"You really expect me to believe that, Ms. Levine?"

"Considering it's the truth, yes. And considering there's nothing even remotely far-fetched about it, yes. You can call the restaurant where we had dinner. We overstayed our welcome, so they're bound to remember us, and remember that we were obviously on a date and having a good time."

"What does that have to do with anything? If you think that means you wouldn't kill—"

"No, I think it means my story is perfectly plausible. We were getting along and trying to work together. He was following a lead I gave him on Cody. He found something. He texted me. I'm sure you've confirmed the message on my phone."

"We will. One of my officers saw you arguing with Detective Kennedy in the street this afternoon."

"We disagreed about a risk I was taking. We parted amicably, with plans for dinner. You can ask Kayla Thompson. She was there."

"My officer caught you sneaking around Renny's Garage, just hours before we found you with Detective Kennedy's body."

"No, he didn't catch me sneaking around. He caught me repairing my bike. You can check with the garage and with the bike shop in Vancouver, where I picked up the tire this evening. With Michael."

"You didn't like him horning in on your job."

"No, I believe *he* was the one complaining. And he got over it. Otherwise why would we be out on a dinner date?"

"It was a setup."

"For what? Is that the motivation you're seriously going with? I killed him because he was interfering with a *job*?"

"I have no idea what your motivation is. I don't care."

It was at that point that I shut up, because I realized he was just fishing for answers, hoping to get a confession he could hand over to the sheriff's department.

When I stopped talking, he was stuck. So he backed up and took another run down the same path, making me repeat my story. When I was done, he hit the wall again. So he had me tell my story again. Killing time until he heard from the doctor or the sheriff's department? Or praying I'd slip up and give him something?

Chief Bruyn wasn't an idiot. Just incompetent, at least when it came to issuing more than a speeding ticket. The town expected him to be tough, yet he wasn't a tough guy by nature. So he overcompensated. Find a private investigator crouched over a dead body? March her down to the station, interrogate her and, hopefully, toss her in jail.

When he was about to make me go through my story a fourth time, I said, "Have you notified the Dallas Police Department?"

"Why would I—?" He stopped. A look of stark "oh, shit" terror, quickly hidden behind a scowl. "Detective Kennedy was off duty. I'll notify them in due course."

"A cop is never off duty." As he glowered, I dropped my gaze, just a fraction, and forced myself to add, "Or that's what I've heard."

The meek approach worked. He stepped out and told his officer to call the Dallas PD. Then he lowered his voice and told the officer to say Detective Kennedy had died of a fall, and they hadn't yet determined whether it was an accident or a homicide. Funny, he hadn't mentioned the accidental possibility to me. Is that why I wasn't with the sheriff's department? They thought it was an accident?

The officer came back and said the Dallas PD wanted to be kept informed. They also wanted to know if Bruyn had notified Detective Kennedy's next of kin.

"That would be his mother," I said, when that familiar look of blind panic hit Bruyn's face. "Not Claire's mother. She was his half sister on his dad's side."

My composure cracked a bit then, thinking of Claire, dead, and now Michael, too. Their poor parents. Michael coming to solve his sister's murder, then murdered himself and—

I took a deep breath. "Now, if you're done with me, I'll go back to my motel to rest."

"Like hell you will."

I fought to keep my voice steady. "You don't have enough to hold me. Your officer can drive me back and can park outside my door, and you have my word that I won't leave."

Bruyn crossed his arms. "You're not going anywhere. You killed a police detective."

"No, she didn't," said a voice from the door.

Jesse strode in, the younger officer at his heels, protesting that he'd tried to stop him. Jesse planted himself in front of Bruyn.

"The doctor's initial report found that Detective Kennedy seems to have died of a broken neck incurred in a fall. He was searching the warehouse, went to that second story, and fell backward off the edge."

"Fell?" Bruyn said. "Or was pushed?"

"Fell. There's only one way up. There's also only one set of prints, which I pointed out to the sheriff's department."

"I saw two sets—"

"On the first few steps. Savannah's prints, as I'm sure she'll confirm. She went up three steps, turned, and came back down." He glanced at me.

I nodded. "I heard a noise below. Turned out it was just a cat."

"The sheriff's department is holding the scene for their lab techs, but I'm sure when they arrive, they'll confirm only one set of prints upstairs. Michael Kennedy's. A tragic accident. But clearly an accident."

The phone rang.

"That would be the sheriff's department telling you to release Savannah," Jesse said.

I heard enough to know that they confirmed Jesse's story— one way up to the second floor and only one set of footprints. I still didn't believe Michael had fallen. Couldn't believe it. But I sure as hell wasn't saying so.

When Bruyn got off the phone, he said, "You're free to go. Just don't leave town. We'll be checking that second story, and if we find your prints up there . . ."

"You won't," I said. "But I'm not leaving town anytime soon. I still have a case to solve."

As we got into Jesse's truck, I said, "Thank you."

"No problem."

"No, really. Thank you. You didn't need to do all that, and I appreciate it."

He fussed with his seat belt, clearly uncomfortable with gratitude, then put on a grin and flashed it my way. "Now you owe me. You realize that, right? If I ever get locked up in a small town, you've gotta come from wherever you are, whatever the hour, and investigate on my behalf."

"And the chances you'll be able to call in that chit someday are pretty good, aren't they?"

His grin widened. "Very good. Why else do you think I got you out of there?"

"Good call." I cracked the window and inhaled the night air, hoping it would settle my stomach. Then I glanced at Jesse. "Speaking of calls, I need to make one when we get to the motel."

"Lucas?"

"No, Adam. I need to keep him in the loop."

He frowned. "Lucas has him supervising you on this?"

"Not really."

"Good, because you clearly don't need it."

He was right. I didn't. And Adam really didn't need a four A.M. update. I just . . . I'd just wanted to speak to him, I guess. It could wait, though.

There was no chance of me sleeping, and Jesse seemed to realize that. He dropped me off at the motel and said he'd be back. I went in and sat on the bed. Just sat. Nothing else, unless you count thinking. Did a lot of that, as the world got too quiet again.

I thought of calling Adam. Bruyn had given me my phone back. I'm sure that wasn't standard procedure, but I hadn't been about to argue.

I won't say how many times I picked up the phone, finger poised over Adam's speed dial. I wanted to talk to him. More than that, I wanted to see him, and I knew that if I told him what had happened, he'd be on the road within the hour, no matter how much I argued.

He'd come, and I wanted that. God, how I wanted that. I wanted someone to hug me and tell me it was okay. Then I wanted to be distracted, to hear a story that would take my mind off Michael's death. Then, when I was ready, I wanted to be cheered up. Sympathy, comfort, support, and laughter. It was a lot to ask of any one person. But Adam could do it. He always did.

Which is why, every time I picked up that phone, I put it back down. If I was going to be the mature investigator Jesse thought I was, then I had to get through this on my own.

Forty-five minutes later, Jesse came back with beer and snacks. I told him I was convinced Michael's death had been murder after stumbling on a ritual in progress. The ritual going on that night might not have been a deadly one, but it had turned out that way.

Bruyn said Michael's cell phone hadn't been found with his body. While it was possible that he'd sent the message—Jesse said that the preliminary report on time of death didn't rule that out—I was betting that the killer sent it right after killing him. Then, when I'd arrived, he—or she—had called Chief Bruyn to report a disturbance at the warehouse. That to me was the most damning piece of evidence. Someone had brought the cops there just in time to catch me with the body.

Jesse absently twisted his beer can, still looking doubtful. "As someone who got arrested twice courtesy of a citizen who reported seeing me break into a place, I gotta say that I'm not convinced it wasn't coincidental. People notice, especially in a small town. But while I think Michael Kennedy's death was an accident, I'll consider the possibility that it wasn't. That possibility, though, means that you're in danger. We need to get this figured out ASAP. I'd like to stay and help. I know you didn't want that, but—"

"No, you're right. When Michael was here I was worried about the three of us tripping over each other, but now . . ."

I trailed off and pulled my legs up, tucking them under me.

Jesse leaned forward, elbows on his knees. "How're you holding up? I know you liked the guy."

"I did." I took a deep breath. "Right now, though, I need to solve this case and catch his killer. So please don't suggest I go home."

"I wasn't going to."

"Good. Okay, next—"

A hard knock at the door.

"Ms. Levine?" a deep voice called.

It was the sheriff's department.

TWENTY-THREE

THE LAB TECHS HAD CONFIRMED WHAT JESSE SAID. ONE SET of stairs. One set of prints going all the way up. One set of prints at the top. Michael's death was being ruled an accident, though they took all my contact information, just in case.

After they left, I kicked Jesse out. If he was working this case, he needed to go home, pack a bag, cancel appointments, whatever. He was reluctant to leave me alone, but I said I was fine. I wasn't, but he didn't know me well enough to tell.

By the time he left, it was after seven, which I figured was late enough to call a few of my shadier supernatural contacts out east. None had heard of either Cody or Tiffany. Never heard of Columbus, Washington. Never heard of Alastair Koppel and his commune. The only one who was any help was the last call I made, to a local witch, Molly Crane, who was up early getting her girls off to school.

Four years ago Molly had tried to kill Jaime Vegas. I'd intervened and left Molly tied up in a swamp. In the underbelly of the supernatural world, that marked the beginning of a working relationship based on mutual respect. A temporary gift of zombies a couple of years ago hadn't hurt matters. Molly liked me. Can't say I felt the same about her, but she was useful.

"If there's a witch living so close to me, then I should know about her," Molly said. "If I don't, she's not just flying under the radar. She's *crawling* under it. You said her magic looks old?"

"That's what I'm thinking. I was going to run it past Paige but . . ."

Molly snorted. "Like Paige would recognize magic that wasn't pure as the driven snow."

Not true, but part of cozying up to Molly meant letting her disparage Paige and Lucas.

"That's kind of what I thought," I said. "And Paige hates me getting involved in anything dark . . ."

Another snort. "E-mail me those pictures. I'll find your ritual."

The motel room got too quiet again after that. I paced, struggling to focus on the case. I couldn't. After a quick shower and change of clothes, I headed out for breakfast.

I walked to the diner. It was a good hike, but I needed the air. As I approached the door, though, I slowed, and my stomach twisted. Word of Michael's death would have spread. There would be questions, probing questions, small-town curiosity spreading its tentacles. I couldn't handle that.

So I walked past. Got ten steps before the door whooshed open and Lorraine called out after me.

"Savannah? Hon? Nothing open down that way. Come on back and get yourself some breakfast."

When I turned to face her, she gave a sympathetic smile.

"Heard you had a rough night. Come and eat. On the house."

I struggled for an excuse. None came.

When I walked through the doors, every eye turned my way. The place was busier than I expected. With the local paper shut down, this was news central. And after finding Michael's body, I was the lead story.

No one said a word, though. After weak smiles and kind nods they all returned to their meals.

I sat at the counter and ordered breakfast. The questions came tentatively. Not "So what happened last night?" but "Are you okay?" and "I'm sorry about Detective Kennedy." They wanted to know what happened and knew it wasn't right to ask, so I told them.

When my meal arrived, they switched to other topics—local and area news, funny personal stories, whatever might take my mind off Michael's death. And over that meal, I mentally took back every nasty thing I'd ever said about small-town folks.

I'd ordered steak and eggs, and was complimenting Lorraine on her hash browns when her gaze moved to the front window. I looked out to see a young woman locking up a bike at the rack. She took an insulated bag from the carrier.

"One of the commune girls," Lorraine said. "We get our eggs and milk from them. This girl has come the last couple of days. She asked about you yesterday, whether you ate breakfast here."

It was the girl who'd seemed like she wanted to talk to me yesterday. Blue-streaked hair cut short and spiky. Studs in her nose and brow. A look that screamed attitude. Her face didn't, though. Soft features and anxious eyes said the tough-girl look was a desperate attempt to find something she lacked.

The girl ignored me as she unloaded the bag for Lorraine and took the money.

"Do you have a minute?" I said. "I'd love to buy you a coffee. Megan said it was okay to talk to me, but I still don't want to get you in trouble."

It was the right thing to say. The tough girl inside her squared her shoulders and lifted her chin. She motioned to Lorraine, who poured her a coffee.

"I'm not afraid of Megan. Alastair said we can talk to you or that detective."

I could tell by the way she said "that detective" that she didn't know Michael was dead. News didn't travel as fast when you lived up on Commune Hill. I didn't see any reason to tell her, so I nodded and sipped my coffee. She did the same, her courage melting again.

"So Alastair said it was okay?" I prodded.

She nodded. "He said if someone's preying on the girls of this town, he wants the guy caught."

"He thinks it's a guy?"

She frowned. "It always is, isn't it?" Her gaze and voice dropped in a way that told me everything I needed to know about this girl's damage.

I asked her name.

"Sylvia," she said. "But I go by Vee."

"Okay, Vee. How long have you been with the group?"

"Just over a year."

Meaning she'd known Tamara, the friend of Claire's who'd left in a hurry. Good.

"Did you know Ginny or Brandi?" I asked.

She shook her head.

"They never came up to the house?" I said. "Talked to Alastair, maybe?"

Her shoulders tightened. "Alastair's a good guy. He's helped me a lot. And, no, I'm not sleeping with him. He wouldn't let me even if I asked. I've—I've had problems. With that . . . kind of thing." She cleared her throat. "His place, it's not what people think. Not what my parents think, that's for sure. Every couple of months they have this cult deprogrammer chick sneak into town to try to talk me out. It's bullshit. No one's holding me against my will. My folks blame Alastair because, otherwise, they'd have to admit that I've got a problem they can't shove under the carpet like they've done all my—" She stopped and took a deep breath. "Sorry."

"No reason to be. It's good to know what the members think of the group and Alastair."

"Alastair's great. Really great."

But I noticed she hadn't answered my original question. Had Ginny gone up to visit him at the house? I broached the subject again with Vee, but she was quick with her denials. Too quick. I filed it and let it go.

"Is there anything about the group that *does* worry you?" I asked.

She chewed her lip enough to flake the skin, then said, "Kind of. It's Megan. She—" She took a deep breath. "Look, I don't like Megan, okay? No one does. She's a bitch. The only reason she's still around is because she runs the business. And because Alastair . . . well, he's kind of attached to her, you know. But I don't like her and I'd be happy to see her tossed out on her skinny ass. I'm telling you that now, because if you find out later that I don't like her, it'll sound like I was making this up."

"Okay."

She didn't go on right away. Drank half her coffee first, and I struggled not to fidget. Sitting for so long reminded me that I'd been up all night, and I found myself swallowing a yawn with every third breath until she finally blurted it out.

"Megan's a voodoo priestess."

I tried to look shocked. Probably did a decent job of it, too, because while I knew someone up there was practicing Santeria, Megan was at the bottom of my list. If there's a type of person who picks up a religion like that, Megan definitely didn't fit it.

Alastair did, though—he might seem distinguished, but he was nothing more than an old hippie, the kind of person who'd be attracted to a mystical religion.

"Voodoo?"

"Kind of. Claire said it wasn't voodoo but something else."

"Santeria?"

"That's it."

"So Claire knew."

"Yeah, but . . . It was weird. She wasn't too fussed about it. She said she'd talked to a friend, who explained that it was just a kind of religion. It freaks me out, though."

"Do all the girls know about it?"

Vee shook her head. "I just told Claire because she was my roommate, and she seemed smart, so I wanted to hear what she thought. I'm the only one who knows. Except Alastair. He . . . he helps Megan sometimes. With the rituals and stuff. They do them in a room behind the shed, late at night, when everyone's sleeping. I saw them once. I think that's why Alastair likes Megan so much. She's cast a spell on him."

I struggled to keep a straight face and nodded. Why are humans so enamored with the myth of love spells? Even at my most desperate, I wouldn't have been tempted by a spell to *make* Adam fall in love with me. My ego is way too healthy for that.

I asked Vee what she'd seen. There was nothing, though, to suggest Megan and Alastair were more than typical adherents doing typical protection rituals, like the one in the shed.

"They do sacrifices," she said, when I didn't seem impressed enough. "That's what Claire told me."

"Animal sacrifices."

"So she said."

"You think Megan had something to do with the murders?"

She shifted in her seat.

"Did you hear anything that might suggest a ritualistic link?"

"No, but . . ."

I waited. Nothing.

"But . . ." I prompted.

"Alastair was gone the night those town girls died." She blurted it as fast as she'd told me about the Santeria. "I got up for a glass of milk. I don't sleep too well. When I was in the kitchen, I heard the door open. It was Alastair. He looked . . . sick. He looked sick."

"Was Megan with him?"

"No, but do you really think she'd take care of the bodies? She had him do it. She killed those girls in a voodoo ritual, then she made him take the bodies into town. It wasn't his fault. He had to protect her."

There were a lot of holes in this theory. Still, it bore investigating.

"Did you tell anyone else?" I asked.

"Just my roommate before Claire. She left after that. I think it freaked her out."

Claire's friend, Tamara. I doubted it was a coincidence that Claire had ended up rooming with Vee. If the cult was as popular as they claimed, Tamara's spot would have been filled before Claire decided to investigate. She must have maneuvered to get the same roommate as her friend.

"What about Claire?" I asked. "Did you tell her what you saw?"

"No." The denial came fast. In other words, yes, she had and she feared that's what got Claire killed.

"Did you know Claire was investigating the group?" I asked.

"Huh?"

"Claire was Tamara's friend from college. Tamara disappeared after she left you, and Claire joined the group trying to find out what happened. She thought it had something to do with Ginny and Brandi's murders."

Vee's eyes shuttered. "I didn't know that."

And she didn't like finding out now. It meant that Claire had been nice to her for a reason.

"Did you ever see Claire with Cody Radu?" I asked. "I heard something about the two of them arguing. If that's true and Claire was investigating, it could mean Alastair had nothing to do with the deaths."

"They did. The day before she died. At the hardware store. Claire went in, saying she needed something. I was with Megan. She looked in the window and saw them go out back together. Later Megan came to our room and told Claire to stay away from Cody. Said he was trouble." She hesitated, then looked at me. "What if Megan *did* kill those girls and she figured out that Claire was snooping around, looking for the killer? That'd be bad for Claire."

Way too many holes in that theory, too, but it confirmed that Claire had been with Cody. And if Megan knew it, maybe there *was* something there.

TWENTY-FOUR

NEXT STOP: PAULA THOMPSON, FOR A LITTLE CHAT ABOUT her dead daughter's paternity. I'd barely gone a block when my cell phone rang.

"Ms. Levine?"

I recognized the woman's voice, but definitely not the meek tone.

"It's Tiffany Radu," she said.

"Yes?"

"I—" A deep breath sighed through the line. "I need to speak to you. Can—can we meet?"

"Sure, how about the diner—"

"No. I mean in private. I heard about Detective Kennedy and . . . oh, God." A broken sob. "Please, can we meet in private, before I change my mind?"

"Okay. My motel—"

A shaky laugh. "The last thing I need is to be seen sneaking into a seedy motel room. There's an empty building downtown that my husband's company owns. Can I meet you there?"

"Sure. My partner should be back any minute. I'll get him to drive me—"

"It's within walking distance, if you're near the diner. And I'd really, really rather you didn't tell anyone you're meeting with me. I don't want Cody to find out."

"Understandable. What's the address?"

Damn, Tiffany was quite the little actress. A bit high school, with all the sighs and sobs, but still pretty damn good.

Yes, I knew it was an act. Come on. The bitch goes from clawing me to begging for help? Sure, something traumatic might have happened. But wanting to meet in an empty building? And not tell anyone? That was a tip-off only a moron would miss.

I picked up my pace.

As I walked, I got another call. "Ship of Fools," meaning it was someone in my secondary address book—the hidden one for contacts Paige and Lucas wouldn't want to know about.

"Druid," Molly announced when I answered.

"What?"

She sighed, and said, more slowly. "*Druid*. That ritual you sent. A pewter ingot in the hand is part of very ancient druidic sacrificial rituals. My source tells me they fell out of use centuries ago."

"You said ritual*s*. Multiple ones then?"

"Right. My source can't narrow it down. You're looking for a druid, though, one who still practices human sacrifice."

"Nasty habit."

She made a noise that could be taken as agreement, but almost certainly wasn't. Molly had likely sacrificed people in protection rituals for her daughters.

I thanked her, hung up, and started hitting speed dial to call Adam and ask him to renew the search, narrowing it down to druidic rituals—

I stopped. I stood there, finger poised over the screen for at least a minute. Then I pocketed the phone and kept walking.

The address Tiffany had given me led to the town's abandoned newspaper building, three blocks from Main Street. It was ugly—shit brown and squat with tiny windows, as if the reporters knew nothing newsworthy would be happening outside, and didn't want to depress themselves by looking.

I tried the front door. Locked. I hit the buzzer, but didn't hear anything. Disconnected, I guessed. I knocked. No answer.

I walked around the side. A door opened and a slender hand gestured frantically.

"I said to be careful," Tiffany hissed as she pulled me inside. "That means *not* using the front door."

"There's no one around," I said. "And even if there was, they just saw me trying to get into an empty building. Typical PI work."

"Did you tell anyone you were coming here?"

"No."

"Good."

The electricity must have been completely disconnected, because the only light filtered in through tiny windows.

"Go left," she said. "Then we'll head downstairs to the presses."

"Who's going to hear us up here?"

"There's something down there I want to show you."

Yeah, right. I only nodded, though, and played along. At the top of the stairs, I paused.

"It's awfully dark down there," I said. "Did you bring a flashlight?"

"There's a lantern down there."

"Huh." I peered into the darkness as I teetered on the top of the steps. Behind me, she cast a binding spell under her breath. Exactly what I expected.

"I can barely see—" I began, then wheeled and hit her with a knockback spell. Or I tried. It failed and as I launched another, she finished hers and I froze in place. I mentally struggled to get free, but the spell held and all I could do was stand there as she ran at me, hands out, and gave me a tremendous shove.

I toppled like a statue, hitting the stairs hard. Pain screamed through me, jolting me out of the spell, and my arms flew out to brace myself before I hit the concrete floor headfirst. I staggered up and wheeled. Tiffany stood at the top of the stairs, casting aloud now, trying to lock me in another binding spell.

I leapt aside and cast an energy bolt. It went off course and hit the wall beside her head with barely a pop.

I raced into the dark basement. I'm sure my battered body complained, but I didn't feel it. All I could think was: *Two failed spells in a row? No way. No fucking way.*

I squelched a bubble of panic. The second had screwed up, not failed. My fault for jumping aside when I should have been concentrating.

I raced into a dark corner, cast a cover spell, and felt the mental click of a successful cast. As for whether I was hidden, that remained to be seen. Hence the really dark corner.

Tiffany's cautious steps sounded on the stairs. I forced myself to relax and focus. Stick to simple spells for now. Defensive magic.

At the bottom of the steps, Tiffany created a light ball, sending it into every corner, including the one I was in. The cover spell worked fine.

When she turned her back on me, I hit her with a knockback that slammed her into the wall. That was more like it.

As I advanced on her, she flipped over and started her binding spell again. I smacked her down with another knockback.

"Your choice of spells leaves a lot to be desired," I said. "In a pinch, skip the binding and go for the knockback. Efficient, effective, fast launching . . . But I'm going to guess you don't know sorcerer magic."

She sat up and her hands shot down. An energy bolt sizzled past me as I stepped aside. It hit the wall with a faint pop, leaving a charred circle the size of a dime.

"Huh, I stand corrected. But that's really more of a party trick. What you need is one of these." I slammed a high-voltage energy bolt into the wall inches from her head. It left a hole the size of my fist.

Still sitting, she started to cast a binding spell. I smacked her with a smaller energy bolt, making her jump.

"You really are a one-trick pony, aren't you?" I said. "Well, two, I guess, if you include that pathetic energy bolt." I leaned down and whispered. "It's really kind of embarrassing."

She lunged. I grabbed her by the front of her shirt and threw her into an ancient printing press.

"Not expecting that?" I said. "Lesson two. Learn some self-defense tricks as well as spell-casting."

Tiffany rose and touched the back of her shoulder. Her fingers came away bloody.

"You bitch," she whispered.

She launched an energy bolt. I darted to the side, but not fast enough. It caught me in the elbow, jolting me enough to make me bite my tongue. Rage rushed through me. My hands flew up. The energy bolt hit her in the shoulder, and scorched through her blouse. She screamed, and I smelled burning flesh.

When her hands rose again, I hit her with a spell Paige and Lucas hadn't taught me, one they didn't know. It pinned her to the wall, her guts on fire, her face contorting in agony.

As I held her there, blood roared in my ears. Seeing her writhing, hearing her mewling . . . I amped it up, just a notch, watching her face, seeing and feeling her terror and—

"Enough, Savannah." Paige's voice, deep in my head. "You have her. You won. That's enough."

The rush evaporated and when I looked at Tiffany again, I saw her terror and panic. I released the spell.

"Now you know what I can do," I said as I stepped toward her. "If you cast any more spells you'll get another taste of that one. Got it?"

"Bitch," she said.

"You keep calling me that. I have a name, you know, though it seems you don't know exactly who I am, so let's try a proper introduction. I'm Savannah—"

"I know who you are." Her lips twisted as she got to her feet. "Daughter of Eve Levine and Kristof Nast. Foster daughter of Paige Winterbourne and Lucas Cortez. The golden girl of the supernatural world. Under the protection of two Cabals and the interracial council."

"Actually, one Cabal. Thomas Nast refuses to recognize me. That'll change when my brother takes over, but in the meantime, I've got the werewolf Pack. For protection, I'll take them over the Nasts any day."

"I suppose you think that makes you special."

"Uh, yeah . . ."

"Well, it doesn't. It makes you privileged. You get your spell power from your parents and your political power from your connections. Take that away, and you're just a smart-ass little girl who thinks she's all grown up. Thinks she can sail into town, intimidate me, stalk me—"

"Stalk you? You're the one who keeps coming after *me*."

"Bullshit. Did you think I wouldn't notice I was being followed? Wouldn't cast perimeter spells and know you're lurking around my house?"

"I don't know what meds you're on, but they're powerful stuff. I've never even been *near* your house. If you saw me there—"

"I didn't need to see you. Someone starts following me and, two days later, Savannah Levine pops up, supposedly investigating the murder of humans. Bullshit. You came here for me. Then you found out we'd had some murders and decided it'd be easier to play private eye."

Twice now *I'd* felt someone watching me, who disappeared when I got close. Two witches in town, both being followed by a mystery stalker. Hmm.

"It wasn't me," I said.

"Like hell. You're investigating me, on behalf of the council."

"How do you know I'm not investigating Cody?" I asked.

She rolled her eyes. "Since when does the council bother with humans?"

Damn. After Molly's call, I'd really been hoping Cody was a druid. It couldn't be that easy, could it? But what exactly did Tiffany think I was investigating her *for*? Let's give her a shake and see what came loose.

"You're in a lot of trouble, Tiffany," I said. "You thought you could just hide out here in Nowhere-ville, but the council has caught up with you."

She crossed her arms. "I haven't done anything wrong."

"No? Let's start with the minor offenses, like sharing your rituals with your human husband. I saw Tommy's Facebook album. If you were going to tell Cody what you are—which isn't advisable, but not a crime—then you should have told him to be more discreet. That's an exposure threat, which attracts the interest of both the council and the Cabals."

"I didn't—" She sucked in breath, rethinking the denial. "It was back when we were dating. He walked in on me doing a healing ritual. I had a big exam and felt a cold coming on.

I told him I was Wiccan. That's what he thinks. He wanted me to show him some magic for his frat party, and I made up a ritual. If you take a good look at Tommy's photos, you'll see it's fake."

"Maybe. But that's just the first of your offenses, isn't it?"

She brushed dust off her slacks. Buying time.

"I'm allowed to use my powers to benefit my family," she said, chin lifting. "As long as I'm careful, I can do that."

"Sure. You can entertain the baby with a light show. You can mix healing teas for your kids. You can set perimeter spells. Hell, if the neighbor's brat was picking on yours, you could wallop him with a knockback . . . if you knew the spell. But that's not what we're talking about, is it?"

"Don't you have better things to do? Bigger crimes to punish?"

"Nope. But I will give you a chance to defend yourself." I glanced at my watch. "Ten minutes. Starting now."

"Go to hell."

I leaned against the wall. "I'm not a crusader, Tiffany. I might help Paige and the council, but I can be reasonable. Them? Not so much. So just tell—"

She spat at me. Missed. That didn't save her from an energy bolt that had her eyes rolling back in her head as she hit the floor, flopping like a beached salmon. I stood over her.

"You want to try again?" I said.

"I have the right to protect—"

"Is someone actually threatening your family?"

"Besides you?"

"I'm only a threat if you or Cody had something to do with those murders. Otherwise, I don't give a shit. Is anyone else threatening them?"

"What the hell do you know about families? You're a spoiled brat who's never had to worry about anyone but herself. If you had children, you'd understand that protecting them is about more than just fighting someone like you."

"In other words, no. What you mean is that you're using your powers to make money. Because, otherwise, your kids might not get the fancy sneakers they want." I leaned over her. "You have no fucking idea what it's like to *need* to put food on the table. You're talking about lifestyle, not survival."

"My children need—"

"Look around you, Tiffany, and you'll see children who *need*. Like Kayla Thompson—"

"That whore's daughter?" Tiffany's lip curled.

I hit her with the internal fireball spell again and she screamed. I let her scream, writhing on the floor, and this time I didn't hear Paige's voice. I waited until she curled up in a ball, gasping. Then I launched it again, this time in her throat. Her eyes rolled, but she could only gag, smoke puffing with each breath. Again, I waited until the fire went out and she lay there, moaning.

"You're going to have a sore throat for a few days," I said. "But if you say one more word against Kayla or Paula Thompson, it'll be the last word you ever say. Understood?"

She glared up at me.

"As for the rest, I'll give you a few hours to think about it. Then I'm knocking on your door and you're either talking to me or—"

"Or you're hauling me in front of the council," she croaked.

"If I'm in a good mood. But right now, Tiffany, I'm not in a good mood. You've got until three o'clock," I said and walked away.

TWENTY-FIVE

WHAT THE HELL HAD HAPPENED WITH MY KNOCKBACK AND energy-bolt spells? My spells didn't fail—not ones I knew so well I could cast them in my sleep.

As I thought about it, though, I remembered that lingering headache and my unsettled stomach. Nothing serious, but put them together and I could be coming down with something. The last time I'd had the flu, it had wiped me out, spell power, too.

But right now, my biggest worry was that I'd made a mistake by walking away and leaving Tiffany with a warning. I'd wanted to push harder, yet I'd realized that I didn't have any leverage. All I knew was that she'd done something she thought worthy of council attention. I needed more information.

Molly said the ritual was druidic. I kind of hoped she was wrong, because that added another complication to a case that didn't need it, not when I was already following leads on witchcraft and Santeria. Did that mean Tiffany Radu wasn't the only supernatural hiding out in Columbus? *Was* she hiding? If so, from what? Was it related to the person stalking her? The person stalking me? Was that person involved in Michael's death?

As I walked toward the Thompson home, I called Paige.

"So, how's the beach?" I said when she answered.

"We saw it."

"Through your resort room window?"

She gave a throaty laugh. "No. We went for a beach walk last night. Today we're touring the volcano. Tomorrow we're going into the rain forest."

"Missing the point, aren't you? You're supposed to be lying on the beach, soaking up the rays . . ."

Paige made a gagging noise. Even on vacation, it would take a binding spell to get her to stay still.

We talked for another couple of minutes. Then, as I was ready to hang up, she suddenly said. "Is everything okay, Savannah?"

"Hmm?"

"You sound a little off. Are you okay?"

My throat clenched and I gripped the phone. *No, I'm not. The guy I went out with last night is dead. I found his body. I spent the night being interrogated by the cops. I don't want to tell you what's happening because you're on vacation, and I can handle this, but I just feel . . . lonely. I feel lonely.*

"Everything's fine," I said.

A pause. "Okay, then, well, if you need us, just call."

"I will."

Next, Jesse checked in to say he'd gotten tied up in Seattle—a client showed up just as he was grabbing stuff from the office. He was on his way now and would call me when he was in town.

I told him about Tiffany. I'm not sure what bothered him most: that she knew who I was or that we both thought someone was spying on us.

"The targeting of two witches doesn't constitute a racially

motivated pattern, as Lucas would say," I said. "We could just have a random peeper."

"Still, I don't like it," he said. "Be careful, okay?"

When I told him about the druidic link, he seemed far less concerned.

"Not many of them practice the old rites these days," he said. "Who's your source?"

"A friend of my mom's."

"We should check it out, but I suspect someone's just trying to get in your good books, Savannah. Have you asked Adam to look into it?"

"Not yet. I thought I'd research it myself."

"Let me handle it, then. I'll send the pics to a druid buddy, see what he says."

I signed off and headed up the walk to confront Paula Thompson.

When I knocked, Kayla answered. She looked up at me, her thin face solemn. "I'm sorry about Detective Kennedy."

"So am I."

She nodded and backed up to let me in.

"Is your grandma—?"

"Right here." Paula rounded the corner, wiping flour-dusted hands on her apron.

"Something smells good," I said.

"It's for you," Kayla said. "When Mom died, people brought food over, so I told Grandma we should make you something. Usually it's casseroles, but Grandma said you won't want that in a motel room, so we're making muffins. Do you like blueberry?"

"I love them," I said. "Thank you."

Damn. This was going to make what I had to do very tough.

"Do you have a minute?" I said to Paula. "I need to speak to you."

"Of course. Come on in."

She waved me through to the kitchen. History books were spread across the table. As Kayla moved them aside, I could see her worksheets, her neat handwriting below her grandma's questions, Paula's writing painfully precise, like a schoolgirl's herself. Homeschooling a child couldn't be easy, but Paula was trying. Anything for her granddaughter.

I turned to Paula. "I should really speak to you alone."

"I'm fine," Kayla said, parking herself in a chair.

"It's about the police file on Ginny's murder," I said. "Did you know they took DNA samples?"

"Course they did," Kayla said. "*Everyone* does these days."

"Actually, no. Someone seems to have gone a little overboard, considering they didn't find any DNA at the scene. They took samples from the victims and they tried to from any possible suspects. Cody wouldn't go for it, but they got them from an old boyfriend of Brandi's, as well as Ginny's landlord, and Alastair Koppel . . ."

Paula froze, oven door open, muffin tray in hand. It took her a second to unstick herself and get the tray in.

"We compared samples," I said.

"With what?" Kayla asked, screwing up her nose. "You said there wasn't any DNA at the scene."

"Kayla," Paula said. "I need some brown sugar."

"Brown sugar?"

"To sprinkle on the tops." She dug in her purse and handed Kayla a ten. "Can you get some from the grocery? And, yes, you can buy yourself something. Remember what the dentist said, though, no hard or sticky candy."

Kayla studied her grandmother's expression, then she scowled at me. She didn't know why her grandma was upset, but I was clearly responsible.

"I'm staying," she said. "Whatever *she* has to say—"

"*Kayla.*" Paula's voice sharpened. "Don't take that tone with Ms. Levine, and don't tell me what you will or won't do. I need you to go to the store. That's not a request."

Kayla shot me an icy look, but she obeyed. Paula went to the front window to watch her go. I stayed in the kitchen. When she came back, she took a seat. I did the same.

"Yes, Alastair is Ginny's father," she said. "But I wasn't lying when I said she didn't know and that she didn't have any contact with him."

"That's splitting a very fine hair, Ms. Thompson. You knew what I meant—was there any relationship between them? I'd consider that a relationship."

"I wouldn't."

She met my eyes, with that same defiant look I'd just seen on her granddaughter. But she couldn't hold it. After a moment, she broke off with a sigh.

"Yes, I'm sure Chief Bruyn would consider it important, too. But I didn't." She caught my gaze again, hers softer now. "Alastair had nothing to do with Ginny, before or after her death. He doesn't know she's his daughter, and I'd like to keep it that way. For Kayla's sake."

"Kayla?"

"I don't want Kayla to grow up in Columbus. She needs schooling—proper schooling, with other children and a teacher who can keep up with her. I go into Battle Ground every week, trying to find work, even head into Portland now and then. But there aren't many openings for a forty-one-year-old cleaning woman with a tenth-grade education. I'm working on my GED. When this recession ends, I'll be ready, and we'll get out. Until then, Kayla is stuck here. With everything she's been through, do you really think she needs the town knowing that her grandfather is the local kook? A dirty old man with a harem?"

"But what if Alastair had something to do with Ginny's death? I know you and Chief Bruyn don't get along—"

"Which is exactly why I didn't tell him. I used to clean the police station. Did reception work, too. Spent four years slapping Bruyn's fingers off my ass, pardon my language. When I found out he was telling people we were having an affair, I quit and everyone knew why. I kept my mouth shut, but that didn't matter. As far as he's concerned, I made a laughingstock of him. If he could tell the town that my daughter's daddy was the local wacko? He would have given himself heart failure racing to the diner to spread the news."

"Well, it looks a lot more suspicious now. Especially when my leads keep taking me back to Alastair's door."

She shook her head. "If they are, then you're looking at someone else in that house. Alastair is a lot of things, but he isn't a killer."

"You didn't want him as the father of your daughter. And that was back when he was, by all accounts, a respectable college student. He got out of town at a damned convenient time. Are you really telling me he didn't know he was about to be a daddy? Because I'm thinking, for a twenty-year-old guy eager to make something of himself, finding out he got a sixteen-year-old girl pregnant would be plenty of incentive to decide it was time to get the hell out of Columbus and never come back."

She didn't answer for a minute. Then she said, "He left before I knew I was pregnant, but I think he suspected it. We'd kept our relationship a secret. His choice. Then I started missing first class every day, sick to my stomach. I wasn't an A student, but I didn't skip. It was a teacher who figured out what might be wrong and persuaded me to take a pregnancy test. That was a month after I started missing classes, and three weeks after Alastair gave me the 'I love you, but I need to grow up, move onto campus, and date girls my own age' speech." She gave a wry smile. "As you can tell, he never quite got to that last part."

"So he left and never looked back. Saved himself a bundle on child support." I looked her in the eye. "Money you could have used."

"Yes," she said quietly. "Maybe I should have asked. He'd have paid. I just— I didn't want to share Ginny with him. I was young and I was hurt, and I was stubborn. By the time things started going wrong with Ginny, Alastair was already on his third wife, so I knew there wouldn't be any money and I couldn't see how bringing her father into her life would help. I'd go from being the whore who got knocked up by a stranger to the bitch who'd kept her daddy away from her. I decided to stick with my first role. I was used to it."

"So twenty-five years later Alastair returns to find his ex with a twenty-five-year-old daughter . . . and doesn't connect the dots?"

She didn't answer. Just sat there until the oven timer chimed, took out the muffins, and began scooping them onto the cooling racks. Then she said, "I imagine the thought crossed his mind. But if he asked, then he'd have to face the truth. Alastair isn't good at facing truths, Ms. Levine. He's built his own world and that's where he chooses to live, blinds drawn to the rest of the universe. In his mind, he's still a twenty-year-old stud. Having a daughter older than the girls he beds up in that farmhouse? That wouldn't do at all."

She pried out a stubborn muffin. "Whatever Alastair is, he still considers himself a therapist. He thinks he's helping those girls and I'm sure sometimes he does, and that makes him feel good. How long would those girls keep coming to him if they found out his own daughter lived a mile away, an alcoholic drug addict who lets her boyfriend use her for a punching bag? No. It wouldn't do at all."

Wasn't that what we'd call motive? Alastair had himself a sweet deal here. What if Ginny figured out who Daddy was and threatened to expose him? I didn't say that to Paula. She might not have wanted Alastair Koppel for her baby's father, but there was obviously still something there, an exasperated affection.

When I made a move to go, though, Paula stopped me.

"Can you wait and talk to Kayla?" she asked.

"I'm not sure she *wants* to talk to me—"

"That's why I'm asking. I need her to know that everything's okay. She likes you, and you're a good role model for her. A smart young woman working at a good job, living on her own in the city. She doesn't see a lot of that here."

"Um, sure. Okay."

"I'll get those muffins ready for you to take. Kayla really wants you to have them."

Kayla showed up shortly after that. Her grandma didn't say anything, but showed by her mood and her actions that we were good, and Kayla relaxed. We talked about her homework and ate a couple of the muffins, and for the first time that day, I forgot about Michael.

It was nice that Paula thought I made a good role model for Kayla, but I couldn't help wishing I could do more. Kayla was a bright kid. She deserved to go to college. I thought about my trust fund. Was there a way to help her without insulting Paula? I'd have to think about that, ask Paige for some ideas.

I had the money. I didn't need all of it. Maybe this was something I could do with the extra. Something good.

TWENTY-SIX

I WAS WALKING AWAY FROM THE HOUSE WHEN MY PHONE started playing "Light My Fire." I grabbed it so fast I nearly sent it flipping onto the sidewalk. Then I took a deep breath and answered.

"Hey," I said.

"Hey yourself," Adam said. "It's 12:01 and I missed my morning update."

I clutched the phone tighter and didn't answer.

"Savannah?"

"Can— Can I call you back?"

"What's wrong?"

I considered going to the motel and phoning him back. That's where I wanted to be when I told him, curled up in a chair, imagining him there, listening. But I couldn't wait that long. I'd been holding back the dam all morning. So I stopped walking and said, "There's been a murder."

"Shit. Another girl?"

"No . . . Michael."

Silence.

"Michael Kennedy," I said. "Claire Kennedy's brother. The Dallas detective—"

"I know who you mean. He's dead?"

I told him what happened.

"So— Wait— You—" He stopped and took a deep breath. "Okay, let me see if I understand. Michael Kennedy called you last night and asked for your help. You went out, found his body, and were accused of his murder. And I'm just finding this out now?"

"I wanted to handle it myself."

"A guy you were working with *died*. You found his body. I don't care if you can handle it yourself. You shouldn't— Damn it. Hold on." A rustle as the phone moved. When a fire half-demon gets mad, things get a little warm, including whatever he happens to be holding at the time. Adam goes through a cell phone a year, usually shorting them out when I'm on the other end.

I resumed walking and forced a light tone. "I keep telling you, you need travel-sized oven mitts."

"Yeah, yeah," he muttered. Another rustle as he wrapped something around the phone.

"That's what I'll get you for your birthday," I said. "Not a new top for your Jeep—"

"Don't change the subject," Adam said. "I'm serious, Savannah. You should have called." He took a deep breath and exhaled. "So how are you making out? No, stupid question. You're not okay, but you sure as hell aren't going to admit it. Where are you? No, that's another stupid question, isn't it? You're working. Haven't slept. Haven't eaten—"

"I ate."

"Nothing good, I'm sure. Stop walking, okay?"

I didn't ask how he knew I was on the move.

"Turn toward your motel," he said. "Then start walking again."

"I don't need—"

"Yes, you do. Michael Kennedy is dead. Possibly murdered by the same killer you're tracking right now. You're running on fumes and you're going to screw up. You'll miss something. Or worse, you'll let your guard down. So get your ass back to that motel and sleep."

"Yes, sir."

"I'm serious, Savannah. Don't pull this shit. Not with me."

"I'm not, okay? You're right. I'm walking back to my motel. You can call my room in ten minutes and I'll be there."

"You'd better."

"I will."

When I got to the motel, Jesse's truck was parked out front. I'd given him a key, so I rapped first. Inside, I could hear him talking on the phone.

"Right." Pause. "Right."

I used my key and quietly opened the door.

"She's here now. Do you want to—?" Pause. "Okay." Pause. "Bye."

Jesse hung up. "That was Adam wondering why I didn't call him about Detective Kennedy. I told him you could handle it, which seemed to be the wrong answer."

I tossed my bag onto the bed. "I should have let him know."

"I thought he wasn't supervising you."

"He's not. He just thinks I could have used a friend last night."

Jesse nodded, but I could tell he wasn't so sure that was why Adam was upset. Seeing his doubts made me wonder myself. Was I really in charge of this case? Or was Adam humoring me? No, he wouldn't do that. Not Adam.

A rap at the door. I glanced out the window to see the woman from the coffee shop, holding a bag.

"I didn't think anyplace around here delivered," Jesse said.

"No, but Adam does." I opened the door and stood in the gap. If she thought my boyfriend was sending me food, seeing Jesse in my room would not help my reputation around town.

"Special delivery?" I said.

She smiled. "Soup and a sandwich. He said to eat it, then get some sleep. That's an order."

Usually, I would have laughed at that. But I could feel the weight of Jesse's gaze on my back, and it didn't seem as funny.

I took the bag. When I closed the door, I waited for Jesse to say something. He didn't. He wasn't that kind of guy. But I saw the scenario through his eyes, and what would have been a sweet gesture seemed a little condescending, like I couldn't be trusted to take care of myself.

"That was nice of Adam," Jesse said finally.

There was no sarcasm in his voice, but my already tender stomach gave an extra twist.

"I'm not really hungry," I said. "Do you want it?"

He shook his head. "No, you should eat." He gave a short laugh. "Sorry. I don't mean to mother you, too. I mean—" He cleared his throat. "I'll go get a room. You can rest if you want. I'll catch up with you later."

I needed to rest, and refusing just because Adam had insisted would be childish. So I set the alarm, laid down, and was asleep in minutes.

I dreamed that I was back in that warehouse, only this time Michael was there, lying on the floor, hurt, and I couldn't find him. I could hear him moaning, the sounds growing softer, slower, his life slipping away, and I yelled for him and I cast spell after spell after spell, but they were useless. I was useless, racing around helpless, no idea where he was.

"Shhh," a voice whispered. "Shhh. It's okay."

But it wasn't okay. I had to find him. I had to—

Suddenly, I couldn't move. I jerked awake to find myself in bed with someone behind me, arms around me. My hands flew up—

"Whoa! It's me. No lethal spells, please."

I twisted to see a familiar figure sitting at the edge of my bed, his boyish face and dark eyes uncharacteristically solemn.

"Adam?"

"Key," he said, holding it up. "From Jesse. And I checked to make sure you were decent before I came in. I was sitting over there—" He pointed to the chair, a textbook now resting on it. "You were having a nightmare. When it wasn't going away, I thought I'd better wake you up."

I blinked and wiped my hand over my face. My fingers came back damp. I glanced across the room and saw my reflection in the mirror, hair snarled, mascara running, face streaked with tears.

"Yep, you look like shit," Adam said. "And I took plenty of pictures, which I will keep until an appropriate opportunity for blackmail arises."

When I turned, he reached over and pulled me into a fierce hug. I resisted, but when he whispered, "It's okay. I won't tell," I collapsed against him. He just held me, and I needed that. God, how I needed that. I knew then that this wasn't about whether or not I could handle the case professionally. It was personal—right now, I needed a friend.

When I got myself under control, he still held me there, and whispered, "Jesse tells me you went out with him last night. The detective. Michael."

I nodded.

"I'm sorry." His arms tightened around me. "I'm so sorry."

I backed up then, wiping my sleeve over my eyes. "It's just . . . He was . . . He was a nice guy. God, that sounds lame but . . . He was just . . . really nice."

"You liked him," Adam said softly.

I lowered my gaze and nodded. "It wasn't— I just . . . I . . ."

"You liked him."

I nodded. "And I feel . . ." I took a deep breath, then blurted out the words I'd been holding in all day. "I feel like I could have stopped it. He wanted to come in last night and I said no. I was goofing around, holding him off and . . . But it's not just that. I gave him a lead about Cody and I think he was following it and I . . . I shouldn't have given him any leads. If I thought there was a supernatural connection, then I was putting him in danger. He walked into something he knew nothing about and got killed for it."

"You had no way of knowing that could happen."

I looked at him. "Didn't I? Sure, it's not like I thought 'hmm, this could be dangerous for a human' and gave him the tip anyway. But I should have stopped and thought about it."

"Do you know for certain that he was following up on the lead you gave him?"

"No, but—"

"Did you think that lead about a delivery had *any* supernatural connection?"

"No, but—"

"Then stop beating yourself up over it."

When I tried to get off the bed, he tugged me back down and turned me to look at him. "You aren't responsible, Savannah. You gave him what you thought was a clean lead. He may or may not have been following it. And as for saving him by inviting him to bed . . ."

I glowered. "I didn't mean it like that. Just that I keep thinking—"

"—of all the things you could have done differently. And for all you know, you could have invited him in, and he would have gone to that warehouse later anyway. Or you would have gone with him and both gotten killed. So the next time you think about letting a guy stay the night, remember that sex probably won't save his life. Even really good sex."

I lifted my fingers, making them spark.

"Hey, two can play that game, remember." He made a fist, then spread his fingers, the tips glowing red. "And mine leave bigger burns."

I flicked sparks at him, then jumped out of the way. My leg caught on the covers, and I stumbled. Adam yanked and I went down, crashing to the floor.

"Hey!" I said, pushing up.

"Hey yourself." He plucked his T-shirt, pointing out the pin-sized holes from my sparks.

"It's an ugly shirt anyway."

His brows arched. "You bought it for me."

"Um, yeah. That's the idea. Give you ugly clothing. Laugh behind your back when you wear it. Been doing it for years. You're a little slow on the uptake."

He hooked my legs and I went down again. When I scrambled to get up, he loomed over me, glowing fingers lowering to a strand of my hair static-stuck to the bed cover.

"Don't you dare—"

The hair sizzled as he lit the ends. I kicked at him, but he leapt out of the way and we goofed around for a few more minutes, until I collapsed on the floor, laughing.

"Better?" he said, standing over me.

"Better. Thanks."

He reached down, grabbed me under the armpits, and hoisted me onto the bed. Then he stretched out beside me, the backs of our hands touching, the silence falling, calm and comfortable, and I closed my eyes, relaxing for the first time since I'd found Michael's body.

"Remember last year, when I was tracking that demi-demon in Ohio?" he said. "The one who possessed—"

"—a teacher who started seducing and killing her students? Oh, yeah. I won't forget that bitch."

"Remember when I realized she was onto me? When she tried to trap me? I told you and you were on the next plane out to help?" He turned me around to face him. "You didn't come because you thought I couldn't handle it."

"Um, actually, yeah. Sorry. I know I said—"

He poked me in the ribs, making me yelp. "Seriously, Savannah. You came because I needed backup and you knew I was too damned stubborn to ask for it. And a few months later, when I was on a case and realized I was tracking two vampires instead of one, I called you in. I'd learned my lesson. *Don't be afraid to ask for backup.*"

I sighed and moved to sit on the edge of the bed. "We aren't just traveling down memory lane here, are we?"

"Nope." He sat up beside me. "I just don't want you to bite my head off when I tell you that I want to stay."

"Okay."

He paused. "You mean okay, you won't bite my head off?"

"No, I mean okay, you can stay."

"Huh, that was easy." He frowned over at me. "Too easy. What's the catch?"

"No catch. I need backup. One investigator is dead. Tiffany Radu pushed me down the stairs, planning to do God-only-knows-what. So that's two reasons—"

"You're forgetting something."

"Hmm?"

"Your bike. I saw it on the way in. And don't tell me you just laid it down. What happened?"

I told him. The acrid smell of burning cloth wafted up and I lifted his hand from the bed.

"No scorching the sheets, okay? They'll charge me a fortune for them."

"Sorry." He made a fist. "The first order of business, I think, is to pay a visit to Cody."

"No, first I need to talk to Tiffany, and that appointment isn't until—" I turned to check the clock. I looked at Adam. "How'd you make it here from Spokane so fast?"

"I was already on my way when I called. And, no, I wasn't heading here to insist on joining the investigation. I *did* plan to stop in, though. See how things were going. Since it was on the way. Sort of."

"Not really, but okay. Let's get moving, then. I've got some ground to cover, and since you're here, I'm starting with Alastair Koppel. His guard dog has been blocking me. I was going to take Jesse. You'll do, though."

"Thanks. Speaking of Jesse . . ." He got to his feet. "I should go talk to him, tell him he can go home and get back to work. I'll just transfer his room over to my card."

I was about to say sure, then I thought about how that would look and said, "Maybe I should just let Jesse help. This *is* his case."

Adam stopped. For a moment, he just stood there. When he finally did turn, his expression was as neutral as he could manage, but I could see the confusion in his eyes, maybe even a little hurt.

"I'd really rather be solo on this, but I can't now," I said. "With Jesse, though, well, he doesn't work with us, so it's not like he'd be supervising me."

"I'm your co-worker, Savannah. And your friend. Not your supervisor or your manager or your boss. I know I joked about that, but I *was* joking. You know that, right?"

"Sorry," I said. "I'm just . . ." I exhaled. "Getting a little territorial, I guess. Too much time spent hanging out with werewolves. It was bound to rub off."

"Well, I don't blame you. I still remember when Lucas and Paige gave me my first solo investigations. I was convinced they were tailing me, watching over my shoulder, making sure I didn't screw up and embarrass the firm."

"No, that was me."

He laughed. "I don't doubt it. Okay, then, speaking of embarrassing, let me take a stab in the dark and guess that you don't want Jesse thinking I've swooped in to take over."

I made a face. "Like I care what anyone—"

He stopped me with a look. "You do. Or your pride does, at least. Okay, I won't give Jesse his walking papers. I'll just tell him I'm bored and want to hang out with you guys."

"Which is the truth."

"Which makes it an even better excuse." He grabbed half my sandwich from the table and pointed at the rest. "Eat or I'll make you pay for it."

"I'll talk to Jesse."

He paused. "You sure?"

I nodded.

"Take the sandwich then. And invite him along to the cookie cult."

TWENTY-SEVEN

I EXPLAINED THE SITUATION TO JESSE, THEN SAID, "IS THAT a problem?"

"Of course not. It's your investigation and he's your co-worker. I think you're handling this case just fine, but when it comes down to it, you represent Lucas and Paige's firm, and if they're more comfortable thinking you're doing legwork on a case for *him* . . ."

"This has nothing to do with Lucas and Paige. Adam doesn't have any cases, so he's going to hang out and help me."

He nodded, slowly, still not convinced. "It's your call. If you aren't worried about Adam trying to take over—"

I cut him short with a laugh. "Believe me, he knows better than to try. He's made it clear that this is totally my case, and he's ready to follow orders." I grinned. "And I'm ready to give them."

"All right then. So where do we start?"

"I want to take another run at the commune. Adam's coming along and you're welcome to join us."

"Mmm, they might feel under siege. You two go. I have work I can do here. We'll meet up later and compare notes."

On the drive to the commune, I asked Adam about the conference and he kept me amused with anecdotes. He had plenty of those. Even picturing him in a roomful of academics was enough to get me smiling.

Adam's stepfather is the most respected supernatural researcher in the country. When he withdrew from his council delegate role and prodded Adam into his place, no one expected Adam to take over the research part, too. In fact, for years, friends would buy him textbooks and journals and reading glasses as a standing joke.

When Adam decided to try filling the research role, too, I remember overhearing Paige and Lucas worrying that Adam was setting himself up for disappointment. Paige and Adam had been friends since childhood, and she knew how tough it was for him to sit still long enough to read a newspaper.

He'd had a few false starts. I'd helped him research things on the side, as he tried to prove himself to the council, getting frustrated when he couldn't find what he needed. But eventually he did prove himself. He'd never be his stepfather, staying on the sidelines lost in his books. But he'd set his mind to it and he'd done it, and I admired him for that.

Speaking of admiration . . .

We'd been inside the commune for less than five minutes before every girl there had checked out the new arrival. Adam isn't drop-dead gorgeous. He's cute, though. Seriously cute. Short, wavy dark blond hair. Perpetual tan. Athletic build. He looks like someone a girl could talk to, who'd flirt and make her laugh and look her in the eye while he's doing it. In other words, he looks like exactly the kind of guy he is, and girls love it.

As usual, Megan was giving us the runaround.

"Alastair is a very busy man," Megan said. "You can't just show up and demand to see him, or he probably won't be around."

"He isn't," Vee piped up from her vantage spot on the stairs. "She's telling the truth. He went out an hour ago."

The front door opened behind us. "But I'm back now." Alastair greeted us with firm handshakes and a smile as warm as a July afternoon.

"They don't have an appointment," Megan said. "I asked her to make one."

"That's all right. I have some time for Ms. Levine and her associate."

"Actually, I can handle the interview. Someone"—I nodded toward Adam—"has been trying to steal my cookies. I'm sure he can be talked into buying a box of his own."

The girls swooped in. While Adam was surrounded, I slipped past to Alastair, who led me to his office. Megan followed. At the door, he motioned me inside, then murmured a few words to her. When he came in, she didn't.

"Megan can be a bit . . ." Alastair smiled, face creasing as he sat behind his desk. "Overprotective. If you need anything more from me after this, call my cell." He handed me a card with the number. "Just don't tell Megan."

He winked and leaned back in his chair, and I got my first good look at him. From his picture, I knew he was a distinguished, handsome older man. But it wasn't until I was sitting across the desk that I really understood why he had a houseful of girls lining up to share his bed.

Guys like Adam have charm. They know how to make a girl feel pretty and special. Alastair probably had that, too, at Adam's age, but by forty-five, it had matured into that rarer variety every good cult leader needs. Charisma.

Two minutes with him and he was acting as if we were co-conspirators, smiling in a way that said he already liked me and was looking forward to spending time with me. I bet that every person who entered Alastair's world got that smile, and few realized he gave it to everyone. That was his gift.

"Don't worry," I said as I pocketed the card. "I won't tell Megan. I don't scare easy, but she does the trick."

He laughed. "Yes, she is a very strong-willed young woman."

"I was thinking more of the Santeria. They have some nasty curses."

The smile froze, then twitched, as he tried to light it again. When it returned, the warmth was definitely more May than July. Early May, with a chance of frost.

"Taking an unguided tour of our property, Ms. Levine?" he said. "Trespassing is illegal. Break and enter even more so."

"Huh. Really? Okay, then. Call Chief Bruyn and show him where you think I broke into. I'd love to see it. I figured it was just a rumor, but it seems not."

His whole face froze now, dismay in his eyes.

"So Megan does practice Santeria." I scribbled in my notebook. "Is she an *iyalorisha* or just a practitioner?"

"A practitioner," he said slowly.

"Seems like an odd choice for someone like Megan, but maybe not. She's here, so she obviously has some yearning for the spiritual. Santeria has a strong role for women, which she'd appreciate, but you should tell her that's more true of the Americanized version. The true Santerian traditions coming from Cuba are definitely slanted toward the guys. If she wanted a more feminist version of voodoo, she would be better off with Candomblé."

As he stared at me, his smooth veneer fell away, his gaze sliding to the door as if mentally willing Megan to barrel through and kick me out. A man with the charisma, but not the balls, to be a leader.

"Actually, I was the one who brought Megan to Santeria," he said, picking his words carefully. "She came to a meeting with a friend of hers, a researcher. Megan and I went home together. And this"—he opened his hands, indicating the house—"was the result. The perfect blending of the spiritual and the commercial."

Spiritual for him. Commercial for her. A fortuitous meeting all around. I doodled in my book as he explained. I already knew what attracted him to Santeria, and I wasn't surprised to hear that despite what Vee said, Alastair was the true devotee, not Megan. As a religion, Santeria suited him. It was mystical and New Age, and slightly shocking. Exactly the image he wanted to project.

Megan would go along with it because Alastair was the Pied Piper who brought girls to her workhouse. It was in her best interests to not only keep him happy, but hold a blackmail-worthy secret over him. Ah, true love.

Time to change the subject. "I saw you gave DNA to the sheriff's department?"

"Of course. If it eliminates me from the list of suspects, then that benefits everyone here. We have enough prejudice to combat without suspicions like that."

"They took samples from the victims, too," I said.

"Yes, I suppose they would, in order to eliminate them from any samples found at the scene."

I nodded. "There wouldn't be any need to compare them to the samples taken from the suspects."

His shoulders tightened, then he forced himself to relax. "I don't know where you're going with this, Ms. Levine. Did they finally find DNA at the scene of Claire's murder? I hope so, if it helps them solve it. She was a lovely girl."

"And Ginny? Was she a lovely girl, too?"

"I'm sure she was. Brandi, too. If they found DNA at the scene, then I'm glad of it, and I hope they've compared it to mine already, because I know it's not a match."

"I have no idea if they have uncovered DNA at Claire's scene. I'm talking about the earlier murder. Your DNA and the victims'. Like I said, no reason to compare them. Not unless you're a private investigator, studying the files, searching for a connection, any connection . . ."

His expression said he knew exactly what I was getting at, but he wasn't about to admit it. Enough beating around the bush, then.

"Are you aware that you're Genevieve Thompson's father?" I asked.

He tried to look shocked, then struggled for surprised, and finally settled for uncomfortable. "I . . . suspected I might be," he finally said. "But Paula never confirmed it."

"Did you ask her?"

"Well, no . . ." He straightened, folding his hands on the desk. "Clearly she didn't think I was a suitable father for her child or she would have told me herself. As much as that pains me, I decided it was best to abide by her wishes."

"That's very noble of you. And, for the record, you're right. She'd like you to stay away from Kayla, too. I'm sure you have no interest in letting your girls here know you're a granddaddy, but if you tell anyone, I'll share your Santeria secret. You and I know it's just a religion, but to folks in Columbus, it would mean you're running a voodoo cult up here."

He fixed me with a look that said he'd decided he didn't like me after all. Didn't like me one bit.

"Did you have any contact with Ginny?" I asked.

"No."

"Brandi?"

"No."

"To your knowledge, did either of them ever come up to the house?"

"No."

"To your knowledge, did Claire have any contact with Cody Radu?"

He opened his mouth, then stopped himself, maybe realizing how unseemly it would be to tattle on the other guy vying for prime-suspect spot.

"You may want to speak to Megan about that," he said.

"I will."

TWENTY-EIGHT

ALASTAIR WAS EAGER ENOUGH TO GET RID OF ME THAT HE didn't escort me to the door, which meant I could sneak over to the kitchen and check out the situation there.

If Adam was charming the girls, I didn't want to interfere. So I slipped into the dining room with a blur spell, then exchanged it for a cover one when I could see the kitchen through the doorway. Adam was leaning against the counter, milk glass in one hand, cookie in the other, crumbs flying as he told a story about our last white-water rafting trip. I noticed he conveniently left out the part where he steered us under a waterfall, trying to get me soaked, and instead ended up getting drenched himself, courtesy of a fast knockback spell.

Planted right in front of him, staring up like a daisy at the sun, was Vee. While he glanced at the other girls as he talked, he kept most of his attention on her. I hadn't thought to tell him that she'd approached me. He was just damned good at reading people. He'd even tailored the story to her, I realized, as she started asking questions about his gear and his favorite spots, and giving him suggestions.

As Adam talked, he glanced at the dining room doorway enough times for me to wonder whether my cover spell had failed. When I heard Megan's footsteps in the hall, I stepped forward. Adam glanced up, eyes meeting mine, and he grinned broadly enough to earn me scowls from the girls.

"Sorry to interrupt," I said. "I'm all done. I'll head outside. Whenever you're ready—"

"Right behind you," he said. Then to the girls, his voice filled with regret, "The boss calls, and I think yours is about to."

On cue, Megan stepped into the kitchen.

Adam turned his grin on her. "Sorry about that. They're all yours."

He thanked them for the cookies. I thanked Megan for letting me speak to Alastair. Then we were off. When we reached the Jeep, I glanced back to see Vee on the porch, watching us go.

"Score," I murmured.

Adam tossed me the keys, then jogged back across the yard, gaze on the ground, as if he didn't see Vee there. Near the porch, he reached down, scooping up some imaginary item he'd dropped, then saw her and gave a start.

"Hey, there," he said. "I was just thinking, I should have asked you about Gray River. Someone mentioned it was great rafting. Ever tried it?"

She came down off the porch to talk to him as I started the Jeep. I revved the engine, in case Vee was worried I'd overhear. They chatted for a while—long enough for me to get warm and put down the top.

"I feel so cheap," Adam said as he climbed into the passenger side.

"You love it." I put the Jeep in drive and rolled out of the yard. "That was probably the best reception you've had in years. Surprising, too. There's some stiff competition in this town. Cookie Cult Al. Sleazeball Cody. And Pickup Dude."

"Pickup Dude?"

I nodded toward the familiar pickup roaring toward us, muffler clattering. The driver waggled his tongue at me, yellow teeth flashing.

"It's close," I said. "But you get my vote."

"So do you want to know what Vee said? Or would you rather keep insulting me?"

"Just keeping that ego of yours in check. It's a full-time job."

"I know what that's like," he said with an arch look my way.

I swerved over just as a garden sprinkler arced our way. Adam swore and ducked, but didn't quite make it. As I veered back onto the road, he ran his hands through his hair, shaking his head, water flecking the dash.

"I'm sure there's a brush in the glove box," I said.

"Yeah, *yours*." He settled for finger-combing his hair, then settled back in his seat.

"So what'd Vee say?" I asked.

He glanced over, brows lifting.

After a moment, I sighed. "Okay, I apologize. Now, *please*, what did she say?"

"Well, she was a little late to the party. Megan sent her looking for the new girl, who seems to be hiding out. Can't blame her. That Alastair guy is seriously creepy."

"Agreed. Now, about Vee . . ."

"She was late joining the others, meaning she walked past the office when you were interviewing the old guy. She heard him tell you that Ginny and Brandi had never come to the house."

"And she said they did."

"Yep. Megan and Alastair caught them snooping around one night when they were out tending to the animals. Vee saw the whole thing. Megan wanted to call the cops. Alastair said he'd handle it. He took Ginny and Brandi aside, talked to them, then came into the house and told Megan they wouldn't have any more problems. She still wanted to report it, but he was adamant. Said it would only cause trouble in the town. She backed down."

"That's not an encounter he's likely to have forgotten," I said.

"Nope. If Megan's saying she never met the girls either, then he's told her to keep her mouth shut."

I parked near the Radu place, and we got out to deal with Tiffany.

"If she recognized you, we should presume she knows who I am, too," Adam said.

"I wouldn't."

"Thanks."

"I didn't mean it like that. The only reason she knows me is because of my parents. As usual."

"And the only way she'd know me is because of my dad. As usual." He shook his head. "Supernaturals overshadowed by their famous parents. We should start a support group."

"I think we already have."

We walked along the sidewalk. Both the officers were hanging around outside the police station. They saw me and peered at Adam, whispering between themselves, then went inside. A second later, Bruyn came out. I waved. He nodded, civil enough, which was all I could hope for at this point.

"Cody lives across from the police station?" Adam said. "That doesn't seem too bright if he's up to his eyeballs in something illegal."

I shrugged. "Another way of pretending he has nothing to hide."

A kid raced between us, nearly knocking Adam off the curb. I glanced over my shoulder to see the sidewalks filling with children.

"Shit!" I said. "What time is it?"

I checked my watch. Three-thirty. I swore again. "I told Tiffany I'd be there before her kids got home. She won't talk to us if they're there."

I picked up the pace. As we approached the Radu house, I heard a baby crying. That wouldn't make things any easier— fussy baby, kids getting home . . .

The Radus' neighbor was out on his porch. An old guy in a housecoat, baggy trousers, and slippers, he looked like he'd just woken up, and from the scowls he was sending next door, I could guess what woke him.

When we started up the walk, he yelled, "Tell that girl to shut her baby up or I swear I'll do it for her."

"I'm sure she's trying to," I said.

"Not very hard. The brat's been wailing for an hour now." He strode to the sidewalk and yelled across the road at Bruyn. "Can't you do something about that? She's disturbing the peace."

Bruyn waved, like he couldn't hear what the old man was saying, then turned and went back inside.

"It's a baby," I said. "It cries. And right now you're making a helluva lot more racket, so how about *you* shut it."

He gaped at me, then glowered at Adam, as if it was his fault for not keeping me in line. Adam rang the bell. The neighbor turned to head inside, then noticed a towheaded girl in pigtails coming along, holding the hand of a smaller, pig-tailed blonde.

"You there," the old man said. "Tell your mother—"

"Zip it, old man," I said. "Go back inside and get dressed before you get arrested for flashing little girls."

Adam chuckled and stepped aside to let the girls get to the door.

"We were just ringing for your mom," he said. "I think she can't hear with the baby crying."

The older girl nodded shyly, eyes down. She tugged on the screen door. Adam held it open for her. The girl turned the knob, but the inside door didn't budge.

"It's locked," she said.

"Mommy must be having her nap," the younger one said as her sister rang the bell. "She takes a nap when Taylor does and she always locks the door. She usually sets her alarm, but if she's really tired, she forgets."

"Do you have a key?" Adam asked.

Both girls shook their heads. "Mom's always home," the older one said.

"Can I try it?" I asked.

The girl nodded. I cast an unlock spell under my breath and turned the knob.

"Huh," I said. "Must have just been stuck. Go on in. Tell your mom we're here."

The older one glanced back to make sure we weren't going to follow them. I let the screen door close. Inside, the baby's howls turned to whimpers as she heard her sisters.

"Mommy!" the younger one said, racing past her sister as she dropped her backpack. "We're home! Did you make the cupcakes? My teacher said I need two dozen for the bake sale and— Mommy? Come on, Mommy. Wake up!" Giggles erupted, punctuated by squeaking springs.

"Don't jump on the bed," her sister said. "Mom?"

There was a pause, a long one, and my heart started thumping. Adam gripped my elbow, reassuring.

The older girl ran into the hall. She saw us and started, like she'd forgotten we were there.

"Is everything okay?" I called through the screen.

"It's Mom. She won't wake up."

TWENTY-NINE

TIFFANY LAY CURLED UP ON HER SIDE, UNDER THE COVERS. Her younger daughter still stood on the bed, uncertain. She gave a tentative bounce, and for a second, I saw myself years ago, bouncing away as my mother sang, *Ten little monkeys bouncing on the bed* . . .

My mom. Their mom. Oh, God. Please no.

I touched Tiffany's neck. She was warm, but I couldn't find a pulse. I shook her shoulder. Her head lolled back, eyes still closed.

I turned. "Adam—"

He was already running back into the hall. "I'll get them."

"Mom?" the older girl said, her voice wobbling.

"She's sick," I said. *Liar, liar.* "Take your sister and—"

I stopped. I wanted them out of that room. God, I wanted them out of that room. But I'd just been found over another dead body. I couldn't stay in there alone. So I scooped up the younger girl and carried her out, motioning for her sister to follow.

"Let's get the baby, okay?" I said. "The doctor is on the way and your mom—"

I stopped myself before I said "your mom will be fine." I wouldn't. When my mother died, they hadn't told me for days, and that only made it worse.

The baby was howling again. When we walked into her room, she was sitting up, face red, chubby body trembling with exhaustion.

The oldest girl snatched a cartoon character pillow out of the crib. "She isn't supposed to have that in bed."

I lifted the baby out. She stopped crying and peered at me through red-rimmed eyes. A hiccup, as if she remembered me. Then a wail. I wasn't a stranger, but I wasn't her mother.

I motioned the older girl to the rocking chair and settled the baby in her lap as Bruyn headed down the hall. Seeing us, he stopped. The older officer, right on his heels, almost ran into him.

Bruyn stared at the girls for a second, winced, then turned toward the front door and yelled, "Mom?"

His mother hurried into the baby's room, clucking and calling the girls by name. I slipped out to follow Bruyn. Adam came up behind me and squeezed my hand. We headed into the master bedroom.

"She's dead," I murmured when I was sure the girls couldn't hear. "I didn't tell her daughters—"

"Good." Bruyn checked for a pulse. "Doc's on the way. We'll tell them she's sick until their dad gets here. I've called him, but he's not answering. Probably sees my number and figures I'm just harassing him." Bruyn straightened and looked at me. "You seem to find a lot of dead bodies, don't you?"

Adam stepped forward, ready to snap something.

I cut him off. "We just got here. You saw us coming up the road. I had an appointment. The girls got here right after we knocked. We didn't go in before them. You can ask the neighbor."

Bruyn picked up a needle that lay beside an open Bible.

So Tiffany Radu had killed herself . . . right after I'd threatened her.

"Did you move anything?" Bruyn said.

I shook my head. Adam slipped out as I recited my steps. As I did my gaze kept going to that Bible. Its edges were so perfect it looked as if this was the first time it had been cracked open.

I glanced down at the page. Exodus 22. Something about that twanged a memory. I could count on one hand the number of times I'd been to church, but I knew that chapter. Why?

"Looking for comfort," Bruyn said, following my gaze. "She wasn't a churchgoing woman, but people do that at the end, wanting proof they're going someplace else. Someplace better."

When the doctor arrived, I went to find Adam. He was looking around the house. As we passed the baby's room, I glanced in. My gaze went to that pillow on the floor, the one the oldest girl had thrown out of the crib. I paused, staring at it like I'd stared at the Bible, not quite knowing why. Adam didn't say a word until we were halfway to the Jeep.

"You had nothing to do with Tiffany Radu's death," he said.

"Never said I did."

"But you're thinking it. That woman didn't kill herself because any threat from you, Savannah."

"So it's just a coincidence that she came home after a fight with me and committed suicide?"

"She didn't commit suicide. She was murdered."

I glanced over sharply. "What'd you see?"

"Not a damn thing. Whoever did it was careful."

"If you're trying to make me feel better—"

"I wouldn't lie to do it." He took my arm and steered me around a pile of dog shit on the sidewalk, then motioned to the scratches on my forearm. "This woman confronted you in the middle of Main Street yesterday. Told you to stay away from her family and clawed you good. This morning she lured you into an empty building and knocked you flying down the stairs. Does that strike you as someone who'd run off and kill herself?"

"She wanted to protect her family."

"By tooth and by claw, not by lying down and dying for them." He unlocked the Jeep's passenger door and opened it for me. "She was lying on her right side, with her left arm on top of the covers. When the coroner gives his report, he'll say the injection site was on her left arm."

"So someone snuck in and injected her while she napped?"

He climbed into the driver's seat, keys in hand, and turned to face me. "The yard is fenced. There's a doghouse, but no sign of a dog. No bowls, nothing. My guess is that it died recently. Maybe not a natural death. There's a vacant house behind theirs, with tall hedges. The killer enters there, hops the fence, picks the lock, and comes in when they know she'll be alone and asleep. Her daughter said she always napped when the baby did. Someone knew that. Someone who knew *her*. Like her lover, who wasn't at home when we got to his place."

"Alastair."

"That's where I'm laying my money, but I'm not ruling out Cody either. Whoever killed Tiffany killed the others, too. She figured out that he killed Ginny, Brandi, and Claire and he realized she had to go—but quietly, so no one would connect the dots."

"Maybe," I said. "But Cody could have found out that *she* was the killer, and killed her quietly before she brought them all down. Or Tiffany's killer could be the person who has been stalking both of us, related or unrelated to the other deaths." I sighed and leaned back in the seat. "Aren't clues supposed to *eliminate* suspects?"

"So you agree that Tiffany was murdered, then?" he said, finally putting the key in the ignition.

I hesitated. It made sense, but I wanted it to make sense.

"I'll wait to hear the coroner's report," I said. "But it's a possibility . . ." When I trailed off, he glanced over.

"The pillow," I said. "There was a pillow in the crib. The oldest girl said it didn't belong there. I just remembered why. When Logan and Kate were little, Elena wouldn't put pillows or stuffed animals in their cribs. They're smothering hazards. Tiffany's baby is a little old for that, but I didn't notice anything else in the crib. Even if Tiffany did decide to start giving her pillows, that one was for decoration, not sleeping on."

"So someone put a pillow in the crib— Shit."

He didn't say what he was thinking. I already knew. I could picture it, the killer standing over the crib, looking down at the screaming baby, pillow in hand, thinking the unthinkable . . .

As we waited to turn onto Main Street, a tow truck drove by. Hoisted on the back was a black BMW. My gut seized, and I stared after it as it disappeared from sight.

"That Michael's car?" Adam asked quietly.

I nodded.

"Okay, we're getting you back to the motel. That's enough for one day. Time for rest, dinner—"

"I'm fine."

"No, you're not."

"I want to be," I said, softly enough that I didn't think he'd hear, but he reached over and squeezed my hand.

"I know," he said. "But let's take a break from toughing it out, okay? We've done a lot this afternoon. Time to back up, give it time to gel, and plan our next move."

I couldn't argue with that. A car honked behind us and Adam pulled onto Main Street.

THIRTY

JESSE WAS ON HIS WAY BACK TO THE MOTEL WHEN I CALLED to tell him about Tiffany. He grabbed takeout from the diner and as we ate, we talked about Tiffany. As with Michael's death, he wasn't convinced it was murder. If Tiffany found out her husband was the killer, it made sense to him that she'd end her own life rather than face the consequences.

"Look at her," he said. "Typical middle-class housewife. Appearances are everything. She couldn't handle it."

I disagreed, but didn't say so. After arguing that Michael had been murdered, I hated to sound paranoid.

Jesse's druid friend had gotten back to him. He was sure the ritual wasn't druidic. So no movement on that front. What he did have was a lead on Cody's illegal activities, but he wasn't ready to share.

"If I'm right, it's the same one Detective Kennedy was following," he said. "Which means I want to tread carefully. I'm pretty sure there's a supernatural link, even if Cody isn't it. I bet that's what his wife was talking about—she was using her powers to protect or promote the business. Anyway, it's pretty vague and you guys have enough to work on, right?"

"Right."

"Then I'll take this, and when I have something, I'll let you know."

I walked Jesse back to his room and we chatted a bit. When I returned, Adam was stretched out on my bed, working on his laptop. He had a box of cookies beside him. Paige's cookies and the commune ones. Paige's were gone. I snatched up the others before he finished those, too.

"You got your own box," I said.

"Yours was open. And I earned them. I found your druidic ritual." He turned the laptop toward me.

"Seriously?"

"Yep. There's a reason Jesse's friend didn't recognize it."

He motioned at the screen, which showed a scanned page from our personal database. I checked it out.

"It's definitely the same ritual," I said. "Everything fits, including the sacrifice of a woman between her twentieth and thirtieth year."

He pointed to the label at the top.

"A hunting ritual?" I said.

"Yep. For boar hunting with spears. You dip the tips into the sacrificial victim's blood and they'll strike the boar in the heart. Not a lot of call for that these days."

"So it's fake," I said.

"It looks real enough . . ."

"No, I mean it's a red herring. Whoever killed those women wanted it to look like a real supernatural ritual. They dug up something so old that any supernatural investigating would know it was real, but would probably never ID it."

"Or a human could have dug it up from an old book and decided it'd be a way to throw investigators off the trail."

"Sure, but my explanation is way more interesting. And

speaking of interesting, I've been thinking about what Ginny Thompson was doing up at the cookie cult . . ."

My theory? Blackmail. Someone might have commented on a resemblance between her and Alastair Koppel. She'd found out when he'd left town all those years ago and put two and two together.

Then she looked at that big farm on the hill and to her, it would seem palatial. Her daddy, who'd never paid a dime in child support, now living the high life with a harem of young women. He owed her, and she was going to collect, and if he didn't like that, she'd tell his secret to the world.

Or Brandi had pushed her into it. From what I heard of their relationship, that seemed more likely. It was Brandi's idea, so she'd gone with Ginny to make sure she carried through.

Blackmail was a good motive for Alastair not to call the cops. And a good motive for Alastair—or Megan—to kill the blackmailers.

Adam had come to the same conclusion about why the young women went there. He wasn't as convinced that it led to Ginny and Brandi's deaths, but agreed there was enough of a possibility that we should get off our asses and head back up to that house for a chat with Megan.

We stopped at the police station first. Adam went in alone to properly introduce himself to Bruyn, chat him up, put him at ease . . . Somehow he thought he could do that last part better without me. Go figure.

When he came out, he said, "Tiffany was injected in the left arm. And it was the back of her arm, which would be easy for someone else to do, but awkward to do yourself."

"They think it's murder then?"

He shook his head. "No, but when I raised the possibility, Bruyn jumped like a starving mutt at a hot dog. He smells Cody all over this one."

"Good. That'll keep Cody busy while Jesse investigates his angle."

I was perfectly willing to throw Adam to the guy-starved girls as a distraction, but he was having none of it. He wanted to snoop around the property on his own, so we switched seats and I dropped him off at the base of the hill.

Once the girls realized I was alone, they were happy to leave me to Megan. And Megan was happy to chat. I think she found me interesting—more of a distraction to her than a cute guy.

And I think the words *Ginny Thompson's late-night visit* helped her decide she'd better talk to me.

"We have an informant, I take it," she said as we sat at the picnic table in the backyard. Her tone was light, amused even. I searched her face for any signs she was covering a sudden panic attack, but she was cool as ice cream. Glass-shard-laced ice cream. Sweet and smooth and deadly.

"Multiple ones," I said, not wanting Vee to bear the brunt of it. "Seems some of your girls aren't too comfortable with the lies they're hearing, like the one where Alastair told me he never met Ginny or Brandi."

"Yes, they were snooping around the property. Yes, I lied and I'm sure Alastair did, too. We caught them ransacking our out-buildings, looking for our secret drug stash. A few weeks later, they turn up dead. Do you really think we were going to share that information?"

"So why not call the cops when you actually caught them?"

"We didn't need that kind of attention."

"From what I heard, it was Alastair who said no cops."

She paused, then said, "Do you know where I grew up, Ms. Levine?"

"No idea."

She smiled. "Liar. I'm sure you did your research. What it didn't tell you, though, is the *kind* of neighborhood I grew up in. I saw a lot of Ginnys and Brandis there. I had some for friends. And one thing they all had in common? No one would ever call the cops on them. People told themselves they were doing those girls a favor, giving them a second chance. They weren't. They were just teaching them what they could get away with. So, yes, I wanted to call the police. Alastair persuaded me not to."

"Because it would call undue attention to the group."

"Particularly so considering what they were looking for. People expect to find two things at a place like this: sex and drugs. But the locals have met the girls and they know we aren't keeping sex slaves. So Ginny and Brandi figured we must have drugs. If those suspicions got out, it would plant a new seed in the townspeople's minds—one that'll worry them more than group sex."

Her explanation made sense. It didn't mean it was the truth, of course. Megan wanted to protect her investment here. She knew exactly what to say.

"I know why Alastair didn't want to call the police," I said. "He was protecting Ginny."

"Maybe." A twist of a smile. "His faith in humanity extends a bit too far sometimes."

"No, I mean Ginny specifically. I know about their connection."

"Connection?" Her confusion seemed genuine.

"He used to live in Columbus."

"I know. That's why he chose it. He knows the town and they know him—at least the older folks do." She paused. "Do you mean he knows her family?"

I said yes, that was it, and she said he hadn't mentioned that to her. I looked hard for some sign of dissembling, but found none. Alastair hadn't told her Ginny was his daughter.

I saw Adam peeking out from behind the barn, so I said my good-byes, and motioned to Adam that I'd meet him at the bottom of the hill.

I pulled the Jeep over to the side of the gravel road. Adam climbed into the passenger seat.

"Find anything?" I asked.

"Nope." He started doing up his seat belt as I pulled off the shoulder. "Got into the shed with the Santeria stuff, but they've taken off the lock and cleared out the back room. Filled it with rakes and—"

The Jeep jumped forward. I slammed against my seat belt. Adam hit the dashboard.

"Shit," he said. "Can you pop the clutch *after* I'm belted in?"

"That wasn't—"

A crunch and another jolt, this one making the Jeep rock. I twisted to look over my shoulder just in time to see the front end of an SUV hit us again, wrenching my neck hard. I caught the grill in the rearview mirror and recognized the emblem.

"Cody Radu," I said.

"Drive," Adam said.

"Like hell."

Cody had pulled back and was idling, waiting. I reached for the door handle. Beside me, Adam cursed as he tried to get his open. The rear impact damaged the frame, making the doors stick. Mine came free first. Cody was driving up alongside the Jeep, moving fast. Making a break for it. An energy bolt in his back tire would stop that.

I started opening the door.

"Savannah!" Adam yelled. "Watch—"

Cody swung the SUV into the side of the Jeep. The door crunched shut, metal squealing as the SUV sheered along it.

"Goddamn it!" I said. "God-fucking-damn it. What the hell is he—?"

"Put it in reverse and go," Adam said. When I didn't answer, he grabbed my shoulder. "Go, Savannah or I'll yank you over here and do it myself."

"I'm not running away," I said as Cody did a three-point turn in front of us.

"I didn't say that, did I? Drive in there."

Adam pointed down two ruts that led into a field. "You want to get him? You can't do it here where anyone can drive by. He's got a 4x4. He'll follow."

I nodded and turned the ignition key. The Jeep clunked as we started forward, but still ran. I turned onto the makeshift road just as Cody roared up.

I hit the gas. The Jeep flew along the path. Jarred a few of my fillings loose, but I kept my foot down, hitting the ruts and sailing over them like a Jet Ski going against the tide.

When I tried to look in the rearview mirror, Adam said, "Eyes on the road. I've got it."

"Can I get a play-by-play?"

"You're winning."

The track crossed a field and continued toward a wooded patch.

"Head in there," Adam said as if reading my thoughts.

"And Cody?"

"Trying valiantly to keep up, and battering the shit out of his fancy SUV."

I smiled.

"I don't think he has the four-wheel drive engaged," Adam said. "If he even knows how to engage it."

I floored it when we hit an open patch. We sailed over a streambed and came down with a crunch that made Adam clasp the grab bars.

I eased off the gas as we hit the woods—a spotty stand of trees with another field visible on the far side. Branches scraped the Jeep and Adam winced, but said nothing.

"I'll cover the damage," I said. "Even throw in a new top."

He didn't smile at that, just kept his gaze on the path behind us. "It's not the Jeep I'm worried about."

"You think I should have gone back to town?"

"And let him think he's spooked you? No. Whatever his problem is, it ends here." He glanced in the mirror. "And it ends now, apparently. Stop the Jeep. He's stuck."

I looked behind me. Cody's SUV was caught in that streambed we'd shot over.

"I'm guessing you want to take the lead on this?" Adam said.

"Please."

"Just watch out," he said. "His truck could come free at any second."

I twisted in my seat and cast my internal fireball, igniting it under the Lexus's hood. A bang. The tires stopped spinning. Smoke curled from the grill.

Adam chuckled. "Or maybe not."

I got out. At first, Cody had his head down as he tried to get the engine running again. I was a few feet away when he saw me.

He threw open his door. I slowed, knockback spell at the ready. He slammed the door and I saw that his hands were empty. I relaxed the spell, but stayed on alert.

"Where's your boyfriend?" he called as he advanced on me.

"Unconscious, thanks to that little stunt of yours."

Cody peered past me. When he didn't see Adam, he gave a humorless smile. "He needs to be a little faster getting his seat belt on."

"Go to hell. If he's hurt—"

"Then that's his own damn fault for having a murdering bitch of a girlfriend. I hope he *is* hurt." He advanced on me as I stood my ground. "In fact, I hope he's dead. That won't bring Tiffany back, but it'll make me feel better. So will this."

He swung so fast I didn't see it coming until the last second. I tried to twist but his fist connected with my shoulder. I fell back, gasping in shock more than pain. Rage filled me and I lashed out with an energy bolt. As the last words left my mouth, I thought *Oh, shit!*

I looked down at my fingertips, expecting to see the bolt flying from them. But they were just outstretched toward Cody, nothing happening. Launching that spell against a human had been reckless—I must have subconsciously sabotaged it.

"You want me to stop?" Cody said, looking at my out-stretched fingers.

Adam had slipped through the trees, out of Cody's sight. Now he rounded the rear of the SUV, his eyes blazing. I waved him back before Cody saw him. Cody swung again. I dodged and lifted my fingers in a knockback, but he charged and kicked my leg out from under me. As I went down, he kneed me in the stomach. Adam rushed forward.

"No," I said, wheezing and shaking my head.

Adam hesitated. I met his gaze and he pulled back behind the SUV, hovering there, waiting.

"No?" Cody said. "You don't like—"

Finally I was able to smack him with a knockback. He stumbled against the SUV.

"Getting clumsy?" I said.

He lunged forward. I hit him again, this one hard enough to knock him to the ground.

"I don't know what you're on," I said. "But it's powerful stuff, Cody. You can barely stand up. Now, what's this about me being a murdering bitch? You think I killed Tiffany? There's a commune full of girls who can testify that I was with them when it happened, so don't—"

"You might not have pushed the plunger," he said, getting to his feet. "But I know you had something to do with her death. You've been following us for days now. Tiffany said it had something to do with that Wiccan shit she used to be into. You stalked her and you harassed her. You lured her into the newspaper building—"

"I lured *her*? She called me. Check her phone records."

"She said you threatened her."

"Yes, I did. I threatened to take action if she didn't stop harassing *me*. She—"

"You lying bitch!"

He swung. I wheeled out of the way. But before I could launch a knockback, he slammed his fist into my gut. I fell, gasping and blinking. Adam ran toward us. Cody drew back his foot to kick me in the stomach. I hit him with an internal fireball.

He screamed and doubled over. Adam stopped. As Cody stumbled back, he saw Adam and realized he was trapped between us.

Cody grabbed the SUV door handle. Adam and I both jumped at him, but Cody was faster, swinging in and slapping the lock closed. Adam reached for the back door. Cody hit the button and all his door locks engaged.

Adam jangled the handle on the driver's side. The metal glowed red hot as he glared at Cody, desperately cranking the engine.

Adam glanced over at me. I was still winded and gasping, pain throbbing through my stomach. The whites of Adam's eyes suffused with red. He pressed his fingers to the door metal. Tendons in his neck popped as he concentrated.

The door shimmered, heat pouring from it. Then it disintegrated in a shower of ash. The safety-glass window dropped, hit the door frame, and shattered.

Cody sat there, gaping at the hole where his door should have been. He looked down at the pile of ash and glass below.

"That's what you get for buying foreign," Adam said. "Barely need to touch it and it falls apart."

Cody lifted his gaze to Adam's, slowly, as if just realizing that nothing now stood between them. Adam reached in, grabbed him by the shirtfront, and hauled him out. Cody's arms windmilled, as he tried to grab something and hold on.

"Not going to take a swing at me?" Adam said. "It's different when it's a guy your own size, isn't it?"

He threw Cody to the ground. Cody started scrambling backward. Adam walked over and kicked him in the stomach, so hard even I winced. Cody yowled and curled up, gasping for air.

"Doesn't tickle, does it?" Adam said. "I've heard you can kill someone doing that. Try to run and we'll test that."

"What do you want?" Cody wheezed.

"First, leave Savannah alone. She had nothing to do with your wife's death. She's here investigating a murder—that's it. You just happen to be the prime suspect. So that's the second thing I want you to do. Confess. Probably too much to ask for, though, so we'll settle for you answering some questions."

I stepped forward. "Let's start at the top. What were you and Claire talking about behind the hardware store?"

"Go to hell, bitch," he sneered.

I lit a fireball in his stomach. Just a little one, but after Adam's kick, it was enough to set him screaming and writhing.

"He kicked you pretty hard, huh?" I said. "I think you need a doctor. The sooner we can get through this, the sooner you can get to an emergency ward. Now, let's try that again. What were you and Claire—"

"A girl, okay? She wanted to talk to me about a girl who'd been at the commune."

"Name?"

"Pammy or Tammy. Something like that." Tamara—Claire's friend.

"And what did you have to do with this girl?"

"Nothing. We talked a few times. I bought her some stuff. She paid me back."

"With sex."

He glared up at me. "No, with seashells. Yes, with sex."

"And the *stuff* you bought was drugs."

"No, candy—"

I ignited another internal fireball. He screamed. Writhed. Called me a whole lotta names.

"I'm not doing anything," I said. "Just standing here trying to talk to you. But obviously you're hurt, so let's say you cut the bullshit. If you gave her drugs for sex, say that, and this will go a lot faster."

He confirmed it. Also confirmed that Tamara had been at the commune trying to get clean. Only she'd ended up whoring herself for a fix.

That conversation seemed to be the only connection between Claire and Cody. Still, it didn't rule out murder. If she'd known he was dealing dope to Tamara, that was a life-ruining kind of accusation. Of course, he wasn't going to admit that.

I tried to get more from Cody. Even used the persuasion spell.

It failed, though, and I fell back on the tried-and-true internal fireball until Adam stepped in, motioning for me to cast a privacy spell so we could talk without Cody hearing.

"That's enough," he said. "He's told you all he's going to—"

"I can get more."

"Sure you can. Keep torturing him and, eventually, he'll admit he killed Ginny, Brandi, Claire, Michael, Tamara, Tiffany, and Jimmy Hoffa. You need more evidence, Savannah, or after a certain point, you can't trust anything he says."

He was right. And, to be honest, I was enjoying tormenting Cody just a little too much. So we left it there. And we left *him* there, on the ground beside his useless SUV.

We got back to the motel to find a half-eaten cold pizza in our room, with a note from Jesse. He'd taken off pursuing a lead and left us the pizza. My stomach wasn't ready for that. I *was* ready to sit down and let Adam dig in, but he insisted on checking out my injuries and getting them cleaned up, and by the time he finished, I was hungry enough for a couple of slices. We took our time eating it, talking and relaxing, and soon it was ten o'clock. Adam yawned and stretched.

"Bedtime already?" I said. "You really are getting old."

He pitched a wadded-up napkin at me. "It was a hint for *you*, the girl who's been stifling her own yawns for the last hour. A short nap this afternoon doesn't make up for a missed night of sleep."

I picked up my laptop. "I just want to check a few—"

He snatched it from me. "That's my job. You get some rest and I'll do the research."

He settled into the armchair and put his feet up on the bed.

"Didn't you say something about getting a room?" I said.

"It's late."

"It's barely ten, and the place is half empty."

"I'm good here." When I started to argue, he said, "I'm pretty sure Cody's not coming back for revenge tonight, but I'm not counting on it. Besides, someone's been following you, and it may be the same someone who killed Tiffany Radu."

"I—"

"You can look after yourself, I know. But someone also might have killed a guy you were working this case with, so something tells me I'm safer here, too."

"Fine, but you're not spending the night in a chair. It's a big bed. Just keep your shorts on and stay on your side this time."

"Hey, the last time *I* was the one who ended up with a fat lip, smacked by you flailing around."

"Um, no. You were flailing. That's why you got a fat lip."

"Go to sleep, Savannah."

I walked to his bag and pulled out a T-shirt, then headed for the bathroom.

"Excuse me?" he said. "That's *my* shirt?"

"I don't own pajamas."

"At least take the one you singed earlier."

"It's ugly, remember? I don't do ugly."

THIRTY-ONE

I DREAMED I WAS BACK IN TIFFANY'S BEDROOM READING that opened Bible. Or trying to. The words kept swimming out of focus. I got so frustrated that it woke me up.

The first thing I heard was Adam's deep breathing. He was sound asleep, lying on his side facing me. He was a respectable distance away, but his fingers rested on my bent knee.

When I moved, he squeezed my knee. I smiled, closed my eyes, and fell back to sleep.

"Exodus 22:18!" I blurted, bolting up in bed.

Adam's eyes snapped open.

"Exodus 22:18," I repeated.

He closed his eyes. "If you're spouting biblical references, I'm definitely dreaming."

I jumped out of bed and yanked my nightstand drawer so hard it flew out, thumping onto my foot—phone book and all. I swore and limped around to the other nightstand. I found the Bible in that drawer and pulled it out.

"You aren't actually going to read that, are you?" Adam said, one eye open. "If it bursts into flames, it's not my fault."

"Tiffany's Bible was open to Exodus 22. I just realized why

that's familiar. It's the one Bible verse I know. Exodus 22:18."
I pointed to the verse. "Thou shalt not suffer a witch to live."

"Shit." Adam scrambled up. He read the verse, then swore
again. "The Bible was open to that page?"

I nodded. "It can't be a coincidence. Maybe it *was* suicide.
She was up to something and was worried I was coming after
her. That might have been her final message."

"To who?"

"Me. She knew I was coming over."

"And she knew no one else would hear the baby crying and
get there first? She knew you'd break in if she missed her
appointment? She knew you'd notice the Bible and realize which
passage she meant?" He shook his head. "No, whoever killed
her left that."

"As a message?"

"Maybe." He sat upright and pointed to the chair. "Hand me
my laptop."

I passed it over, then sat on the edge of the bed as he opened
the database and started typing. When the chapter reference
didn't work, he tried the text itself.

"I've heard that verse," he murmured as he kept looking.

"Yeah, it's a famous one."

"No, I mean—" He glanced up at me. "How do you know
it? Your mother doesn't strike me as the Bible study sort. Paige
might respect all religious faiths, but that's one passage she
wouldn't repeat. Was it the Coven? It sounds like something
they'd use."

"As a motto, no doubt. Proof that the world hates us and we
have to hide. But I don't remember hearing it there. I don't remember where I heard it at all. But it stuck in the back of my mind."

"Let me call my dad." He grabbed his cell phone, then stopped.
"No, last resort."

His dad had a stroke a few months ago—Robert was in his seventies—and Adam hated bugging him with anything that wasn't life or death.

"If it's about witches, then Paige—" I glanced at the clock. Nearly six . . . and three hours earlier in Hawaii.

"Let's hold on to the 'call a friend' card for a minute. Tiffany dies with a Bible opened to a verse about killing witches. Yesterday she said someone's been spying on her. You said someone's watched you a couple of times. What do you and Tiffany have in common?"

"We're both young and hot. Well, in her case, less so on both counts, but close enough." I caught his look. "Oh, you meant the witch part. Okay, so there's a chance we have someone in town out to kill witches. Big surprise. Not like we haven't been dealing with that for the last few centuries. Totally unfair, when there are much worse things running around out there. Mass murderers, serial rapists, half-demons . . ."

"Thanks."

"I'm just saying, in general, one would think demon blood would inspire more persecution than being able to make healing potions. But if we do have a killer targeting witches, how does that tie into the other murders? Sure they're young women, but they aren't—" I stopped. "Or are they?"

Adam shook his head. "Ginny's file shows she's got an uncle in jail, and he's her mom's twin brother, which means Paula Thompson is no witch, ergo, neither is Ginny. We already know Claire had a brother, so no witch there either."

"Michael was her half brother on their dad's side. And if she was a practicing witch, that might explain why she investigated the commune. Her friend mentions something that sounds supernatural and she gets worried. Turns out to be Santeria, but by then, she's already been targeted by the killer."

"Okay, but Ginny . . . ?"

"There were two people killed that night—a fact we keep over-looking because Ginny comes with her own obvious suspect."

"Brandi." He nodded. "Brandi is a witch. The killer goes after her. Ginny and Brandi are inseparable so he takes Ginny out, too, then laughs as everyone zeroes in on the abusive boy-friend theory."

"Time to get to know a lot more about Brandi Degas."

Great idea. But as soon as we started the research, I was reminded why we'd overlooked Brandi from the beginning. Because Mr. Mulligan had been right—she was little more than Ginny Thompson's shadow. I hadn't been able to form a single theory where the target was Brandi alone. But now I had one, and my bio check showed no brothers or uncles, which would have ruled out witch-hood.

We needed to chat with Brandi's mom.

It was still way too early for an interview.

"I'll grab breakfast," Adam said when I headed for the shower. "I'll get it at that coffee shop so I can thank the server for running stuff over for me."

"Good idea. Oh, wait. When you talk to her, you're my boyfriend."

"Huh?"

"She jumped to that conclusion and I figured she might not bring the food if she wasn't aiding the cause of true love, so . . ."

"You lied to get room service. Well, considering I'm walking out of your room at seven in the morning, we'd better not straighten *anyone* out. If I grab your ass in public, then, I'm just playing my part."

"And if you get your fingers broken for it, I'm just playing mine."

He laughed and left.

The Jeep wasn't running well, but it *was* running. Good enough. Jesse was gone when we set out, so I texted him to say we'd catch up later. When we arrived at Carol Degas's house, I double-checked the address. It was on the outskirts of town, and I expected to see a dump. The house was tiny, yes, and it showed its age, but it was as well kept and tidy as Paula's mobile home, with fresh yellow paint, flowers in the tended garden, and a multicolored wooden Welcome! sign on the door.

"Carol must have moved out after Brandi died. Probably couldn't afford the upkeep without her daughter's rent money. Shit."

"She might have left a forwarding address with these folks." Adam rapped the door. "Wouldn't want those welfare checks to get lost."

I could hear gospel music playing inside. At least we weren't waking up the new owners. Adam knocked again, and finally the door opened. There stood a tiny old woman, with a deeply lined face and hands that trembled as she clutched the door.

"We're looking for Carol Degas," I said. "She used to live here."

"Still does," the woman said in a reedy voice. "I'm her."

According to the file, Carol was fifty-two. No matter how hard I looked at this woman, she didn't appear a day under seventy.

"We're in town investigating—"

"Brandi's murder. I figured that was who you were. I've been wondering when you'd come see me." She held open the screen and ushered us in.

We followed her into a hall lined with cheap religious prints. Gospel music boomed from deep in the house. I squinted at a needlepoint hanging on the wall. A Bible verse of some kind, but damned if I could read it—half the stitches were out of place.

"I've found Jesus," Carol said, beaming.

"Huh," I murmured under my breath. "I didn't know he was lost."

Adam gave me a look, his eyes telling me to watch it, his lips holding back a smile.

She waved us into what must have been the living room, but looked more like a Vegas chapel, every inch of space crammed with cheap china Madonnas and butt-ugly cherubs.

"Do you know Christ our Savior, child?" Carol said as we sat.

"Not personally."

I got another look from Adam, who prodded me onto the loveseat, then sat beside me, close enough to elbow me if I got out of line.

I have nothing against organized religion. Well, not much. But if you're going to have a religious conversion and clean up your life, then do it when your child is born, not after she dies.

"How about you, young man?" Carol said, turning to Adam. "Have you accepted Christ into your life?"

"I'm still . . ." Adam gave a sheepish shrug. "Looking, you know? Trying to find the right church. Which one do you belong to?"

"Our Holy Savior in Battle Ground. It's a very old church. Small, but old."

"Can't say I've heard of it. Maybe I'll check it out. How does it feel about . . . ?" He squirmed. "I've got this problem. More of a question, really, and I'm having a hard time finding the right answer from the churches I've tried." He glanced sharply at me. "Don't give me that look."

I wasn't giving him any look, but I rolled my eyes on cue, murmuring, "Not this again."

"It's bugging me, okay?" He turned back to Carol. "I've got this good friend who's been dating this girl and she's into . . . stuff. Occult stuff."

"Occult?" Carol's eyes widened.

"It's not occult," I said. "I keep telling you it's—"

"Witchcraft, I know. She says she's a witch."

Carol frowned. "Wiccan?"

"No, this one says she's a real witch."

Carol looked genuinely confused. "You don't mean devil worship, do you?"

"It *is* Wiccan," I said. "A branch of it anyway. And I keep telling him it's not occult; it's an earth-based religion."

"I don't think I'd call it a religion myself," Carol said slowly. "But if they do, then maybe . . ."

"What does your church say about stuff like that?" Adam asked.

"I don't know. I'd have to ask. Personally, I don't agree with it."

"See?" Adam said to me.

"She said she doesn't agree with it. She didn't say she thinks 'something should be done about those people.'"

"I was kidding."

"No, you weren't."

"I'd had a few beers."

"So which was it? You were drunk or you were kidding?"

As we faced off, Carol said timidly, "I might not agree with it, but the Bible teaches us to respect the customs of others."

"No, the Bible says 'Thou shalt not suffer a witch to live,'" Adam said. "It's right there in black and white."

"I can't believe the Bible would say . . ." She stopped herself and nodded. "No, our pastor does teach us that the Bible includes passages that have been misinterpreted. The teachings of Christ are clear. We must respect others, even if we disagree with them. That's what my pastor said about homosexuals. I might not agree with their choices, but Christ would want me to treat them the way I want to be treated. I think he'd say the same about witches."

"We'd like to ask you a few questions about Brandi," I said.

If there was one word to describe Carol Degas, it was vague. Not evasive just, well, not entirely present. It was as if all those bottles of whiskey had washed away both her personality and her memory, and she was just struggling to hold on, clinging to her new religion with a death grip.

She could talk about Christ, and that's really all she could talk about. Seemed to know him better than the daughter she'd lived with for twenty-five years.

"I wasn't a good mother," she said, finally. "I know that and I accept my share of the blame, but it's like Pastor Williams says—no one is entirely responsible for another person, even a child. They grow as they will. Look at Ginny Thompson. Paula is a fine woman. She might not be a churchgoing Christian, but she's a Christian at heart. Look at how her daughter turned out, in spite of that. I do feel guilty about Brandi, though. The dreams prove that, Pastor Williams says."

"Okay, so about that night—"

"The dreams prove that," she continued, as if I hadn't spoken.

Personally, I had no interest in Carol Degas's dream life, but obviously she wanted to tell me.

"I dreamed that the little girl died," she said.

"Little girl?"

"Ginny's daughter. I dreamed that I heard Ginny and Brandi planning to kill Kayla, so Cody would take Ginny back. They were right in this house, in the basement, gathering up supplies. I heard them, and they then left and I knew I had to do something. So I tried calling Paula. She always knows what to do. Only I couldn't finish dialing the number. I kept trying and trying, but I couldn't do it, and then I passed out and when I came to the little girl was dead and I cried and cried, because it was all my fault."

She looked at me expectantly.

"Okay . . ." I said.

"The little girl was Brandi," Adam said.

I turned to him. "What?"

"Subconsciously, it was Brandi. *Her* little girl."

Carol nodded emphatically. "That's exactly what Pastor Williams said. When we dream, things aren't always as they seem. Kayla was Brandi. Brandi and Ginny represented evil in the world. They conspired to kill my little girl and I didn't do anything to stop them. I wanted to, but I was too drunk, too . . ." She searched for a word. "Ineffectual. That's what the pastor says. It proves that I felt guilty."

"Okay . . ." I said.

"I even dreamed they were going to kill her in the same place where they died," Carol leaned forward. "They were going to drug her and take her there and make it look like a pervert did it. And that's exactly what happened to *my* baby, isn't it?"

"Except for the pervert part," I said. "There was no sign of—"

Adam nudged me to shut up, then said to Carol, "Your pastor is right. It's your subconscious speaking. You feel guilty, but you've used it to turn your life around, and that's the important thing."

She nodded, satisfied.

I wasn't.

Maybe that was the humane thing to do—give the old woman some peace. But I couldn't cut her any slack. If she'd cared, she should have done something *before* her daughter died. If she felt guilty now, she should be out volunteering at a day care or soup kitchen, not sitting around listening to gospel music and moaning about how guilty she felt.

THIRTY-TWO

AFTER WE LEFT, I SAID, "WERE YOU SERIOUS ABOUT THAT dream crap?"

Adam shrugged. "It makes sense. Her psyche can't deal with the guilt, so it displaces it with a dream about the death of someone else's daughter."

"It's not just her psyche that can't deal. Carol Degas is a human ostrich. And that dream? I think it's bullshit."

"Well, one thing I'm ninety-nine percent sure on is that Brandi wasn't a witch. Nor did Carol somehow find out that Tiffany Radu *was* one and kill her, thinking she was following a Christian precept. Seeing all the religious stuff in her house made me think we might be onto something, but there's no witch-hunter—" He stopped, frowning.

"What?" I said.

"Nothing. Just . . ." He shook his head. "Nothing. Anyway, back to the dream, I'm wondering if it's more than a garden-variety guilty conscience."

"You think she had something to do with her daughter's death?"

"Not overtly, but maybe there's something she's not telling us. Or something she isn't really aware of herself."

"If she does remember something, we'd better hope it comes in another dream, because short of hypnosis, that woman isn't going to . . ."

When I trailed off, it was his turn to look over and say, "What?"

"I need to trace a call," I said.

I connected to the office database and dug up the number of a half-demon phone company exec who helped us whenever she could, repayment for Paige getting her out of a Cabal commitment uglier than any cell phone contract.

"Lina," I said when she answered. "It's Savannah Levine. Can you check a phone record for me?"

"Absolutely. Do you have the number?"

I gave it to her, then said, "I need to know if any calls were placed from that number on the night of November 18 last year."

"There's one." She rattled it off. "Do you want me to check the source?"

"No, I recognize it. Any other calls after that?"

"No." Keyboard tapping chattered across the line. "But there is one from the second number, made just over an hour later to a cell phone." She gave me the number. "Do you want me to check with the cell company for the registered owner?"

"Maybe not. Hold on." I pulled up my contact list and entered the number. "No, seems I already know it."

I thanked her, then signed off and told Adam what I'd found.

"Shit," he said.

"Do you remember what caliber of gun was used in the murders? Thirty-eight, wasn't it?"

"Right."

"The kind of gun a guy in Columbus might keep under his mattress, wave around when he's drunk, get confiscated if it's not properly registered . . ."

He frowned, but didn't ask, just drove as I explained my theory.

Paula and Kayla were at home, Paula clearing away the break-fast dishes as Kayla got out her books for the first lesson of the day. I introduced Adam. Kayla sized him up.

"You're a private eye?" she asked.

"I don't look like one?" he said.

"No."

He laughed. "How about Savannah? Does she?"

"More than you."

"It's all about the edge," I said. "I have one. You don't."

"All right," Adam said to Kayla. "Forget the lock-picking lesson, then."

"Lock-picking?" she said.

He took a lock-pick gun from his pocket and her eyes rounded.

"I was going to give you a lesson while Savannah talks to your grandma," he said. "But if I'm not proper PI material, then I wouldn't be a proper teacher . . ."

"What's this?" Paula said, wiping her hands on a dishtowel.

I introduced Adam as my co-worker and friend, then said, "I need to talk to you alone, Paula. Is it okay if Adam takes Kayla outside, shows her how to use the lock pick?"

She looked at Adam. "I don't think—"

"Please, Grandma?"

"They'll be right at the front door," I said. "If we sit in the living room, you can see them through the window."

"I suppose so . . ."

They left. We went into the living room, and Paula positioned her chair where she could see the front steps as they worked on the lock.

"There's been a major development in the investigation," I said. "I wanted you to be the first to hear it. As you know, the gun used to kill Ginny and Brandi was never found."

"Has it been?"

"No, but it's been identified as a gun that was stolen from the police station's evidence locker a few years ago."

Paula glanced at me and I kept my eyes as wide as possible, giving no sign I was bullshitting her. I was good at that.

I continued, "That's when you worked at the station. Do you remember it?"

"Vaguely," she said. "It wasn't in the evidence locker, though. Just in the office. Confiscated from Bill Martin—a local no-good. They figured he'd broken in and gotten his gun back."

"Maybe, but that's not what they think now. In fact, Chief Bruyn swears he knew who took it, he's just not telling me."

Paula swallowed.

"Of course, whoever took the gun isn't necessarily Ginny's killer," I said.

Paula nodded.

"But the person who did take it should come forward before Bruyn comes knocking. I'm sure whoever took it had a good reason. But then, when it went missing, she couldn't exactly report it, since it was stolen goods in the first place." I caught and held Paula's gaze. "That gun must have been taken by someone who had access at night. Someone like the cleaner."

She shook her head. "It wasn't me. It . . ." She hesitated, then said, "It was Ginny. She came to see me one night. Brought me coffee. I knew something was up, but I thought she just wanted money. Then, a week later, when Bill came back for his gun and it was gone, I knew what Ginny had come for. Everyone in town knew the gun was in that office. I confronted her and she admitted it. Said she'd run into some trouble with a dealer and she needed it to scare him off. She wouldn't let me give it back, so I bought her a lockbox and made her keep it in that, away from Kayla."

"And it never occurred to you she might use it *on* Kayla?"

She should have jumped at that, shocked. But she only shook her head, her gaze once again fixed on the girl outside the window.

"No," she said, barely over a whisper. "It never did."

"But that changed at 12:38 on November 18 last year, didn't it?"

Now she glanced over sharply. "What?"

"November 18. The night Ginny and Brandi died. You got a call at 12:38 from Carol Degas."

"Did I?" She shrugged. "I suppose I might have. Carol would sober up at all hours of the night and call me, suddenly concerned about where Brandi was."

"Except that night she knew exactly where Brandi was. Going to Ginny's apartment to take Kayla, already drugged, to an abandoned building where they planned to kill her and make it look like the work of a sexual predator."

"N-no. Ginny—Ginny would never . . ." Paula shook her head. "Kayla was her daughter."

"Which makes it all the more reprehensible. Especially when her motive was to get back her abusive asshole boyfriend. Cody told Ginny he didn't want her because she had a kid. She decided to remove that obstacle. Carol overheard and called you. She passed out while she was still on the phone, woke up the next day, and convinced herself it was all a dream because Kayla wasn't dead, and Brandi and Ginny were."

"Carol Degas is a drunk," Paula said. "I don't care if she's cleaned up and found religion. She still has a brain like Swiss cheese. Have you talked to her? She can barely remember what day it is. Kayla is alive. So whatever Carol imagined never happened."

"Because you stopped it. Carol called. You got hold of that gun and you tracked them to that abandoned building and you shot them—"

"No! It wasn't like—" She stopped short and glanced at the phone. "I think I need to call my lawyer."

"Sure. You do that and I'll call the sheriff's department and they can continue this conversation."

Paula looked out the window. She crossed her legs. Uncrossed them. Glanced toward the phone. Then said, "Why *isn't* Chief Bruyn or the sheriff's department here?"

"Because I haven't told them."

She peered at me, trying to gauge my motives.

"It wasn't like that," she said finally. "Carol called to tell me what she'd heard. I didn't believe her. Ginny would never do such a thing. Clearly Carol was dead drunk. I almost went back to bed."

"But you didn't."

"No, I didn't."

I let the silence drag on for half a minute before saying, "You told yourself Ginny would never do it, but you couldn't rest until you made sure."

Paula nodded. "I knew the building. When I got there and saw Brandi's car out back—" She sucked in a deep breath. "I didn't have the gun. Obviously Ginny was drunk or stoned and not thinking straight and all I had to do was snap her out of it."

She stopped again. I waited her out.

"I found them in the basement. Kayla . . ." Her voice cracked, gaze shooting back to the window. "Kayla was on the floor. They'd pulled off her pajama bottoms and her panties and . . ."

She couldn't finish. Couldn't go on for another minute, then said, "They were fighting. Brandi thought they needed to make it look as if she'd been violated . . ." Another crack in her voice. "That's when Ginny started having second thoughts. But Brandi had the gun. Ginny's gun. She turned it on Kayla, and I thought—I thought Ginny would stop her. This was her daughter. Kill her own child? For a man? How could I raise—?"

She shook her head and took another deep breath. "I thought she'd do something, but when Brandi pointed that gun at Kayla's head, Ginny stopped arguing and closed her eyes. Just closed her eyes. I screamed. I ran forward and there was a shot. It went past me. I hit Brandi. She fell and I jumped on her to get the gun and we were struggling and I saw Ginny standing there over us.

"I got hold of the gun, but Brandi wouldn't let go. It fired. I don't know who pulled the trigger. I yanked the gun away and I got up, and Brandi was lying there, dead, blood pumping out. I heard this sound and I thought it was Kayla waking up and I turned and there was Ginny, bent over, hands to her chest, blood running through her fingers. The bullet had gone right through Brandi and into her.

"Ginny was still alive. I told her I was going to get help, that she'd be okay, but she started crying, saying she was sorry, it was Brandi's idea, she begged me not to leave her. I tried to calm her down so I could get help, but she kept crying and then . . ." Paula looked away and brushed a hand over her eyes. "And then she was gone."

"So you called the only person you thought you could count on. Ginny's father."

She looked up sharply.

"Phone records," I said. "One of the girls at the house saw him coming in late that night. He'd gotten a call on his cell from you."

"Alastair's a smart man," she said. "I thought he'd know what to do. He knew Ginny was his daughter—he'd already figured it out and we'd agreed to keep it a secret. But for this . . ."

"He owed you."

She nodded. "I wanted to turn myself in. It was an accident. But Alastair said I'd lose custody of Kayla. I couldn't bear that. So we left Ginny and Brandi there and he helped me take Kayla home. I hated doing that—leaving her in that apartment alone— but Alastair said I had to. We put her to bed and locked the doors. Alastair took the gun and my clothes. He said he'd burn the clothing and get rid of the gun. Then I sat up all night and waited for Kayla to call me when she woke up and her mom wasn't there."

"And then you sat back and watched as Bruyn zeroed in on an innocent man."

She gave a harsh laugh. "Innocent? That's one word I wouldn't use to describe Cody. Do you want me to say I felt bad about that?"

"You decided he deserved it. He gave Ginny the ultimatum that started everything."

"No. Cody didn't expect her to do that. He wanted to get rid of her, so he said the problem was the one thing she couldn't change. Or so he thought. But would I feel guilty if he went to jail? Not for a minute. Did I push Chief Bruyn in his direction?" She met my gaze. "I did not. You know that as well as anyone. I told you the truth about Cody and how he treated my daughter. That's it."

"But then Claire found out the truth. You had to kill her, and when her brother got too close—"

"No. Absolutely not." Paula's eyes blazed. "I had nothing to do with that young woman's death or her brother's. The night Claire Kennedy died, I was at a friend's in Portland. I had a job interview the next morning. Kayla was with me. And the night Detective Kennedy died, I was right here, playing bridge with my sister, Dorothy, and Lorraine from the diner. We heard the sirens when the police went by."

I pressed her, but I knew she was telling the truth. It would be too easy to check her alibis. Besides, I'd never seriously thought she was responsible for Claire and Michael's deaths. Even intentionally killing Ginny and Brandi to save Kayla had been a stretch.

"Alastair says whoever killed Claire Kennedy staged it to look like Ginny and Brandi's deaths," she said. "They wanted it to seem like we had a serial killer. Probably hoped Cody would be charged with Ginny and Brandi so they could pin Claire's death on him, too."

"Then it has to be someone who knew that Alastair planted that occult stuff at the original site. That was never released to the media."

"Occult?" Paula looked genuinely confused.

I took the photos from my bag and pointed out the ritual circle and other signs. "Alastair must have done that after you left."

"No, those things weren't there."

"You must not have noticed them. They're too subtle—"

"No, I would have seen them. When I went to confront Chief Bruyn about his grandson showing those photos to Kayla, he tried to say they'd been in his desk all along. He shoved them in my face, the bastard. Made me take a good look at them, too. Those things weren't there."

THIRTY-THREE

AS I STOOD, PAULA EYED ME WARILY. "NOW WHAT? DO I need to call a lawyer?"

"Not unless you killed Claire or Michael Kennedy. Claire's mother is my client, so her death is my professional concern. Her brother's death is my personal concern. As far as I can see, you had nothing to do with either, so . . ." I shrugged and put my notebook into my bag. "Not my concern."

"What about the gun? If Chief Bruyn suspects I stole it—"

"He doesn't. I lied. You're in the clear."

She let me get to the hall, then she called, "Savannah."

I glanced back.

"Thank you," she said.

"If it'd been me," I said, "I'd have shot Brandi, and it wouldn't have been an accident."

I went outside and said good-bye to Kayla, then watched as Paula threw open the door and bent to hug her.

As Adam drove, I relayed Paula's story.

"I can see how it happened," Adam said when I was done. "It's Alastair who's full of shit. They wouldn't take Kayla away for a clear self-defense case."

I shrugged. "It might not have looked all that clear to him. But she's wrong about the photos. She just didn't see the signs—the cops didn't, remember? If Alastair is into Santeria, he knows enough about rituals to fake one and give the murders a satanic cult angle."

Adam's fingers tapped the steering wheel, his gaze distant.

"What?" I said.

"He could, but would he? Wouldn't anything cult-like have them looking in his direction? Then, if they found the Santeria—which he wasn't hiding very well—he'd be the new prime suspect. Maybe the cops never noticed those ritual signs because they *weren't* there. Where did Jesse get his set?"

"From a contact. A friend—" I swore. "They were doctored before Jesse got them."

We could verify that theory easily enough—just look at the real photos. But when I called the station, Bruyn was out. I wanted to stop by anyway, but Adam eased me off, not wanting us to jump to conclusions so fast.

"Remember Claire did have that pewter bead in her hand," he said as he drove. "Sure, I think it would be dumb for Alastair to stage it, but maybe he didn't see that."

"He was panicked and did the first thing he could think of. But if that's true, then it seriously cuts down on the suspects for Claire's murder."

"Let's say Claire found evidence that Paula killed Ginny and Brandi. She goes to Alastair to get his advice. He kills her."

"Then Michael starts getting close. Alastair lures him to a warehouse staged for a ritual—"

The Jeep thumped into a pothole. My stomach heaved and I grabbed the dashboard. Adam hit the brakes and my breakfast almost hit the windshield.

"Shit! I'm sorry." He eased the Jeep to the side as I bent forward, eyes closed.

"Kleenex," I mumbled, trying not to open my mouth too far.

"Right. Okay. I've got napkins."

He passed them to me and I spat out the stuff in my mouth. As I wadded up the tissues, an opened pack of gum appeared in front of me. I took a piece, and chewed before saying, "I think I'm coming down with something."

"You haven't been feeling well?"

"A bit nauseated." I glanced over. "And no, it isn't morning sickness. Somehow I doubt I'm a suitable candidate for the next immaculate conception."

"I was feeling a little off myself first thing, and it's definitely not morning sickness for me. Could be the flu. Any other symptoms?"

I told him about the headaches and the spell-casting.

"You're having trouble casting spells?"

"Just a few misfires. It's nothing."

"You should have told me. If I'm watching your back, I need to know that your spells are on the fritz."

"Let's just get to the motel and talk to Jesse about the photos. Avoid the potholes if you can."

He pulled back onto the road.

"Maybe whoever gave Jesse those photos did the doctoring himself," I said. "He wanted Jesse to investigate Claire's death, so he Photoshopped the others. I keep going back to that witch theory. If Ginny and Brandi's deaths weren't connected to Claire's, then that makes even more sense. Claire could be a witch. She's killed. Two weeks later, I'm being stalked and Tiffany—who we know is a witch—is killed."

Adam didn't say anything. When I looked over, he was staring straight ahead.

"What?" I said.

"I just keep . . ." An angry shake of his head. "About the witch thing. It's tweaking a memory, and it's driving me crazy because I can't figure it out. I'm going to check a few more things in the database, then I may have to break down and call Dad."

The first order of business at the motel was to talk to Jesse and get specifics on where he got the crime-scene photos. When we pulled in, though, the parking spot in front of his room was still empty.

"Shit," I said. "I gave him the file." I walked to Jesse's door. "Time for a little B&E. Not like he hasn't done the same to me . . ." I murmured an unlock spell under my breath, then grabbed the handle and—

The knob didn't turn. I tried again. Then tried harder.

Adam shouldered me aside and used the lock-pick gun. The door opened.

We went in. As Adam retrieved the folder, I closed and relocked the door, then started to cast.

"Savannah." Adam sighed.

"It's bugging me, okay?"

I cast the spell. The door stayed locked. I focused harder and cast a fourth time and felt a whisper of relief as I heard that familiar click. The door opened.

I held out my hand and cast a light ball. When nothing happened, a weird sensation like panic settled into the pit of my stomach. As I started to cast again, my fingers trembled. I stopped and made a fist.

"Savannah . . ." Adam said. "You aren't feeling well. We'll deal with it."

"Just give me a sec, okay?"

I concentrated and cast. The light ball shimmered, then went out. Another cast. It returned and stayed. Weak, but steady. "Damn it, damn it, *damn it*."

Adam reached out, as if he was going to put his arms around me, but stopped short.

"No need to keep your distance," I muttered. "Apparently, I'm not that dangerous today."

"Apparently you're *sick* today."

"I need my spells."

"They help, but you don't need them. Not as much as you think you do."

"Let's get back and check out that file."

"Changing the subject and completely ignoring the point I'm making."

I shook my head and grabbed the file.

I leafed through the file. The crime-scene photos—and other pages—weren't there. I read the rest, looking for anything that disagreed with Paula's story. Nothing did. Good. As I read, Adam searched his database.

"*Fuck,*" he said. I jumped, papers sliding to the floor. By the time I'd gathered them back up, he was on his feet, still holding his laptop, reading it as he paced, mouth set, forehead furrowed.

"Found something, I take it."

"Witch-hunters," he said.

"Ah, an old and noble profession, a mere step down from that most esteemed position: Grand Inquisitor. Hate to break it to you, but the witch hunts ended a few hundred years ago."

"Not for some people." He turned his laptop around to show me. "These ones date back even further than the Inquisition. Very rare. Very elusive. Young women who are trained from birth."

"To hunt witches?" I shook my head. "If such a thing existed, I think I'd know about it."

"Did I mention the rare and elusive part? They usually kill in a way that looks like suicide or natural death, which is what was tweaking my memory. I was searching on the Bible verse, though, and they don't usually leave such an obvious sign."

I bent to read the screen, then tapped the database title. "It's filed under myths and legends. Meaning it's bullshit. Mysterious trained assassins secretly killing witches?" I shook my head. "Just the kind of bogeyman a Coven—or sorcerers—would create to turn us into the cowering mice they want us to be."

"Okay."

"No, it's not okay. First, the Inquisition. Then the witch hunts. Then centuries of quaking in the dark, too damn scared to cast a light ball, terrorized by our *own* kind. Nobody does this to werewolves or vampires or half-demons. Why witches?"

"Um, because no one believes in werewolves or vampires or half-demons." Adam put the laptop aside. "You're preaching to the guy who's heard the same sermon from Paige for the last twenty years. Witches get a bum deal. Always have. Personally, I'd blame sorcerers, but considering you're a sorcerer, too . . ."

"Blame *male* sorcerers. Or maybe just males in general. Inquisitors, judges, hangmen . . . they were all male."

"Are your spells still on the fritz? Or should I slink from the room while I still can?"

"I'm kidding. You know that. There are just as many bitches out there as bastards. Equal opportunity asshole-ism."

I plunked onto the bed, picked up his laptop, and read the entry.

According to the myth, witch-hunters had begun as an actual supernatural race. The Benandanti. I'd heard of them. A small race of Italian *demon*-hunters, not witch-hunters, although they'd been known to go after any supernaturals who used their power for evil. They were extinct now. No one seemed to know why. According to this legend, though, they'd been wiped out and replaced by witch-hunters.

Witch-hunters had been priestesses who'd held absolute power over their people with garden-variety magic—the kind every street magician knows. Then their people started trading with a nomadic tribe, which included families of Benandanti.

The Benandanti, true to their nature, didn't much like the priestesses. When the priestesses realized the Benandanti had real supernatural powers, they cried foul . . . and accused them of being exactly the kind of evil the Benandanti fought. When people wouldn't listen, the priestesses decided to eradicate the Benandanti. That took a few generations, and by the time they succeeded, they'd ironically slid into the role of the Benandanti, convincing themselves that *they* were the righteous ones ridding the world of evil spell-casters. So, when the Benandanti were gone, they moved on to a more ambitious target: witches.

The entry described a secret society of women who spent their childhood and adolescence preparing for the day when they would kill a witch or two. When they "came of age," they finally got their chance. It reminded me of religions where the young adults spend a few years traveling, spreading the word and making converts. Only these girls hit the road in hopes of killing a few witches before rejoining civilian life, marrying and raising the next generation of assassins.

Like your standard myth, it made a good story, which is why my gut reaction was to treat it as such. And yet . . .

According to the legend, there were very few of these families remaining, as elusive as snow leopards. When they killed, they did it in a way that wouldn't raise any alarms, even among witches. Wasn't that exactly how Claire and Tiffany died? One the apparent victim of a serial killer. The other likely a suicide.

Witch-hunters were said to recognize witches on sight—as sorcerers do—then stalk their victims until they found exactly the right circumstances. What if one had been following Claire Kennedy? That witch-hunter comes to Columbus, and discovers another witch . . . then another. She'd think she'd struck the jackpot.

Kill Claire and link her death to the first two crimes. Kill Michael when he got too close. Kill Tiffany in an apparent suicide. And then? Well, there's one witch left . . .

"If this is right, you're in deep shit," Adam said, around the time I came to the same conclusion.

"I'm not backing off."

"I don't expect you to. Just don't blast me with an energy bolt if I dog your steps until this investigation is done."

"I won't." I eased back on the bed, pulling my feet up. "My spell-casting has fizzled, remember? Damned inconvenient time for the flu."

Adam went still. Too still. I was about to ask if he was okay, when he grabbed his laptop and began typing furiously. When he looked up, his eyes were dark with worry.

"What have you been eating?" he asked.

"Um, lots of stuff. As usual. Most of it bad for me."

"No, what have you been eating *regularly*? In the last few days. Something I might have had, too." His gaze shot to the door. "The coffee shop. You had three meals from them, and I've had one . . . No, I was feeling a little off before that. Something else then. What have you been eating a lot of? Especially something given to you by someone else—"

His gaze swung to the table and he let out an oath. I grabbed the box of cult cookies.

"You weren't eating these, though," I said. "You finished off Paige's."

He shook his head. "No, I swiped a cult one, too. I had to see if they lived up to the advertising. I liked Paige's better, so I finished hers."

"Witch-hunters are young women, right?"

"Yep, and there's a whole house of them on the hill, making cookies. Who gave you the box?"

"Megan, but it was sitting on the counter before that. I'd stepped outside with one of the girls. Anyone could have come in and dosed it." I thought back to every contact I'd had with the young women at the cult. "It could be Megan, could be Deirdre, could be Vee . . ."

I remembered someone else. Someone I'd had far less contact with. "The new girl. She was watching me, and she saw me talking to Tiffany. Remember when we were at the house while Tiffany was being killed? Megan was asking where she was."

"Looks like we've got our—"

"Except for one thing. She was Claire's *replacement*. She arrived in town at the same time I did."

"Doesn't mean she wasn't here before. But, yeah, that makes it a little less clear cut. We need to take a closer look at *all* those girls. I can't say for sure that it's the cookies, but that's my guess. There are a bunch of poisons that can inhibit spell-casting."

"Poisons?"

"That's why I'm worried. I know you're going to hate this, but I want to get you to Portland, pay a visit to Dr. Lee."

Lee was the physician used by most area supernaturals when they had a health concern that went beyond a cold or flu. In an emergency, we can use a regular hospital, but whenever possible we avoid it—there are things in our systems that can give wonky test results and raise eyebrows.

"So the theory would be that this witch-hunter poisoned me to reduce my spell-casting so she can get the jump on me," I said as we prepared to leave.

"Could be. Or she might just be protecting herself *against* you. That Bible was left out for a reason. She knew you'd be involved in the case, and I can't see why she'd tip her hand like that unless it was a warning."

"So she's *not* targeting me, just telling me to back off? Mmm, not so sure. I see it more as a challenge."

Adam's look said he didn't like that explanation. A challenge said she intended to kill me no matter how hard I fought.

My cell phone rang. It was Bruyn.

"You were looking for me?" he said.

"I was. I wanted to get a look at the crime-scene photos if you have them."

"Sure do. If you've got a minute, swing by now. I've got some news you might want to hear."

THIRTY-FOUR

ADAM CALLED DR. LEE FIRST, CHECKING TO MAKE SURE HE would be in when we got there. He talked to the doctor, who agreed it sounded like one of the poisons Adam listed.

Dr. Lee said there were about a half-dozen toxins that could affect spell-casting and induce nausea. None would be immediately detectable in a cookie, if the dose was low enough. Most were mild and all I had to do was stop eating the cookies. Two of the poisons, though . . . Well, I don't know exactly what Dr. Lee said to Adam, but when he hung up, he insisted that our visit to Bruyn had to be very short.

Adam started fidgeting within sixty seconds of getting to the police station. I don't blame him. Bruyn's big "news" was that the results from the lab were finally in and the bullet that killed Claire hadn't been fired from the same gun as the one that killed Ginny and Brandi.

That would have been far more useful to know a day ago. Now it only confirmed Paula's story, though I guess it also meant Alastair hadn't killed Claire using the same gun. Right now, though, the case wasn't at the top of my priority list.

I did, however, want those crime-scene photos. Bruyn wanted an update first. I gave him some tidbits that would in no way implicate Paula. He seemed satisfied with that, and we were about to leave when his mother came in.

"I just got a call, sir. Bob Thorne is reporting a truck parked over by the sawmill since last night and he—"

"I'll look into it as soon as I'm done this meeting," Bruyn said, waving at us.

"There's a *reason* I interrupted your meeting, dear." She turned to us. "The vehicle Bob is reporting is a 1992 Dodge pickup, registered to Jesse Aanes from Seattle. Isn't that the other young detective you've been working with?"

Adam waited until the Jeep doors were shut before he blasted me. "Why the hell did you say we'd look into it? They were perfectly willing to send a cop to check it out—"

"*When* those cops returned from a call. In other words, it's not a priority. And if we suspect anything supernatural, then we can't let them go out there, can we?"

"You need to get—"

"First, we don't know for sure that I've been poisoned. Second, there's only a one in three chance that it's fatal."

"*Only* one in three. Well, that's okay then."

"I never said—"

"I don't care if it's one in three thousand, Savannah. I'm taking you to the doctor."

"Yes, right after we stop at the sawmill, which is on the way out of town, Adam. I'm not being reckless. If Dr. Lee said I was in serious danger, we'd be halfway to Portland by now. If you want, you can drop me off at the motel and I'll ride to the clinic while you check up on Jesse."

"I'm not sending you off on your motorcycle if you're sick."

"Then we're stopping at the sawmill unless you can give me one valid reason why Jesse would be parked in that neighborhood all night." I met his gaze. "Michael Kennedy almost certainly got killed because of a lead I sent him on. Are you honestly asking me to leave, knowing Jesse could be in trouble?"

The anger fell from his voice. "No. I'm just . . ." He looked at me. "I'm worried about you, Savannah. First a killer targeting investigators. Then a killer targeting witches. Now you're almost certainly poisoned, and I'm worried."

"I know. And I appreciate it."

He blinked then, like he'd expected me to come back with a smart-ass rejoinder. When I didn't, he didn't seem to know how to answer, just took out his keys, jiggled them for a second, then said, gruffly, "A quick check. Very quick," and started the Jeep.

We found Jesse's truck a quarter-mile from the sawmill gates. We parked behind it. I tried his cell one last time—I'd been calling it since before we said good-bye to Bruyn—and got his voice mail again.

As Adam got out of the Jeep, I tested a light-ball spell. It took two tries, but if I concentrated it would work. When I tried moving on to a fireball, Adam opened the passenger door.

"I'm just—" I began.

"Fretting about your spells."

"I'm not fretting. I'm heading into a potentially dangerous situation. Just give me a minute—"

He hauled me out. "You're quite capable of taking care of yourself, spells or no spells, Savannah."

I wish I could agree. With my spells failing, I felt like a knight walking around in his long underwear. I reminded myself that I wasn't completely naked. I just needed to conserve spell power, which meant letting Adam bring a flashlight and lock picks.

The sawmill was surrounded by an eight-foot-tall barbwire-topped fence, plastered with Keep Out signs and security company warnings. That would have been a lot more impressive if those signs didn't appear to have been printed on a home computer. They were barely legible, the laminate weather-beaten and cracked.

All I could make out was the company: R. G. Ballard out of Columbus. There was certainly no sign of a patrolling guard. The entrance into the parking lot was locked, but the gates didn't close properly and we easily slipped through the gap.

The sawmill was short and sprawling, with a few small outbuildings. A lot of square footage to cover. Adam looked from building to building, scowl deepening.

"We'll start at the midpoint, behind the sawmill," I said. "I'll cast my sensing spell." I stopped. "Shit."

"It might not have done much good anyway," he said, and I didn't know if he meant there was just too much space here . . . or that my spell only applied to the living.

As we rounded the corner, we saw an old sedan pulled up near a back door to the sawmill. Someone had slapped a magnetic sign on the door. R. G. Ballard Security.

"Seems we have security after all," Adam said. "No need to worry, then. We can get back in the Jeep . . ." He caught my look and sighed.

"Cut it out, okay?" I said. "A security car doesn't mean a security guard. The owner probably stuck that magnet on a clunker, and parked it here to make it look like the place was guarded."

"Easy enough to check." Adam took out his cell. He dialed the number on the magnet, frowned, then swore. "No signal."

"Seriously?" I tried mine. Same thing. "It worked out by the road. I'll run back and—"

He caught my arm. "Let's just get this over with."

The receiving doors were open. We stepped into a big room with an old metal desk and a whiteboard covered with the ghosts of words and numbers. A pair of work boots sat forlornly in one corner, one tipped over and filled with shredded paper and baby mice.

The next door opened into a hall dotted with security lights and papered with yellowed motivational posters. Beside one someone had written in black marker: "You know what really motivates workers? A fucking job."

Most of the posters had been defaced. Parting words from the employees. If I had to face rainbow posters exhorting me to have a positive attitude, I'd add my own commentary, too. And I wouldn't wait until *after* I was laid off.

Most of the office doors were closed, empty nameplates on each. The last one, though, stood partly open, light seeping into the hall. When I headed toward it, Adam passed me. I grabbed his arm. We faced off, but only for a moment. He wasn't happy to be here, meaning he was spoiling for a fight. Best not to give him one. I let him go.

He cleared his throat loudly as he approached the door. The sound echoed through the empty hall. He slowed, listening for any sounds of movement. Nothing. He pushed open the door and looked inside. I trailed him.

It was a big wood-paneled office. Clearly executive level, the dented metal desk looking as out of place as the old lunch box and dog-eared magazines scattered across it. The security guard had taken the best office the sawmill had to offer, dragging in abandoned furniture from other offices.

A half-smoked cigarette rested on the edge of an old company mug, the smell of it still permeating the room. The magazines were car ones. None I read. I prefer mine without half-naked women. A partially eaten sandwich lay on an open magazine.

The cigarette was out. Adam touched the end of it.

"Cold," he said.

I picked up another mug and stuck my finger into the contents. "Coffee is, too." I pulled my finger out and sniffed it. "Coffee with a kick. Whiskey, I think. Definitely cold, though."

As I went to put it down, I realized the mug was new, unlike everything else in the office. A matching extra one sat on a shelf. Both bore the same logo. Radu Developments.

"Cody's family company," I said, showing Adam. "Two brand-new mugs."

"Jacket, too," Adam said.

He nodded to the coat hanging off the back of the chair. I picked it up. A new, fleece-lined windbreaker with the Radu company logo on the breast pocket.

"Coincidence?" I said. "Or does Mr. R. G. Ballard rate corporate gifts for a reason?"

"One thing's for sure. The security guard was here earlier."

"And now he's not."

THIRTY-FIVE

WE BACKED UP AND CHECKED ALL THE OFFICES, JUST TO BE sure. They were empty.

The door at the end of the hall opened into a big room with tables and folding chairs. It had whiteboards, all wiped clean. Meeting room or quality control, I guessed.

A set of steel double doors probably led to the sawmill floor. Adam started heading that way, but I wanted to search systematically.

A glance inside the other two doors identified both rooms as storage. One was mostly empty. The other was jam-packed with crap.

Adam walked into the nearly empty one and shone his light around.

"Boxes," he murmured. "Doesn't look like they've been touched in months so—"

I stopped him and tilted his flashlight until it illuminated the dusty floor. It was covered in footprints.

I walked over to the nearest box. While it was battered and dirty, little of that dirt was actual dust. If the sawmill had been closed more than a year, there should be dust. According to the label, it was filled with office supplies.

"Explains the footprints," Adam said. "Someone's been swiping paper and pens. The security guard probably has a deal going with that real estate agent who runs the copy shop. Maybe she gives him the Radu company swag. They're developers, so she probably gets tons of it."

"Maybe. But why leave office supplies behind in the first place? I doubt the workers would have had any compunctions about stripping the place clean after they got their pink slips."

The box was taped shut with shiny new packing tape, but the cardboard showed signs that tape had been applied and ripped off many times. I opened it. Inside I found another box, newer, with a logo for a company called Pharma-Link at a Canadian address. I tore it open. Inside were drugs. Prescription drugs.

"You're shitting me," I murmured.

I walked to the next box and opened it. More drugs. Adam ripped open another. Same thing. We went into the other storage one. It was packed with boxes.

"Guess we know what brought Jesse here," Adam said. "He tracked down the destination for those deliveries Cody was getting."

"His big illegal enterprise is importing prescription drugs from Canada? No wonder he was so worried about anyone finding out. After the white slavery rumors, this would have been such a disappointment." I shook my head. "So the security guard is in on the scheme, letting Cody and his buddies store their stock here. Considering that the place is up for sale, no one would think it odd if they saw Cody driving into the sawmill. He probably has more stashed in the warehouses down the road, which is why Michael was checking them out. Only Jesse came straight to the source."

So where *was* the security guard? And, more important, where was Jesse?

We split up to pick paths through the crap, just doing a quick check to make sure the room was vacant. I was moving aside a chair when I saw a boot sticking out from between two crates.

"Got something," I whispered. I leaned over the crate to see a leg protruding from the boot. "Or someone."

I could tell by the boot that it wasn't Jesse—not his style. Nor were the ugly work pants.

A tarp lay across the body. I peeled it back as Adam came over. Underneath was a guy in his fifties, with greasy gray hair. Adam checked for a pulse and shook his head.

I leaned over and saw the pool of blood under the body. He'd been shot in the back.

When I glanced up, Adam had his phone out. He glowered at it.

"Still no service?" I said.

He nodded.

I had no desire to be caught with another corpse. Yet I knew better than to suggest one of us run back to the Jeep and call for help. We couldn't separate when my powers weren't up to par.

"We'll call as soon as we can," I said. "We need to find—"

"Shit."

Adam was staring at something on the other side of the boxes. I walked over and followed his gaze to another body, this one sitting against the wall, gun in his hand, wall behind him splattered with blood and brain. His face was covered in more blood, but I recognized it.

"Cody."

"Guess we know who killed the guard," Adam said. "And Claire. I just really hope Jesse didn't do anything dumb like call him here, confront him, and send him over the deep end."

"He didn't commit suicide," I said. "I had a hard time believing Tiffany would, but I absolutely cannot believe Cody did. The guy has the survival instincts of a barracuda. He'd never flip out, kill Jesse, kill the guard, then kill himself. Someone just wants to make it look as if he did."

I headed for the door. "We need to find him."

The big set of doors did indeed lead onto the sawmill floor—a huge open space filled with crap. Not crap, I guess. Machinery mostly. Here and there were blank spaces, as if those pieces had been sold. The remainder looked as if it dated from the sawmill's opening.

Rooms were easy to search systematically while keeping an eye on the exit. This would be like searching an open forest, treacherous terrain filled with ambush spots.

"I'm going to cast my sensing spell," I whispered.

Adam hesitated, then nodded.

The problem was knowing whether the spell was coming back negative because nothing was there or because it was shorting out. I could pick up faint pulses, though—rats, cats, or other critters. When I faced east, I caught the distant signs of a human-sized presence.

I pointed and nodded. Adam let out a sigh of relief. However much he'd been grumbling, he had been concerned about Jesse. Just *more* concerned about me.

I only hoped it was Jesse, and not the person who'd killed Cody and the guard.

I let Adam take the lead. He carefully picked his way past the machinery, avoiding stepping on any debris and announcing his presence.

As we passed a saw, blades covered, I heard the scuffle of a shoe on the concrete and spun, hands flying up in a spell.

It failed. Someone knocked me to the ground. I caught a whiff of overwhelming BO.

Before I could fight back, Adam hauled the figure off me. Another stink filled the air—burning fabric. Adam threw my attacker aside. I leapt to my feet. There lay a middle-aged guy in a jacket so filthy I couldn't guess at the color. Same went for the guy's hair, and even the guy himself.

He scuttled back, gaze fixed on Adam looming over him.

"This is my spot," the man whined. "Randy promised he wouldn't give it to anyone else."

I directed Adam's attention to a nest of rags and boxes in the corner. Adam swore under his breath and reached into his back pocket.

"Is Randy the security guard?" I asked the homeless guy.

He nodded, still watching Adam.

"When did you last see him?" I asked.

"Yesterday. He brought me a sandwich."

Adam plucked out a twenty and handed it to the guy. "We've been looking for a friend of ours who came in here. Have you seen anyone today?"

The man shook his head and took the money. "I just got here. I was down at the diner. They give me day-olds and yesterday's newspapers if I come by at ten."

"Did you see anyone here last night?"

"Wasn't here last night. I've got another place in town. It's better, but the lady in the building beside it calls the cops if she sees me there, so I don't stay during the day."

"We need you to get out of here," Adam said. "It's not safe right now."

"This is my—"

"—spot. We know that. And you can come back in the morning, but right now it's not safe."

The man crossed his arms. "You'll take my stuff."

I motioned to Adam that we needed to get going.

"Fine," he said to the man. "Just stay put, okay? Don't come out, no matter what you hear."

"Is it a delivery?"

Adam nodded. "Yes, it's another delivery, but we've got new guys and they're nervous, so stay here and be quiet or they won't let you stay, no matter what Randy says."

We started to walk away.

"Hey!" the guy yelled, making us both cringe.

Adam wheeled, shushing him.

The man plucked at his jacket sleeve. "You burnt my coat."

Adam frowned. "How would I do that?"

I took the wallet and gave the guy two more twenties.

"No incinerating the homeless," I whispered as we walked away.

"Yeah, yeah."

We walked a few more steps, then he glanced over at me.

"Back there, when the guy jumped you . . ."

"Swing first, cast later. I know."

"If I ask how you're feeling, can I hope for an honest answer?"

"Not great, not bad. I'll—"

"—be okay. I know." He sighed. I pretended not to notice.

"I'm going to try my sensing spell again," I said.

Adam nodded. I cast. It failed. I was midway through a second try when I caught a flicker out of the corner of my eye. Something flew straight at me, so fast I saw only a fastball blur. It hit the side of my head and everything went black.

THIRTY-SIX

I WOKE UP LYING ON THE DUSTY FLOOR. MY ARM THROBBED. My head throbbed even worse.

"Adam," I croaked.

Silence. When I tried to rise, my stomach lurched and I gagged, mouth filling with bile. I spit it out and had to take a second to steady myself, head and stomach both spinning.

When I could finally lift my head again, even looking around made my gorge rise.

I was alone. Beside me, I saw the outline of a body in the dust, then drag marks.

They'd gotten the muscular guy out of the way first, planning to come back for the helpless girl next. That was a mistake. I lifted my fingers and cast a sensing spell. Nothing happened.

Shit.

I fought welling panic. I was fine. I just needed to conserve my energy for one good lethal blast.

I pushed up on all fours. My stomach lurched and I retched. My arm throbbed. I looked down to see an angry red bump. I'd seen marks like that after every shot I'd had in my life. A reaction to needles.

I'd been injected with a sedative.

It took a minute more for me to get to my feet. Another to get steady enough to stay upright. The whole time my brain was screaming at me to get moving. Follow the drag marks. Find Adam.

Logically, I knew if our attacker wanted Adam dead, he wouldn't have gone to the trouble of dragging him off. Still, as I stood there, fighting to keep from curling up in a ball and spilling my guts on the floor, I felt weak. Useless, powerless, and weak.

I finally managed to start lurching forward, straining for any sound of my attacker's return. The sawmill was completely silent.

I thought about the homeless guy. Had he left? Was he dead? Or was there a better explanation for his sudden appearance and now his silence?

Wasn't that the perfect disguise for a killer? Roll a real homeless guy, steal his clothes?

I followed the drag marks down a passage that ended at a wider one where the floor had been recently swept.

No more tracks to follow.

As much as I wanted to conserve spell power, I needed to find Adam. I closed my eyes and cast the sensing spell. On the third try, I gave up.

I looked at the puncture wound in my arm. Not a sedative. More of whatever poison I'd been dosed with for the last few days. That's why I could barely walk without upchucking on my shoes.

I managed three more steps. Then I heard a low moan. I froze, prepping a cover spell before I realized what I was doing. I stopped casting and looked around. Off to my left, a denim-clad leg peeked from between two pieces of machinery.

I raced over, stomach forgotten. As I flew around a processing table, I caught a glimpse of light hair and my heart fluttered with relief. Then I realized it was too long to be Adam's.

Jesse lay on his back, eyes closed. When he moaned again, I touched his arm and his eyes opened.

"Sav—" He swallowed. "Savannah."

I shushed him and helped him sit up. He winced and put his hand to the back of his head. Dried blood plastered his hair to his skull.

"Something hit me," he whispered.

"I know the feeling."

"I think . . ." He made a face. "I think I've been drugged."

He was still wearing his denim jacket, but the bottom of his T-shirt had been shoved up. He pulled it up further and found a pinprick of blood on his abs.

"How's your stomach?" I whispered. "Do you feel sick?"

"Queasy, but I think that's from my head."

I told him what happened. When I finished, his eyes widened.

"The homeless guy. Shit! I found him just after I got here. Even gave him some money trying to get him to leave." He shook his head. "You said the guard's dead?"

I nodded. "Cody, too."

"Cody? I never even saw him. The guard was alive when I got here. I had to sneak around to avoid him. I got a lead on those pharmaceuticals. That's not only Cody's illegal enterprise—it's his supernatural connection. He's selling cut-rate drugs to supernaturals and raking in a massive profit."

"Taking advantage of our problems visiting doctors."

"Right. That's where Tiffany came in. She set everything up. Her and another supernatural named Timothy Greer. I'm guessing he's playing the homeless guy. He must have killed Ginny and Brandi because—"

"Not Ginny and Brandi. They were— Never mind. It's not important now. We need to find Adam."

"Right."

I tried to help him to his feet, but lost my balance, and he had to grab and steady *me*.

"Are you okay?" he whispered. "I've never seen anyone actually look green."

"Poison, I think."

"*What?*"

I told him what Adam and I thought was happening, then warned him not to count on my spells.

"Okay," he said. "We need to find Adam and get you to a doctor."

We'd gone about ten feet when Jesse pointed at smudged grease on a machine.

"Someone brushed against that," he said. "This way."

I bent to examine the spot. "There's dust on it. Someone brushed against it awhile ago."

He leaned over and frowned. "I don't see any dust."

"It's— Never mind."

Jesse led the way, picking up more signs, most too faint for me to see. I stayed behind him. He tried a few times to get me to go ahead. "I should be watching your back if your spells are failing." But I said no, and we kept going.

We'd been searching for about ten minutes when he froze.

"Did you hear that?" he whispered.

I shook my head.

"Over there." He waved into the darkness under a conveyer belt.

"You hide there," he said. "I'm going to check it out."

I crawled into the space. Once he'd slipped around the corner, I snuck across the aisle, and ducked behind another piece of machinery, something with knobs and dials.

I was squeezing behind it, my stomach protesting, when I caught a flicker of motion across the way. A crate resting atop the conveyer belt wiggled. Then it toppled, hitting the floor with a resounding crash . . . and blocking the space I'd just crawled out of.

I peeked out to see Jesse at the end of the aisle. He stared at the box. It jiggled again, then shifted, better blocking the hole. Twenty seconds passed, then he broke into a run, boots slapping the concrete as loud as he could manage as he raced to where I was apparently trapped.

"Savannah!" He stopped. "Shit! Are you okay?"

He didn't wait for an answer. He grabbed the crate, but it wouldn't budge.

"Fuck! What is in this thing? I'm going to get something to move it, okay? Hang tight. I'll be right back."

He ran loudly back down the aisle. Then he stopped, sat on a crate, and leaned back against a table, getting comfortable as he waited for the poison to do its work.

THIRTY-SEVEN

JESSE HAD SET US UP.

I'd started suspecting him when I'd thought about that object flying at my head. Then I became more certain when he'd kept leading me with invisible "signs." But even now, after witnessing proof, I couldn't believe it. I just didn't see a motivation.

Had he enticed me on this case to kill me and collect a bounty from the Nasts? I'd love to think they hated me that much—somehow it was better to be feared than to be ignored. But if they'd offered a bounty, I would have heard of it. Lucas always knows when there's one on him.

Could Jesse be a witch-hunter? With legends, there were always nuggets of truth surrounded by layers of bullshit. Maybe the part about them always being women was part of the bullshit. Jesse entices me onto a case where he thinks witches are involved, gets me to sniff out Tiffany, kills her, then comes after me.

I knew now how Michael had fallen from that balcony. Jesse lured him up there, probably by rattling stuff around, then telekinetically shoved him over the edge. I hadn't considered him before because he'd been on the phone with me when I got

Michael's text. More important, no Agito could send a guy flying like that.

But if Jesse killed Michael, what better way to throw off suspicion than call me while texting me from Michael's phone? As for his powers, he had to be a Volo. I wasn't sure how that was possible. There were only a few in the world, and at his age, he shouldn't have full control over his powers yet.

I peered out at Jesse again. Too far to launch a deadly spell . . . if I could even manage one. I needed to get closer.

I cast the blur three times and failed. On the fourth, it caught and I slid out the other side—away from Jesse. Then the spell broke.

I took a deep breath. Sweat trickled down my forehead. When I wiped it away, I realized my skin was burning. Fever, coming on fast and strong.

Less than ten feet to my left, the aisle branched off. I could run that way and escape. Not fight. Escape.

No, maybe a blur spell would get me far enough to cast—

Far enough to cast, maybe. Far enough to cast until something worked, while Jesse threw God-knew-what at me? No.

Escape it was.

I closed my eyes, focused hard, and cast again. It clicked on the first try. I was so intent on escape that I didn't hear the patter of my own sneakers until it was too late. I dove out of the way, managing to get into that branching aisle just as Jesse leapt up, crate clattering.

I looked around. The spell was still holding, but it was only a blur one, so he could see me if he looked hard enough. I held my breath and ran again, not caring how much noise I made, just getting as far as I could.

I darted into the first hiding spot I found, wedging myself between two pieces of equipment. I resisted the urge to try a cover spell. Unless he shone a flashlight right at me, I was safe.

Great. Sure. Just wait until he decides to leave. Not like you could be poisoned or anything.

No, I couldn't hide for long, but I *could* hide long enough for him to get closer.

"Savannah?"

I closed my eyes, tracking his voice.

"Come out, come out, wherever you are." A chuckle. "Guess it couldn't be that easy. Luckily for you, I am chock-full of contingency plans. Or, I suppose, that's *not* so lucky for you."

It didn't sound like Jesse. The voice was his, but the tone, the cadence, even the chuckle . . . The singsong sarcasm poked at a deep memory.

No, it's Jesse. You confirmed the photo. Adam knows him. That's clearly Jesse. He was just playing a role before, for you and for Adam and probably for Lucas. Worming his way into your confidences. But why?

"I wouldn't hide too long," he said. "Or when they finally raze this building, they're going to find your corpse, kiddo."

Kiddo. Another memory twitch.

It's the fever talking. Ignore it and be ready.

Jesse walked past me. I cast an energy bolt. Nothing happened. I closed my eyes and cast again. Nothing. Cast. Nothing.

A squeak of his boots. I opened my eyes. He'd turned back my way.

I looked around wildly and saw a pencil perched on top of a metal table just behind him. I remembered one of the first spells I'd learned. The simplest spell.

I cast. The pencil levitated on the first try. I moved it to the edge of the table and let it go. As it clattered to the floor, Jesse spun. His left hand formed a fist at his side and a rusty hammer rose from under the table. He maneuvered it out, watching and listening for me to make a move. My gaze stayed fixed on that fisted hand still at his side.

Every telekinetic half-demon has a "tell." A physical tic that precedes an attack. The other day, in activating his powers, Jesse had flexed his right hand, hiding his left . . . because it was a tell I'd recognize.

I heard Paige's voice from eight years ago. *She'd make a fist with her left hand. She was good at covering it, but I figured it out about two seconds before she sent a twenty-pound pot sailing at my head.*

The day before that I'd found out who my father was. I heard *that* voice now. *Trust me, kiddo, you're gonna love this one. You've hit the genetic jackpot.*

Leah O'Donnell.

My elbow bumped the machine beside me, and I realized I was shivering.

No way. No fucking way.

I blinked hard. It was the fever. I was losing it. I was remembering Jesse talking about Leah so I'd hallucinated that fisting left hand. Or maybe all Volos had that tell. And "kiddo" wasn't exactly a rare endearment.

But as outrageous as it sounded, it made sense, too. Jaime had sounded freaked out when I called. She'd been trying to contact Paige, and she'd been very happy to hear that I wasn't staying at home alone. Because she knew Leah had escaped her hell dimension? Feared she might come after me and thought I was safe if I wasn't in Portland?

Crazy, yes, but in my world, the most bizarre explanation is usually the right one.

Now if I could only figure out what possible reason Leah would have to take over Jesse and try to kill me, I'd be set.

That brainpower, though, was better spent sending the bitch

on a one-way trip back to hell. I concentrated, pouring everything I had into a lethal spell—

If the killer was really Jesse, I could justify killing him. But if it was Leah in his body?

Oh, shit.

I didn't have a clue how to exorcise her. I needed to get Jaime.

Sure, just run outside and call her. Hope you don't die of poison in the meantime. Hope Leah doesn't kill Adam in the meantime.

For now, just incapacitate Leah, find Adam, and go. And do it without my spells.

Shit.

Jesse was moving down the aisle, hammer hovering in the air as he searched for the source of the noise. When he slowed, I mentally lifted the pencil and dropped it again. I couldn't get it high enough, though, and the rolling sound was unmistakable.

Jesse crouched and spotted it. I cast a binding spell. It fizzled. I closed my eyes and tried again.

"Someone doing a little telekinesis of her own?" Jesse said. "Why don't you come out and we'll play—"

He stopped as the spell clicked. I leapt out from my hiding spot. My stomach shot up on a wave of bile. I ignored it and barreled into him. As my hands made contact, the spell snapped. He ducked. I stumbled. A power-drive to the side of my skull sent me to the floor.

I tried to scramble up. The hammer appeared, hovering over me.

"Move, and I'll knock you back down," Jesse said. "And this will hurt a lot more than my fist, kiddo."

"So what happened, Leah?" I said. "Did your hell dimension kick you out? Not nearly the badass you thought you were?"

Jesse blinked. Then sputtered a laugh. "I beg your pardon?"

I pushed onto my elbows. "Did you really think I wouldn't recognize you?"

A pause. He tilted his head, considering, then said, "Actually, I'm surprised I pulled it off this long. But I shouldn't be. No offense. You're a great kid. Just none too quick on the uptake."

I started to rise. The hammer readied itself to strike and I stopped.

"Good girl," Jesse—Leah—said. "I wouldn't want to mess up that pretty face. You grew up nice, kiddo. If I were a guy, I'd totally go for you. But I'm not, which was part of the problem. It would have made things so much easier."

"Would have made *what* easier?"

"Oooh, do I get to reveal my nefarious motives now? I love this part. Okay, cue the sinister music. The villain is about to tell all."

She stepped toward me. While it was clearly still Jesse's body, my fevered mind saw Leah.

"It started in my childhood. My brother used to torment me . . ." She frowned, tilting her head. "No, I did the torment-ing. Huh. That doesn't make nearly as good a story."

"Can we get on with it?" I said. "I'm dying here."

"Oh, it's all about you, isn't it? You aren't going to die, Savannah. Well, I hope not, because I'm really kinda fond of you. Always was. As I recall, you're the one who snubbed—"

"You poisoned the cookies."

"So you figured that out? Good girl. Probably thought it was that evil commune, didn't you? Nope. The cookies were just convenient—like the commune itself."

"You knew I'd find the Santeria and think it suggested something supernatural *was* going on in Columbus, when it was just a New Age cult guy practicing what he considered a cool religion."

"Pretty clever, huh? The cookies were just a bonus. See, to zap your spell-casting, the poison has to be administered slowly, which would have been much easier if ol' Jesse could have just seduced you and popped in a needle now and then when you were sleeping. But it was clear from the start *that* wasn't happening. So on to contingency plan A. Poison something you were munching on. Start draining your spell power while being taken into your confidence, lowering your defenses on all fronts. First part worked smashingly. Second, not so much."

She was standing so close now that I could reach out and grab her foot. Yank her down. And I would have, if I wasn't more likely to puke on her than punch her. Just keep her talking. God knows, Leah loved to talk.

"You weren't interested in poor Jesse as *any* kind of partner. First you team up with the detective. A human? Never thought I'd see the day. You used to have nothing but contempt for humans. A girl after my own heart. So I get rid of the human—"

"You did kill Michael."

She sighed. "You're interrupting. Fine, let's get this over with. My list of crimes against humanity. I didn't kill Ginny and Brandi, but you already knew that. Gotta give you credit, kiddo—I wasn't sure you'd figure that one out. I was actually kind of proud of you, putting together the pieces. Had some trouble with the follow-through, though, didn't you? Couldn't bear to take little motherless Kayla away from her grandma. Nothing says a killer can't be a good mama. You know that from experience."

I opened my mouth.

Leah cut me off. "Sorry, got off track there. I was listing my crimes, wasn't I? Killed Claire—that was the setup to get you on the case, so Jesse could get close. Didn't kill Tiffany. Figured the twit offed herself when you started sniffing around. Killed the security guard and Cody, and, yes, killed Michael. He was in the way. Added a nice twist to the case, too. And a serious bonus—Jesse swoops in to save the day, bringing you two closer. Then who shows up? Adam Vasic. After I timed it just right, killing Claire when I knew Paige, Lucas, and Adam would be away for the week, he had to cut out of his conference early. I remember Adam, you know. That last day at the compound. You were already giving him big puppy dog eyes. Too cute. Between you and me, though, what's cute at twelve is kind of sad at twenty-one."

"Go to hell. Oh, sorry. Go *back* to hell."

She laughed. "No, thanks. Do you know how tough it is to get out of there? And that's just escaping. Then I needed to track down a necromancer who owed me a favor, and use my poltergeisting skills to torture him until he agreed to get me into a new body. Which is *not* easy either, let me tell you. And now that I'm here, I intend to stay, which is where you come in."

"To do what? Cast a super Krazy Glue spell to keep you in Jesse's body?"

"Um, no. Sorry. Once again, it seems, it's not about you—it's about Mom, who is one relentless bounty-hunting bitch, dead set on bouncing my ass back into my hell dimension."

"You want me to ask her to back off?" I laughed. "Not likely."

"Um, no. Wrong again. I don't need you to ask her anything. Your only job here is to play daughter-in-distress. You've had some practice at it, I'm sure. You call Mom. She comes running. I cut her a deal—if I get to stay in the living world so do you. I'll release you, with the name of the poison, which will be the only way any doctor can treat you in time. Haul me off to hell . . . and you die a slow, painful death." She grinned. "A brilliant scheme, if I do say so—"

She stopped as I disappeared under a blur spell. She swung

the hammer, but I'd caught her off-guard. I scrambled out of the way, then leapt to my feet.

I won't say I ran—it took all my power just to lurch, and even then my brain kept screaming at me to slow down, conserve energy to cast, not escape. I ducked into an aisle, then another, as Leah whipped who-knew-what at my blur. Finally, when I was far enough ahead, I slid into a shadowy corner and hunkered down.

Leah needed me alive. As much as I raged at being used as a pawn—and not for the first time—I clung to that as proof that I wasn't as close to death as I felt. Save Adam. Save myself. Then come back, hunt the bitch down, and send her back to hell.

THIRTY-EIGHT

"DO YOU THINK THIS IS GOING TO HELP?" LEAH YELLED. "You've been poisoned. You have no idea what it is. You get that, don't you? Please don't tell me you're going to get all noble and sacrifice yourself to save the countless innocents I might kill if I'm allowed to live."

She laughed. "No, Paige hasn't rubbed off on you that much. You're still your mother's daughter. You don't give a damn about my future victims."

I held my breath as she walked past me.

"Do you really think I'm going to go on a killing rampage?" she continued. "You know me better than that, Savannah. I don't enjoy killing. I just don't mind it. If no one gets in my way, I'll be happy to live a nice, boring, murder-free life. I even tossed you a bone with Cody, by killing him and making it look like a suicide. I left evidence at his house that'll finger him as Claire's killer, and will suggest he offed the trailer trash twins, Ginny and Brandi. Then he came here and shot the guard before killing himself. He'll get blamed for everything—hell, probably even for his wife—and he won't be around to argue. All the murders are solved and little Kayla can stay with Granny. That's what you want, right?"

She walked a few more steps.

"You don't believe me about the poison, do you? You think it's not fatal. You think you have enough time to get away."

Her voice kept moving away. I tensed, ready to dart out and get farther away. Just get far enough away to start my sensing spell and find Adam.

She'd stopped talking, though, so I couldn't tell where she was. I strained for the clomp of Jesse's boots on the concrete. Then I heard the swish of fabric moving along the floor. A thump. Then another. Leah was dragging someone.

My heart stopped. She passed me, dragging the bound-and-gagged body of the homeless guy. I could breathe again and sucked in air a little too hard. She stopped and looked around.

"Close by, I think. Close enough to watch a demonstration? I hope so."

She pulled a syringe from her pocket. I knew what was coming. And I knew I shouldn't do anything about it.

Paige would do something without a second thought. Lucas would pause to analyze the situation, but he wouldn't sit by and watch an innocent man die.

But I *was* my mother's daughter and I could analyze this situation in the cold light of reason and say, "There's nothing I can do. Nothing I *should* do." I was too sick and too helpless without my spells.

Save myself. Save Adam. Whoever this guy was, I couldn't save him.

It was so simple. Logically, it was so simple. And yet, as the man struggled, his eyes rolling in terror, I realized I wasn't completely my mother's daughter. Not anymore.

She pushed the needle into the man's neck. I leapt forward. The blur spell broke and she twisted out of the way, fingers still on the syringe, pressing down the plunger as I cast a binding spell. It failed. I cast again. It failed.

I ran at Leah. She backhanded me, sending me flying off my feet again.

"Damn," she said as she walked over to me, lying on the floor. "As much as I liked being a chick, there are definitely advantages to having a guy's strength."

She stomped on my stomach and I let out a howl. She hauled me up by my hair and I threw up, splattering the floor with everything in my stomach.

"That might make you feel better, but the poison's in your bloodstream."

She whipped me around to see the homeless guy convulsing on the floor. His eyes rolled and I was sure he was screaming, but all that escaped the gag was a horrible mewling sound.

"Doesn't look too comfortable, does he? It'll all be over soon, though. For him, at least. That was a double dose."

I fought to get up. She let me, then delivered a right hook to my stomach and I went down again, doubled over in agony.

She grabbed my hair again and forced me to look at the homeless guy, dead now, wild eyes staring, face and body contorted.

"Kids these days don't take anyone's word for anything," she said. "You need proof. So I provided it. I'm hoping that will be enough, but if it isn't, I'm willing to indulge you with a second lesson. I have someone else in the back room just dying to help me out."

Adam. I looked at the homeless guy and threw up again.

"Don't like that idea, I see," Leah said. "Really got it bad for Fire Boy, don't you? Can't see the attraction myself. A nice guy, but nice isn't right for you, Savannah. Too vanilla. I'd be doing you a favor, you know, getting rid of—"

"What do you want?" I rasped, throat raw from retching.

"I've already told you. Call Mommy Dearest."

"My cell doesn't work in here."

"Still haven't lost your bite, huh? You're right. It doesn't. Handy thing, a cell phone blocker. But this call will get right past it."

"If you think I have a spell to contact my mother—"

"Then draining your spell power would have been really dumb, wouldn't it? Just concentrate really, really hard and call Mommy."

"You're nuts."

"Mmm, possibly. But I'm pretty sure it will work. Eve is out there right now, looking for me, and she's always looking out for you. That made things tough, I'll tell you—getting close to you while she's hunting me. Luckily, I have two addresses these days. Jesse Aanes and a gal in Connecticut. I let Eve find hideout number two, and she's been chasing that body . . . while I keep popping back here. Now it's time to give her the forwarding address. You call, she comes, we negotiate."

"What if she doesn't hear me?"

"Then you'd better try harder."

When I said nothing, she yanked my hair again. "Don't even think about getting noble on me, Savannah. I've got Adam, remember?"

I squeezed my eyes shut as I doubled over, concentrating with everything I had.

She relaxed her grip on my hair a little. "That's better. Now just let out a big old mental distress call and Mommy will come—"

The chattering of metal cut her short. I didn't open my eyes to see what was happening, just kept focusing, drawing on my power the way I had only once before, when Leah had told me my father had had Paige killed. I pretend that I don't remember that day, but I do. All of it, as much as I try to forget.

Now I needed to draw on that power again.

More clattering and chattering. Then a squeal as some piece of machinery moved. A crash as something fell over.

"Damn, girl," Leah said. "Even doped up, you can set a room shaking. You just have to put your mind to it."

I kept focusing, feeling the energy fill me. Around us, everything rattled and shook. A wind whipped up. Then came an awful, spine-twanging wail. Something whipped past me. Leah sucked in her breath.

"I do believe that's Mommy," she said with a chuckle.

The wailing grew louder, coming from every side now. Ghosts? Demons? Earth spirits? I didn't know. Didn't care. They were just a by-product of what I was trying to do. I kept my eyes shut as my power rose.

"Savannah?" Leah's voice quavered just a little. "Um, you might want to take it down a notch, kiddo. You're calling up every—"

I leapt up and hit her with a knockback spell. She flew into a metal rack. As she tried to recover, I hit her again and she went down. Around us, spirits whistled and moaned. The very building seemed to shake.

"What the hell are you doing?" she shouted over the din.

"Sending you back where you belong."

"Then you'd better pack your own bags, kiddo, because if I go, you do, too. There's no way you'll make it to a hospital in time. Even if you did, by the time they figure out which poison it is, you'll be dead."

"That's a chance I'm willing to take."

My voice was eerily calm. *I* was eerily calm. I could hear my mother's voice, telling me not to be stupid. Save myself. But the voice was faint, overruled by my own.

If Leah was given a free pass, she'd use it. She'd kill anyone who got in her way, and when the day came that she got in trouble again, she'd know how to get help. Come after me. Threaten my friends and my family.

I knew what I had to do.

Leah leapt at me. I hit her with another knockback. I could feel my energy ebbing, the fever burning so hot I could barely see. Around me, the spirits started to fade, my power fading with them.

No time to delay. I'd made my choice. Now finish it.

I cast a binding spell. Leah froze. While holding her, I closed my eyes and concentrated until sweat poured down my face, dripping onto the floor.

Mom? Are you out there? I need you.

I bent over, fists clenched, calling and calling and calling, as I had that day all those years ago, feeling the house shaking around me, the spirits rising, every spirit but the one I wanted and I'd kept calling until finally . . .

A faint whisper. "Savannah . . ."

My head jerked up, eyes flying open.

"Mom?"

I struggled to focus. My eyes burned. My legs ached holding me up. The building seemed to sway.

"Savannah . . ."

A shape appeared, so faint I could see only an outline with a weird blue glow dangling at its side. But I knew it was her. I knew.

"I heard you were looking for someone." I waved at Leah. "I got her for you, Mom."

I struggled to smile. The room flickered, like the lights were about to go out. Beside me, Leah's eyes blazed and it took everything I had to hold the binding spell as she fought to get free, to tell my mom about the poison, to make the deal.

"Don't listen to anything she says, Mom," I said, my voice

hoarse, every word a struggle. "She's going to lie and tell you I'm in trouble. I'm okay. Adam's here. He'll get me help. We figured everything out and foiled her plan. So don't listen to anything she says. Just take her away."

The figure moved toward me. I called on every ounce of strength I had to stand tall, not to let her see how sick I was. She leaned toward me, embracing me, and I felt it. I swore I felt it.

"So proud of you," she whispered.

"Take her," I said. "My spells aren't working so good—something she gave me. But I'm fine. Just take her before the binding breaks. And whatever she says, don't listen."

My mother moved away then, and that weird blue glow rose. Leah's eyes rolled. Absolute terror filled them and I drank that in, let it fill *me*. The glow sliced down like a blade, passing right through Jesse's body, leaving no mark. A scream. A terrible scream. Then Jesse's body fell over, Leah's spirit gone.

"I'm okay, Mom," I said again, barely above a whisper. "Don't listen to anything she—"

I hit the floor and the world went dark.

THIRTY-NINE

"SAVANNAH?" THE VOICE WAS UNRECOGNIZABLE, CHOKED with panic. Hands gripped my shoulders. "Come on, Savannah. Wake *up*. Just open your eyes. Please open your eyes."

I tried. I really tried. But the most I could do was flutter my eyelids enough to see Adam bent over me.

"That's it. Just stay with me. Please stay with me."

"Jesse . . ."

"He's fine. He's gone to call an ambulance."

"I . . ."

"Don't talk. Just stay with me, baby, okay? Stay with me."

Everything went dark again.

I felt like I'd been dropped ten stories onto the subway tracks, electrocuted, then run over by a half-dozen trains. My muscles ached. My head pounded. Each breath took effort. I could hear the *blip-blip* of machines and smell the stink of overcooked lasagna, laced with antiseptic. Even with my eyes closed, the light scorched my eyeballs. Cold air blew over me, freezing everything except one hand, which was warm, cupped in someone's. Fingers brushed hair from my forehead. Touched my cheek. Rested there a moment, then brushed the hair back again, lulling me to sleep.

When I woke again, someone was rubbing my shoulder, murmuring something I couldn't make out.

With effort, I cracked open my eyes. It was Adam, pale under his tan, eyes bleary, hair standing up, like he'd been running his hands through it.

"You look like hell," I whispered, throat aching with the strain.

He let out a shaky laugh, hand tightening on my shoulder.

"Not going to tell me I look worse?" I whispered.

"No." He bent down, lips brushing my forehead. "You look great."

I squeezed my eyes shut against a different ache. I wished he'd joked back. And I was glad he hadn't.

"Guess Dr. Lee found an antidote, huh?" I said.

"He always had it. We just needed to know which poison it was. He figured it out from your symptoms and had it ready when we arrived. It was close, though. Too close."

I craned my head to take in the room. I was in Dr. Lee's clinic in Portland.

"Paige and Lucas aren't here," he said as he straightened. "I called a few times, but they must have been out for the day. They're probably back by now. I'll go call—"

I gripped his hand as he tried to walk away. "No."

"They should know."

I shook my head. "If Dr. Lee says I'll be fine, then let them finish their vacation."

His mouth tightened. "They *should* know, Savannah."

"They will, when they get back." I managed a smile. "If they get mad, blame me."

Blame me.

I thought about Michael. About Claire. About that security guard. About the homeless guy.

"Savannah?" Adam leaned over me, face drawn with fresh worry.

"Just tired. Don't call them, okay?" I tightened my grip on his hand. "Just stay."

I drifted off into nightmares. I was back on the scenic lookout with Michael. He was kissing me, telling me he wanted a third date, and over his shoulder, I could see Leah ready to push him over the cliff, and I tried to tell Michael to run, to get as far from me as he could, but he only laughed and kept kissing me.

The scene changed and I was in the sawmill with Adam, searching for Jesse. I told Adam to let me handle this, that it was my problem and he needed to get out, get away from me, but he just kept saying he'd protect me. Only he was the one who needed protecting . . . *from* me.

I knew what happened wasn't my fault, but I felt like it was, like I should have figured out something was up with Jesse.

Leah had chosen her target perfectly. Jesse was telekinetic, so she could use her powers and I'd never be the wiser. Lucas knew him and trusted him, which was an instant stamp of approval for me. And, in life, Leah had been a deputy sheriff, meaning she could pull off even the PI parts with ease. She'd found the perfect disguise and there was no reason I shouldn't have fallen for it. No way I could have stopped her sooner. No way I could have saved Michael. But I couldn't stop thinking it.

Every time I opened my eyes, though, Adam was there. Nothing I could say would make him leave my bedside. Finally, one of the nurses must have heard us arguing about that. She came in and said she had to work on me and he couldn't be there. It'd be about an hour, so he should go get something to eat, and she'd have someone notify him when he could come back up.

I drifted off again as soon as Adam left. I couldn't rest with him gone, though. I started dreaming that Leah was in my room, and I kept screaming at myself to wake up, but I couldn't.

Rage boiled up inside me, impotent rage at Leah for everything she'd done. It roiled until it exploded and the room flashed against my eyelids. A cry of pain. A crash. Then the sound of running feet, a nurse saying "You can't be here," a voice protesting, not Leah's, but a young woman's, insisting she was a friend. The nurse hauled her out, and the dream slid away.

Jesse came by, and we pieced together what had happened to him. He didn't stay long. It was awkward, because I kept thinking of him as the guy I'd worked with, only he wasn't. This was the first time I'd met the real Jesse Aanes. It felt weird talking to him now. But I was glad he was okay.

"I'm ready to go," I announced the next afternoon as I brushed my hair. Given how long my hair was—and that I'd been tossing and turning for almost twenty-four hours—the brushing was a major chore. I figured if I could accomplish that, I was ready for anything.

"When you can stay awake for more than an hour, we'll consider it," Adam said.

I swung my legs out of bed. "It's been sixty-five minutes. Bring the Jeep around front—"

He grabbed my legs and pushed them back under the covers. "I was being sarcastic."

"Too bad, I'm holding you to it. Now let go—"

"If you can't make me, then you're clearly not ready."

"It's always easy to find you two," a voice said from the door. "Just follow the sounds of bickering."

A red-haired woman in her late forties walked in, garnering a double take from a passing orderly half her age. If I pointed it out, she'd say it was only because he recognized her from her TV spots, but the truth is that Jaime Vegas is gorgeous. Even in a casual blouse and slacks, she exudes glamour.

She sailed over to my bedside, giving me a hug. She'd called Adam when he was still in the ambulance, and between them—and with Jesse's help—they'd pieced together the story. She'd been checking in every few hours since, undoubtedly relaying the updates to my mom. I didn't ask if Mom was with her now. There are rules about that sort of thing, and we were careful not to bend them too often or the Fates would *ensure* my mother couldn't make contact with me.

"So Leah's back in her hell dimension?" I asked as Jaime settled on the edge of my bed.

"Nope. She got an upgrade to a worse one."

"And Mom?"

Jaime's grin faltered. "She's . . . not in the best place right now. Kicking herself silly. You know Eve. She can pull the whole 'I don't give a shit' routine, but when she makes a mistake, she beats herself up worse than anyone else could."

"Sounds familiar," Adam said, giving me a look I ignored.

"We'd argued about telling you that Leah was out," Jaime said. "I wanted to. Eve didn't. We had Leah in our sights—or so we thought—and she was a thousand miles from you, so Eve didn't want to freak you out, freak Paige and Lucas out, spoil their vacation . . ."

"Tell Mom it wouldn't have made a difference. Even if I'd known Leah was free, I'd never have seen her in this until it was too late."

"I'll tell her. And she has a message of her own to pass along. She says that what you did was incredibly selfless and brave, and if you're ever tempted to do anything like that again, remember she's waiting on the other side to kick your ass for the rest of eternity."

I laughed, but it came out a little ragged, my gaze sliding to the safety of the window.

"Did I miss something?" Adam asked.

"She's warning me not to tangle with psychotic hell-escapees," I said. "Which is good advice in general, and—"

"What'd Savannah do?" he said, cutting me off as he turned to Jaime.

I tried to protest, but Jaime told him. As Adam realized what she was saying, his face went rigid, eyes blazing, his fingers heating on my arm. When she finished, though, he turned to look at me, and his expression . . . It was respect and it was pride and it was anger and it was something more, too, but before I could figure out exactly what it was, he glanced down, rubbing his chin, the fingers rasping against his beard stubble.

"Yes, you need a shave," I said.

The corner of his mouth twitched a little, but he still didn't look at me.

"Your mom's right," he finally said, voice gruff. "It was an insanely brave and insanely stupid thing to do, and if you ever consider it again, remember I'm on *this* side, and if you survive, I'll kick your ass for the next fifty years, okay?"

"Okay."

I smiled and he looked at me, and our eyes met, and my heart started beating so fast I could barely breathe.

"Oh, would you look at the time?" Jaime said, jumping up. "I promised Elena I'd call with an update before three."

"I'll call her myself," I said quickly, and Adam looked away just as fast, saying he'd get my phone, then go grab us all something to eat from a café across the road.

"They have chocolate-chip cookies," he said as he handed me my phone. "They look *really* good."

I made a gagging noise and he laughed, and whatever had been in the room a moment ago had passed.

As he teased me, though, a nurse stopped and popped her head into the room.

"You got the cookies, then?" she said.

We all stared at her.

"I heard you talking about cookies . . ." Her gaze moved down the hall. "No, they're still here. Just a moment."

She came back carrying a box that made my stomach clench. Taste of Heaven cookies.

"Your friend dropped these off earlier," the nurse said as Adam took the box.

"Friend?"

"A young woman. She came in to see Savannah. She knocked over the bed tray and Linda gave her quite the tongue-lashing, I'm afraid. She left these and took off."

"When did this happen?" Adam demanded.

"When you went for dinner last night," I murmured. "I thought I dreamed it." I turned to the nurse. "What did she look like?"

"Mousy little thing." She colored. "I shouldn't say that. She was very sweet."

"Did she leave a name?"

"No. She was about your age. Long dark blond hair. Turned-up nose."

I thanked the nurse. When she left, I turned to Adam. "The new girl at the commune."

He frowned. "I thought Leah . . ."

"Killed Tiffany? She said she didn't—and she wouldn't bother to lie. Seems we have a witch-hunter after all. So can we leave now? Before she comes back and kills me in my sleep?"

He grabbed my shoes and jacket from the closet.

FORTY

GETTING DISCHARGED FROM THE CLINIC WASN'T EASY, SO WE took the express route . . . out the nearest exit door. Jaime covered for us. I gave her my house key and said we'd meet her there tonight. An hour later, we were pulling up to the commune gates.

I let Adam help me out. When he tried putting my arm around his waist, I pushed him away.

"I'm fine," I said.

"No, you're barely walking." He put his arm around me for support. "Enough with the heroics, okay? You've earned enough brownie points to last you a lifetime."

My cheeks heated. I tried stepping away again, but he only tightened his grip.

"Either I help you or we go back to the hospital and get you a cane. Better yet, a walker." He grinned at me. "Now that, I'd pay to see."

I lifted my fingers, tips sparking.

He laughed. "You don't scare me, Savannah Levine. You might have your spell power back, but you're liable to keel over before you can cast."

A figure appeared on the porch. Megan, bringing out a basket of laundry. She shaded her eyes and looked our way. A hand raised in halfhearted greeting, then she came out to meet us.

I had to remind myself I'd been gone only a day. Not long enough for people to notice I'd left, I hoped. The fewer questions I had to answer, the better.

"We're looking for the new girl, Amy," I said.

"That makes two of us," Megan said.

"She's not here, I take it," Adam said.

"Packed and left last night. Didn't even ask for her final wages." She hefted the basket on her hip. "I should have notified the police. I just thought . . . well, I thought with Cody dead and the murders solved, she wasn't likely to turn up dead."

"What the hell are you doing on my property?" boomed a voice.

We turned as Alastair strode toward us, his face red with fury. Behind him, girls watched from the house, accusing glares fixed on me.

"I cannot believe you would have the nerve to set your foot on my property after what you did."

"What did I—?" I began.

"You're a lying, hypocritical little bitch, Ms. Levine."

"Whoa!" Adam stepped forward. "I don't know what you think Savannah did—"

"She came to my house and she pretended to care about that little girl—"

"If you mean Kayla—"

"Of course, I mean Kayla. You told Paula you weren't going to do anything. You promised her. She trusted you. You lied because you didn't have the guts to look her in the face and tell her you were turning her in."

"What? I never—"

"You saw what kind of mother she was to Kayla. You saw

how much that little girl needed her. But you turned her in. And for what? That wasn't even your case—you were hired by Claire's mother. You had nothing to gain by accusing Paula."

"Civic duty," Megan murmured. "She's a detective. Whether Ginny's death was her job or not, it was still her responsibility—"

"I don't know what's going on here," I said. "Did someone accuse Paula—?"

"*You* accused Paula," Alastair said. "And not only that, you didn't have the guts to do it to her face. You didn't even have the guts to make the accusation in person. Or to give it to Chief Bruyn, because God forbid, he might show some mercy."

"We have no idea what you're talking about," Adam said. "But Savannah didn't accuse anyone of anything. She's been in a hospital for the last twenty-four—"

"Who was called?" I cut in.

"The state police," Megan murmured when Alastair wouldn't answer. "Early this morning. Bruyn arrested Paula a few hours ago, and called social services for Kayla."

FORTY-ONE

WE WENT STRAIGHT TO THE POLICE STATION. ON THE DRIVE, Adam ranted about Alastair's sudden show of concern for the benefit of the girls watching. I barely listened. Two sheriff's department cars sat out front. Adam parked behind them and I took off ahead of him, jogging to the door.

I felt the chill as soon as I opened it. Bruyn's mother and the local officers were crowded in the front room. All three stared at me and none said a word. The old woman pointed to Bruyn's office, where I could hear him talking.

I threw open the door.

Bruyn turned sharply, and saw me. "Looks like you don't need to track her down after all. Here's the source of your information. Savannah Levine."

Bruyn left me with the two detectives—a man and a woman. They weren't the officers who'd come to the motel to question me after Michael's death.

"Come in," the woman said. "We have some questions for you."

"Me first. Who told you I accused Paula Thompson?"

The detective looked at her partner. They exchanged a confused frown.

"You did," the other one said.

"No, I did not. I've been in Portland since yesterday afternoon."

"Ah, that explains the delivery. You sent it from there?"

"If someone sent you something, it wasn't me, and I know nothing about it. What did you get?"

A package, they explained. Delivered directly to the sheriff's department first thing this morning. Apparently from me. Inside, they'd found all my supposed case evidence—copies of my notes, my interviews, plus some notes that *weren't* mine. All of it led to a single conclusion. Paula Thompson had shot Ginny and Brandi, whom she believed were plotting to kill Kayla. According to the extra notes, though, I'd found no evidence to support that, and personally thought she just wanted a way to get custody of her granddaughter and rid herself of her embarrassment of a daughter.

"We've verified most of the details," the detective said. "We have phone records showing the calls from the Degas home to Paula Thompson, and to Alastair Koppel. We've confirmed your DNA findings—he is the girl's grandfather, which speaks to his motive in helping Thompson. We expect to charge him as an accessory after the fact."

She beamed at me. "You're an excellent investigator, Ms. Levine. If you've ever considered going legit, we're always looking for recruits."

Her partner cleared his throat. "Oh, and this was in the package," he said, handing me an envelope. "You must have left it in the file by accident."

I took the envelope. On the front was my name, with *Confidential* below it. I ripped it open and read.

Hey, kiddo. If you're reading this, then I guess you won. Good job. I know I should be gracious, but I can't help it—I'm a sore loser. I want a little payback. And my hell will be a little cozier, knowing I got it. Say hi to little Kayla for me. Tell her she has every right to hate your guts and hate the world and grow up just like Mommy, as every little girl should.

I crumpled the letter, rage filling me.

Adam's hand tightened on my shoulder and he leaned to my ear, whispering, "We'll fix this."

How could we? The damage was done. My own work, used to do exactly what I'd tried to avoid.

"You'll have to excuse us," Adam said. "Savannah's been ill and she's very tired. If you need to speak to her, can we do this another time?" He passed them his card. "I'm going to get her home."

The first thing I saw when I barreled out of the police station was Cody Radu's house. Empty now, every window dark, a swing on the front lawn swaying forlornly in the wind. I thought of their three little girls. Orphans now. I don't know what kind of father Cody had been, but I knew one thing—three young witches were going to grow up thinking they were the daughters of a serial killer. Being treated like the daughters of a serial killer.

I turned away. As Adam fumbled to get my door open, I noticed Kayla down the street, coming out of a building. I blinked, sure I was seeing wrong. A woman in a business suit stepped out behind her. A social worker.

I saw the backpack over Kayla's thin shoulders and the battered suitcase the woman carried. With her free hand, she guided Kayla to a sedan idling in front of the building. Kayla walked with her head down, gaze fixed on the sidewalk.

"Kayla!" I shouted as I ran toward her.

She glanced up. Then she looked away, opened the back door to the car, and got in. When I called again, the social worker shielded her eyes and squinted at me.

"This is a mistake," I said as the woman put Kayla's suitcase in the trunk.

"Are you a relative?" the woman asked.

"No, but it's a mistake. You don't need to take her. Paula will get out on bail and it'll all be cleared up—"

"Paula Thompson has been charged with her daughter's murder. Bail or not, the girl can hardly stay with her, can she?" The woman handed me a card. "You can contact my agency if you have any concerns. Right now, I need to get this little girl to a home."

"You have a placement for her already?"

"I meant a residential facility."

She brushed past me and got into the car.

"Savannah," Adam called.

I glanced over to see him a few yards away. I hurried to Kayla's door. She sat rigid, staring forward, backpack on her lap.

I rapped on the window. She ignored me.

"Kayla," I said. "Please. It's a mistake. I never meant—"

The car started rolling away. I jogged alongside it. Adam started walking fast, closing the gap between us.

"Kayla, *please*. I can explain. I didn't do this. I'd never—"

The woman hit the gas. I lurched forward. Adam caught me. I pushed him away, but the car was already too far gone to catch.

"Savannah," Adam said, reaching for me.

I circled around him and headed back toward the Jeep. I passed it and kept walking. Adam jogged after me.

"For a sick woman, you're running away pretty good," he said.

"I'm not—"

"Running away?" He caught my arm and pulled me up short. "You're running as fast as you can, which, thankfully, isn't very fast." He didn't even try for a smile. "I know how bad you feel right now, but—"

"Do you? Do you really? That little girl finally got exactly what she needed, and now she's lost it."

"You tried to make sure that didn't happen—"

"But apparently I didn't try hard enough, did I?"

"What the hell else could you have done?"

I didn't answer that. Couldn't. I could only feel it, in my gut, guilt blazing through common sense. I should have stopped Leah sooner. Anticipated this final attack.

"Stayed away," I murmured. "That's what I should have done. I should never have gotten involved in this damned case in the first place. All I did was screw it up. Got Michael killed. Ruined Tiffany's daughters' lives. Ruined Paula's. Ruined Kayla's." I gave a bitter laugh. "Par for the course, isn't it? Everything I touch turns to dust. Everything dies. Everyone."

"Don't be—"

"Melodramatic? Am I? Too bad, because I'm feeling a little melodramatic right now, and I'm sick to death of pretending I don't ruin everything I touch. I got my mother killed—"

"You had nothing to do with—"

"Yes, I did. They came for her, and I was there, playing sick, wanting a day home from school. She would have escaped if they hadn't grabbed me. I got her captured, and that got her killed. Then Paige takes me in. Am I grateful? Do I smarten up and behave for her? No, I just kept plowing along, turning the Coven against her, getting her house burned down, getting her run out of town, ruining her reputation, killing her dream of leading the Coven—"

"Do you think she cares? If it wasn't for you, she wouldn't have Lucas. She'd gladly have traded her old life for him. You know that. You didn't—"

"I killed my father."

His mouth opened. Closed.

"Can't argue with that one, can you?" I said.

"No, I'm just trying to figure out what you're talking about."

"Don't lie to me."

"I'm not. Your father died when the house collapsed. Maybe that collapse started with your magic, but you certainly didn't kill—"

"*Don't lie to me!*"

Sparks sizzled from my fingertips. My hair snapped with electricity. I stepped toward Adam, but he stood firm, holding my gaze, not even flinching when the sparks singed his shirt.

"I know what happened that night," I said. "I've pretended not to know what happened because that was what you all wanted. I lashed out at my father. I threw him into a wall. I killed him. I know that. I've always known that."

The look on his face then—the sympathy and the pain—was almost enough to make me break down completely, and when he reached for me, I imagined myself collapsing against him, how good it would feel—eight years of pain washing away. But I couldn't. I stepped back, teeth gritting, sparks flying.

"Go away."

"No, Savannah."

He stepped forward again.

"I said go away!"

My hands flew up to ward him off, and he sailed off his feet, chin jerking up like he'd been hit with an invisible uppercut. He crashed to the ground, keys sailing from his hand, blood gushing from his nose.

I ran over. "I didn't mean—" I stopped. Swayed. Looked down at him, dazed and bleeding. I stepped back. "Don't you see? I never mean it. Never. But it doesn't matter. My mother. My father. Paige. Michael. Paula. Kayla. Everything I touch, everyone I touch."

"Not me." He pushed to his feet. "I'm not going anywhere, Savannah."

"No, you're not," I whispered. "You're staying right where you are. Because you know not to come any closer."

He screwed up his face. His nose gushed again and he swiped the blood aside, impatient. "What?"

"Nothing."

He moved in front of me. "There, is this close enough?"

I said nothing. He took another step, so close I could smell the blood.

"Still seems safe," he said.

"Don't."

"Don't what?"

I lifted my gaze to his. "Don't mock me."

He looked me in the eye. "I'd never mock you, Savannah. I know you're hurting and you're going to lash out, and if you need to do that, then I'm right here. Lash away. I can handle it. Just don't do this to yourself. You want a target? Use me."

I started to shake. I clenched my hands to stop it. Waves of energy pulsed from my fists. Sparks popped, singeing his clothes, burning his skin. He only stepped closer, eyes locking on mine.

I stumbled back. Then I ran. I scooped up the keys and I ran, and I didn't care how immature it looked, what he thought of me for it. I took his keys and I ran because if I stayed, he'd get hurt. Or I would.

I ran to the Jeep, leapt inside, and pulled away from the curb, tires chirping, dust flying, seeing him out of the corner of my eye, but not daring to look. Just get away. Get away fast. Get away far.

FORTY-TWO

I DROVE TO THE MOTEL. I GRABBED MY THINGS, STUFFED them into my bag, and took off on my bike, leaving the Jeep behind, keys on the bed where Adam could find them.

By the time I was pulling out of the lot, I could see him, coming toward the motel. His arm lifted, hailing me. But he didn't pick up the pace, knew it wouldn't do any good.

Get away fast. Get away far.

The last part didn't work out so well. I'd barely gone twenty miles on the highway before I began shaking again, this time from exhaustion. Then the rain started, a thunderstorm whipping up in the distance.

I stopped at the first motel I found. By the time I left the office with my key, the thunder was crashing, lightning splitting the sky, rain pelting, hard as hail. I trudged along, getting soaked, bone-cold soaked, and not caring.

When the key stuck in the lock, I was too exhausted to make the trek back to the office. I cast an unlock spell. It worked the first time. I went inside. Cast a lock spell on the door. Tested it, not quite trusting that my powers were back. They were—my temper tantrum earlier proved that.

I flicked on the light. It came on, then went off, every light in the parking lot following as the power failed. I cast my light ball.

Thank God for my spells.

I squeezed my eyes shut, forcing back the prickle of tears. I still had my spells, but I'd give them up to fix what I'd done. I couldn't bring my mother back, or my father, or Michael, but if I could fix even one thing and give Kayla back her grandmother, I'd gladly give up my powers.

I stripped off my wet clothing and crawled into bed, the light ball still blazing on the night table beside me. I fell asleep as soon as my head hit the pillow.

I slept through the storm. What woke me was a much quieter noise: soft snoring. I opened my eyes. The room was still pitch black, parking lot lights out.

I blinked and lifted my head, following the snoring to a chair beside the bed. In the dim glow of cloudy moonlight, I could make out a familiar figure asleep in the chair.

"You don't take a hint, do you?" I murmured. I smiled, but tears tickled my eyes, and I blinked them back.

I still felt like shit. Exhausted and achy. But more than that, I felt ashamed of my breakdown. I don't do pity parties. Never have. Shouldn't start now. So what if I'd stumbled? I needed to haul myself up by my bootstraps, and keep moving. Do what I could for Paula and Kayla, get Lucas's help.

I had another problem to solve, too: the small matter of a witch-hunter on my tail. I couldn't let Paige come home to that or she might join me on the hit list.

I sat up and took a deep breath. I should do some work, quietly, letting Adam catch up on his sleep. Now, where had I dumped my laptop?

I cast my light ball, trying to keep the power on low. When nothing happened, I tried again, and didn't even feel the mental click that told me it worked. I cast again, and again, and again. Then I remembered my last thought before I'd climbed into bed.

If I could fix even one thing, and give Kayla back her grand-mother, I'd gladly give up my powers.

Oh, shit.